BEAR CHILD

RICK CHURCH

ARCHWAY
PUBLISHING

Archway Publishing books may be ordered through booksellers or by contacting:

Archway Publishing
1663 Liberty Drive
Bloomington, IN 47403
www.archwaypublishing.com
844-669-3957

ISBN: 978-1-6657-1418-1 (sc)
ISBN: 978-1-6657-1420-4 (hc)
ISBN: 978-1-6657-1419-8 (e)

Library of Congress Control Number: 2021921443

Print information available on the last page.

Archway Publishing rev. date: 11/16/2021

PROLOGUE

MOST PEOPLE ARE FAMILIAR WITH MALE BEAR CUBS. CUTE LITTLE BEARS who fight with each other, they stand on their hind legs, wrestle, and fall down like little boys the world over. They eventually leave home and fend for themselves. Bears do not have a herd mentality where the herd takes its cues from the leader in times of danger, so the mama bear does not try teaching her young that way of life. She teaches them to be a bear.

Folks on Native American reservations located in bear country know what bear scat smells like. Grandmas use berry picking as an opportunity to teach that it smells like the pig crap in yards, and dads reinforce it while hunting with their offspring. It would not do any good to try to teach someone that bear scat smells like pig crap if that person did not know what pig crap smells like.

Most young adults are self-absorbed. It is said that with age comes the wisdom which is often lacking in the early stages of life. Like the bear, each person will have to endure falls, fights, and beatings, both emotional and physical. In bear families, mothers assume the teaching responsibility. In human families, fathers play an equally important role. If there is no dad at home to teach life lessons because dad is in the county jail or was never in the home to begin with, that makes it rough going for any young person, especially males.

CHAPTER 1

THE MURDER OCCURRED SOMETIME DURING THE EARLY FALL OF THE year according to soil and insect forensic evidence on the body at the burial site, (drainage ditch) according to the Cook County Medical Examiner's office. The deceased was described as an adult male, possibly in his fifties, who at one time suffered a fracture of his jaw and of his left clavicle. These were old injuries and not related to the cause of his death. The apparent cause of death was one 9mm shot to the chest and two 9mm shots to the forehead area. Three 9 mm shell casings were located at the scene.

The second body was discovered in an underground parking garage in Chicago. Apparently, the body had been wedged between two parked vehicles. The victim was the owner of one of the vehicles while the other car was registered to a long-term parker who used the garage while in Europe seven months out of the year. It was badly decayed but maintained throughout the cold Chicago winter. Cause of death was one 9mm gunshot wound to the chest and one 9mm wound to the frontal lobe of the head. Two 9 mm shell casings were recovered at the scene.

The third body was discovered on its back in the entryway of the victim's home. An estranged wife discovered the body during a welfare check on the victim. A cardboard pizza container was on the victim's chest with a baked pizza inside. The victim's telephone records indicated the last call placed by someone using the victim's phone was to a local pizza shop thirty days prior to the discovery of the body. The cause of death was a 9 mm gunshot wound to the facial area of the victim. One shell casing was located at the scene.

Due to the addresses of the victims and the locations of the shootings, the three cases were investigated by three different geographical units of the Chicago Police Department. This may have contributed to linkage blindness due to a lack of shared information or interest by those units. Another factor was that no one had tried to match the spent cartridge casings recovered at the scenes. There was an obvious reason for this; Chicago was averaging well over three hundred gunshot deaths per year for several years straight. Because of drive-by shootings and other gang-related gun deaths, the Chicago police were swamped with forensic ballistic examination requests.

The examiner normally would fire the suspect weapon into a tank of water or forensic fiber to collect the spent round. This round would then be matched to recovered rounds from a victim or victims of other crimes. In this case, there was no weapon recovered as of a year after the three murders. No weapon or matching rounds. The weapon of choice for most gang shooters is a 9 mm due to low cost and ease of ownership or possession. During most gang shootings dozens of 9 mm shells are fired, thus dozens of shell casings per shooting. An extractor on a semi-automatic weapon would normally leave identical marks on each shell casing. The sheer volume of casings to compare between crimes inhibited the ability to perform the task, however. The shell casings in the three murders could have been matched if they had been compared to each other.

Eventually the Chicago P.D. did link the three homicide victims as serial killings. After many months of research and interviews, the three victims were identified as Mr. Ira Stover, Mr. Edward Shelf, and Mr. John Terry. A brief computer check placed all three as City of Chicago employees on leave from city services and participants in a contract behavior therapy group for anger management. All three victims were under city human resource-mandated participation. The Health Insurance Portability and Accountability Act of 1996 (HIPAA) privacy rules made investigation inquiries difficult at best. HIPAA mandated that patient names, patient treatment information, diagnoses, medication, medical histories, and corresponding physicians be kept private. Barrier after bureaucratic barrier delayed and prevented vital information to flow into the investigative channel. However, HIPAA is a federal law, and fingerprinting is a federal investigative tool. Submission of fingerprints go directly to the FBI, so it was only natural that the FBI were the first to get fingerprint results. This was important in this case.

The fact is, normally it would have been finally determined that all three were ordered into anger management sessions by their employer, the City of Chicago, and all three had surviving spouses who would bring wrongful death suits against the city for placing their partners directly in harm's way, ultimately causing their deaths. All three families would have retained the same law firm. They would have collected millions of dollars in settlement agreements. Normally - but these three men who were killed around the same time never had family members who came forward to bring any lawsuit against the city. The families did not become monetized, although this did not raise eyebrows.

It was discovered by the FBI that the three sets of fingerprints belonged to three people who were already on the FBI radar and who had been using their spouses' last names to conceal their identities. Regular old-fashioned fingerprinting of the three victims taken postmortem helped to make the identification from prints already in the system as employees of the City of Chicago. Well, partial identification anyway, until the determination that the men had misspelled and/or reversed spelling of their three spouses' names, Revotos, (A.K.A. Stover) Fleahs, (A.K.A. Shelf) and Yeret, (A.K.A. Terry). With a little more help from the FBI, it became apparent that all three men were important members of three Mexican cartel crime families and were living in the United States while dealing in human trafficking trade, drug smuggling, and money laundering in a real barn-raising spirit.

The most interesting fact was that none of this information was immediately shared with the Chicago Police Department; in fact, it was never shared with them. Some federal investigations are considered too sensitive for even limited information sharing with local law enforcement murder investigations. This would fall under the heading of "Concealed Intelligence." This information would not be shared for several reasons, the most important being the belief that federal drug-interdiction funding for major drug investigations should be given to federal agents rather than providing smaller drug investigations with federal funds. Smaller as in police and sheriff departments also referred to by federal agents as "Whack-a-mole" in the war on drugs approach.

CHAPTER 2

TIMOTHY BEAR CHILD WAS BORN AND RAISED ON A WISCONSIN INDIAN reservation. He was ten years old when he became aware that kids from other cultures who did not necessarily approve of his family. He was at a school function, a sporting event. A wrestling match to be exact, and the kids and parents from a school outside of his reservation had to sit in the gymnasium bleachers with the kids and parents from his school district. Most of the cheering and support for the opposing school came in the form of derogatory shouts and yells that reflected a strong dislike for the reservation team members. Specifically, the team's cultural image, "Blanket Ass," and "Cheat'n Injun" were the terms shouted out in public.

The only reason he was there was because an older cousin who came to live with his family was rapidly becoming a state wrestling champ. Timothy did not know anything about wrestling and came to resent the sport he didn't understand. He was expected to act as a wrestling partner for his cousin even though he was out-gunned, out-weighed, and out-wrestled every time. It seemed that almost every time he was trying to spend time with or groom his favorite horse at home, his uncle would always call him into the house to wrestle with his cousin. He blamed this sport for the negative feelings he developed toward his cousin. When he became a teenager, his cousin was no longer the state champion but had transitioned into a United States Marine.

Tim had become Tim, not Timothy, any longer. He became mature enough to realize his cousin and the sport of wrestling were not the issues. The way white people demeaned his cousin, a member of his family, and a member of his all-native school team was an issue, a deeply felt issue. When he was a ten-year-old kid, he did not have the intellectual insight to realize what had taken place. His negative feelings about wrestling were related to the way his culture was treated at that public wrestling meet. Tim was proud of his cousin becoming a U.S. Marine, but he noticed that his cousin's name never appeared in the community paper like other local military recruit names did when they finished training. This was not unusual. Wedding announcements for Indian folks never appeared in the local paper like they did for white folks. Indian death notices never showed up in the local press unless that person was the cause of a fatal traffic accident.

Bear Child accepted the name "T. Bear" from his friends while in high school. That was during the days of nicknames used in T.V. shows and Hollywood movies. He had become comfortable with the internet and the various computer devices like most people his age. Although he did not want a career in the computer or I.T. field, his expertise with the internet soon offered him a future in criminal investigation and crime analysis.

When he was a freshman in college, he was invited by Tori Scott, a friend of his, to go to an open house which was really an affirmative action recruiting event put on by the Chicago Police Department. One of the white officers behind a table indicated that the department was opening the door to minority recruits. The white officer was polite to him and answered many of the questions he posed. What impressed him the most was when the white officer told him that if he did not have an answer for him, he would find out and get back to him with correct information. Never had any white person offered to be so responsive to him.

Later that evening Bear Child had a conversation with Tori and implied that he would consider applying while he was still enrolled in school. His friend found it hard to believe that he would ever drop out of school instead of waiting to go into law enforcement with a degree of sorts. "Any degree, any field," said Tori.

Bear Child spoke very clearly and said, "Why struggle in college when you already have the internet and Google? Look at it this way,

Tori, they already have a Chief of Police in every police department in America. They already have a Sheriff in every sheriff department in America. They already have a Director of the FBI. Maybe leave now and start where most cops start, at the bottom. You probably didn't notice but it was entry level, they didn't hold this event to find a Police Chief. You don't need a degree for this."

There was a long pause before Tori spoke. When he did, he said, "You know, when you see the old black and white silent films about piano movers hoisting those upright pianos on a rope and the rope breaks? Or when a piano gets away from them, and they end up chasing a runaway piano down a hill in San Francisco? You know, the old silent films shot during the depression? Bear, those pianos belonged to white folks. All I'm saying is Indian folks didn't have piano movers and pianos. With a college degree we can earn good money and buy our families a piano."

"No Indians had pianos or movers. Not until one of those pianos fell on an Indian, and the Indian sued the movers and the piano owner," replied Bear Child. "You don't need a degree to sue anyone and recover damages. Then you can buy all the pianos you want." It was clear that Bear Child's immature response was due to his inability to appreciate the value of an education. He also hadn't had a father in his home.

A few minutes later the two were silent but still walking together when Bear Child's friend said, "That guy was the most professional person I have met in years." Bear Child thought maybe his friend had read his mind. He never shared his thoughts on being treated like someone who was deemed suitable, just like a white person, but, somehow, he felt elevated to a status he never held before. He had been accepted by a white man. A white cop.

Several days later both Bear Child and Tori applied for positions with the police department. Then they both received letters accepting them and offering them positions after the mandatory written test, background check, physical agility, and oral board. However, months later when Bear Child had to confront white folks on the job, he was still looked upon in disfavor. He never really knew if it was his sworn position as a cop or his race that was more objectionable to them.

One particular time he and another officer had to investigate a complaint. A white homeowner came to the door after they knocked and informed them that his partner should come in, but Bear Child could not. Bear Child's partner was a white man, so Bear Child naturally felt angry and rejected. He immediately wanted to assert himself and shame the homeowner.

Bear Child asked, "Excuse me, but you don't want me inside your house because of the color of my skin? You're kidding, right?" The homeowner never turned around to address Bear Child but instead continued to walk back into his house. He said loudly over his shoulder, "You may have stepped in dog crap and have it on your shoe, Officer." After that embarrassing incident, Bear Child measured his response before becoming aggressive to people, both white and minority, but he continued to be uncomfortable when it came to racial snubs or disparaging remarks even after four years on the job.

At the start of his fifth year of service, Bear Child was enjoying a day off at a local shopping mall when he noticed someone was following him around inside a sporting goods store. At first Bear Child thought maybe he was imagining this strange person stalking him, but as he progressed from one display and department to another, the stranger clung to him like a shadow. When Bear Child heard the squawk of a handheld radio, he knew what was happening. He quickly headed for the exit near the last register in the store, knowing this person would follow and confront him, believing he shoplifted. Bear Child stepped out of the store only to be immediately grabbed by the collar of his shirt by another fellow waiting for his arrival and in the company of another man.

"Not so fast, Senor Jesus! I am a police officer, and you are under arrest," said one.

"Si, Federales, Poncho," said the guy who had him by his collar.

By this time, the fellow who was following Bear Child around the interior of the sporting goods store had joined his two friends. They were then provided the opportunity to witness an off-duty cop render all three of them harmless and inoperative.

As Bear Child removed the hand that held onto his shirt collar, he began cupping his right hand around the guy's arm and following it down to the left wrist and hand. Bear Child then twisted the wrist backward and began to break his wrist and two fingers telling him,

"This is for 'Jesus.'"

crack! went one finger.

"And this is for 'Poncho.'"

crack! went the other finger.

"Ass Wipe," added Bear Child under his breath.

The sound of the finger bones breaking sounded like a big dog chewing on a chicken bone and caused the other two guys' eyes to widen in disbelief. Bear Child took advantage of this and immediately went to an almost-sitting position which automatically dropped his weight and center of gravity. Using a sweeping motion, his right leg struck the closest guy just above the ankles, knocking him to the tile floor like a bowling pin. The back of his head struck the tiles, cracking his skull. The poor fellow immediately grabbed his head, as if holding it between his hands would repair it. He rolled onto his side and curled up into a fetal position. The fellow with the handheld radio started to backstep with his free hand in an open palm position toward Bear Child, indicating that he wanted no part of the fight going on.

Bear Child said, "Come over here and give me that piece of shit" while taking the radio without waiting for him to comply to his demand. Bear Child smashed the radio into the left temple of the guy and then threw it to the floor, knocking the battery loose and breaking the radio's plastic case into several pieces. Bear Child asked him, "What department are you bad- ass cops working for?" He demanded that the guy get on the floor and lay down next to his buddy.

Bear Child looked over at the first guy he tackled and ordered, "You, too, and take your fingers with you. Do it now!" After the three had complied, Bear Child had the presence of mind to look for the placement of mall security cameras. He counted two of them pointed in his direction. One of them was approximately 100 feet from his position, spanning the mall from one second-story walkway to another. With any kind of luck, the camera would not pick up his facial features. He had several options available to him, but none of them were appealing. Bear Child left the mall and went to his car, where he immediately did the wisest thing he ever thought of doing in his life. He called his department's dispatcher and requested an on-duty squad to respond to the mall because he wanted to report an assault.

CHAPTER 3

AFTER SIX MONTHS OF DEALING WITH THE POLICE DEPARTMENT'S JUS-
tice system regarding the mall assault, Bear Child realized that maybe
he could be charged in the criminal court system and who knows, even
sued in the civil court system, too. He was looking at a possible one to
three years in the joint, serving time for possible manslaughter if the guy
died, who knows how many years on adult probation if the guy lived.
Would he get time served or just a flat-out screw job?

It was during this period that Bear Child was on the receiving end
of a very fortunate event. One day he received an unexpected telephone
call. A law firm representing the shopping mall where the incident occurred wanted to make him an offer of over $60,000 for signing off on
any possible torts or damages from the mall's security company that
employed the three that may have assaulted Bear Child.

Suddenly the crap that he had stepped into started to smell fresher,
more like an ocean breeze, although Bear Child had never seen or
smelled an ocean. $60,000 for not doing anything but sign on the dotted
line? If they were willing to give away that kind of money without him
having an attorney, what would they do if he had an attorney? The living room of his small, rented apartment filled with the scent of flowers;
flowers were something he had smelled.

The department was in the process of suspending him, but the union
told his supervisor that they would fight the suspension based upon the
three identifying themselves as "Police Officers" while attacking Bear
Child. The department relented but wanted to force Bear Child to attend

anger management sessions. They had learned that the store detective who had his head bounce onto the mall floor had suffered a fractured skull and later an aneurysm, although he lived. The union thought Tim should agree to it. But like everything in his life, the truth was hidden at times. There was a rumor kicking around that the department had responded to the mall before. It seems that someone had filed a prior complaint that the store detectives posed as police there.

Bear Child investigated this bit of information during his spare time and learned that his sergeant had family on the mall security payroll. In the meantime, he had to spend his afternoons in the plush office of a contracted psychiatrist as required for four weeks. This Performance Improvement Management Process was really part of a progressive discipline plan to fire him. In street terminology, if there were an acronym for Performance Improvement Management Program, PIMP would apply. He was being pimped by the system: Mandatory attendance in a program which would end in termination because he was in the program. A real Catch 22 approach to employee purging.

After his four weeks with the psychiatrist, he was assigned to a group engaged in anger management sessions at a local hotel meeting room for a half year. They met at the hotel because the psychiatrist's office was too small to accommodate the group. He collected his full pay, and while at the hotel he was eligible to have his lunch cost reimbursed by his department. So, he joined the other group members in the hotel bar drinking lunch on the city once a week for twenty-six weeks. At the end of those weeks of conferring with some self-proclaimed and tipsy legal experts he got to know and dislike immensely, Bear Child had a very good idea what he was going to do.

There was a lot to say about a man and his liquor when the man has been drinking and he was bitter. If that man is multiplied by four, some real insight was shown because those four were loose with their tongues and not guarded about their true feelings. Names like "darkie," "nigger" and "big black buck" got tossed around in their company. Once on his way into the men's room, Bear Child caught the abrupt ending of an exchange with the last words being "Fuck'n Indian in our group."

Nevertheless, at the suggestion of fellow group members, he decided to bring a legal action against his department. He was advised to find a recent law school grad who passed the state bar and was licensed to practice law, the thinking being that the new lawyer would be hungry for money to help pay off his or her student loan debt.

"Look for a lawyer with office furniture that looks like used IKEA bookcases and desks," offered one fellow group member while another suggested finding a new female attorney who wanted to "blaze a feminist path in the legal system." Bear Child thought he knew what this guy meant to say but did not correct him in public because it would have been disrespectful. This was not about gender; this was about police administrative abuse. Another group member suggested not retaining, "a guy with facial hair that makes him look like a satanic goat." Bear Child figured that this suggestion was just about personal choice and would not be of benefit to his strategy at the time, but he would keep it under advisement.

One group member, an older, more sophisticated fellow, suggested finding a "hard-ass attorney. One who doesn't like anybody. Ya know, an attorney who had a judge that has called him a Rat Bastard in court. Now that is a hard-ass attorney."

Of course, this was the same fellow who said his neighbor was caught in "vagrant delicto" vs. flagrant delicto. But who was judging? More important, Bear Child didn't know where to find a "Rat Bastard" attorney.

This act of bringing any legal action against a department was a career killer. Bear Child felt his career was over anyway. He had a sense that his time as a cop would be coming to an end when he first conferred with his union representative. As he gathered more intelligence about the department's hidden history with the mall issues and the phony police that worked there, he knew someone was smelling up the profile he had built as a regular copper, being accepted by his co-workers on the street and his supervisors. He was now disposable. But he wasn't going to let this happen.

CHAPTER 4

BEAR CHILD HAD NOT BEEN HOME IN SEVERAL YEARS. HE DECIDED TO take a few days during a three-day weekend to travel home, visit his family, and talk to his uncles. Some of his uncles had been in the military and had seen the world. Sometimes going off the Reservation provided insight into different cultures. He had an uncle who was a Marine in Vietnam. He had done a few days in the Brig while in the Marine Corps and a few months of jail time after he was discharged. Out of respect, Bear Child did not ask about the specific charges whiles others were there but did solicit his help in finding a "Rat Bastard" attorney.

After explaining his situation to his uncle, he was referred to a family friend, Noel Two Horses. "He is a former cop and has his own private eye business in Arizona." In confidence his uncle informed him that if it were not for Two Horses, he would have been in prison.

"Seriously, it was that serious of an offense, Unk?" asked Bear Child in disbelief.

"Serious as hell, nephew."

Bear Child asked his uncle, "He's that good?"

"Well, if Two Horses tells you that you will wind up in prison, you better take some makeup and high heels with you or toughen up, nephew."

Bear Child thought about that for a minute and asked, "Where would a person find Noel Two Horses?"

Bear Child did not have a great amount of cash, but he knew he had enough available to begin his quest. With his cousin's computer he was able to locate Two Horses' investigative agency in Prescott, Arizona. He booked a roundtrip flight to Prescott and paid for it online with a pre-paid credit card that very same afternoon.

After clumsily making it safely into and out of TSA, Bear Child put his belt and his shoes back on and followed the others into his departure gate. He didn't know what to expect, but he listened to his flight attendant's instructions and even located his barf bag.

Bear Child arrived in Prescott, rented a car at the small airport, and drove it directly to downtown Prescott. As it turned out, Noel Two Horses was not that difficult to locate; well, his bookshop anyway. It was right on a corner in downtown Prescott, inside an old building named the Saint Gregory Hotel. Walking through the front door of the book-shop, Bear Child was amazed at the interior. There was an old-fashioned parlor with a fireplace and ornate wooden paneling with framed old pho-tographs on the wall, even a spittoon. Bear Child immediately gravitated toward the parlor where, on a table next to a Meerschaum pipe, was an unopened telegram for Dr. John Watson.

As Bear Child was taking in the interior of the shop, he was ap-proached by a heavy-set guy who asked if he could help him.

"Yes, I am looking for Mr. Two Horses."

"That's me, what can I do for you?"

"My uncle told me that you might be able to help me find some help for a civil action in Chicago, against Chicago P.D. He said you helped him a long time ago."

Noel Two Horses crossed his arms in front of him and asked, "I'm sorry, you are?"

Bear Child submissively responded, "I'm sorry, I'm Tim Bear Child, and my uncle is Lee Tousey." Two Horses replied with a big smile and unfolded his arms. "Well, wow! How is Lee? Please come sit down, Mr. Bear Child. What can I do for you? Can I call you Tim?"

Noel Two Horses listened to Bear Child recite his recent unfortunate history, but it was getting late in the morning. Noel had skipped break-fast and was getting hungry. He offered Tim lunch at the restaurant located at the hotel. Normally Noel would have his lunch at his better half's restaurant in town, but Rebecca's place was casual. He wanted to impress Bear Child with linen and waiters. At lunch that day, Bear Child followed Noel's lead to order from the menu. The same meal was served to both by a very polite waiter who happened to know Noel's last name. During the meal, he returned and asked, "Mr. Two Horses, I hope everything was to your satisfaction?" Noel replied in the positive and hoped Bear Child caught the Mr. Two Horses name. The men seemed to enjoy each other's company, and the meal served to them was pleasant enough, but what Noel thought Bear Child bathed in was being with Noel Two Horses. During the meal Noel came up with an idea, so he started to test the waters with Bear Child while both were in a candid mood.

"Tim, what did you like about traveling into Arizona for the first time? How did you get here, plane, car?"

"Well, I flew for the first time today."

"Did you like it?"

Bear Child thought about his response for a brief, few seconds and said, "I loved it, I wished I would have done it earlier in my life."

Two Horses giggled and said, "That is what I wanted to hear. You know, Tim, experience is great, don't get me wrong, but new adventure is what gives you that experience."

"I watched you think before you answered my question, and that told me something, also. You don't appear to be rash or impulsive. I think I'm going to share some of my sage advice with you, but I will also explain my rationale behind this."

"Tim, sometimes we make quick decisions. Your idea of suing your police department is really not suing the department; you will be suing the city who employed you. The city has insurance money you will end up with when you win, and you will win. In short, you will be suing an insurance company, a company that is under contract with the city to provide resources in the event of a legal suit. You will not be avenged, and your crap sergeant will not be touched. He will maintain, his buddies and his job will remain until he retires."

"Tim, I think you need to consider your future before you bring suit. Not your future with Chicago P.D. because as soon as you file the complaint requesting the right to sue, your future is gone with that department. Now I am not going to say' if I were you', because I am not you, and Chicago P.D. did not crap on my blanket. If it were my choice, I would settle with these various insurance companies, the mall's insurance carrier, the security company insurance carrier, the city's insurance carrier, but I would demand a letter of recommendation from my police department."

"I would stay in the criminal justice field but on my own terms, maybe here in Arizona. Hell, I have friends who could assist you in getting on a department here if you wanted it. Sleep on it tonight, and you and I can get together tomorrow to talk. I will tell you something else. If it were my choice, I would get my degree either before starting with a new department or while you are working in that new department. Today's educational system and the technology available to you is unbelievable; you could go online and get your degree in no time."

The next morning over breakfast at the Saint Gregory Hotel, Bear Child listened to Noel's instructions about gathering up his college records and his employment and training history prior to returning to Arizona. "Get a jump on the enrollment process," offered Noel. "In the meantime, I can connect you with an Arizona attorney who would gladly communicate with the various insurance companies for you. Should they refuse to communicate with your attorney, he can have a Chicago attorney take it from there."

"I can and will send you some contact information on some Arizona departments along with a few names to use, people I know personally. You may even want to get some vocational testing to see if there is another field you could excel in other than law enforcement. I would be happy to arrange that for you, too."

Bear Child returned to Chicago and seemed to enjoy the return flight with a little less anxiety than the flight into Arizona. He exited the aircraft in Chicago with an air of confidence that is usually exhibited by more experienced travelers. He had the opportunity to fly commercially in the past but never did, instead traveling by car to all his relatively close destinations. Home to the reservation for a visit, from the reservation to his college campus. From his college campus dorm room to Chicago by car for his police department training, and finally, after securing the job and finding an apartment, to his job. No exposure to TSA, although he knew what TSA was from his training and from chatter on the job.

Noel shared his thoughts and Bear Child's information with Rebecca the same evening Bear Child flew back to Chicago. She listened intently as she often did and, as Noel got further into his tale, the tempo began to slow, revealing that perhaps Noel was rethinking his actions. Before too long Noel stopped the telling of the visit from Bear Child and said, "I know I must be sounding rather narcissistic but..." Rebecca smiled before she nodded her head in agreement and tactfully saved his vanity by saying, "Mr. Two Horses, not everyone wants to follow your path to stardom, so do not be offended if this young man changes your agenda."

Noel responded by joking and yelling, "Who would pass up fame and fortune? Fast women and fast cars?" Rebecca responded with the same volume level, "Your car is pretty pokey! But your women are still fast," as she slapped him on top of his head and ran from the room with Noel in pursuit.

Rebecca was a woman who Noel admired and treated with much respect. She usually initiated their romantic interludes. He was wel-traveled but not experienced in the manly art of seduction and romance. He was still learning and not yet able to bring himself to open up entirely with her. He held back displaying his true feelings through conversa-tion. His ability to engage her in romantic conversation eluded him. He viewed himself as being in the Neanderthal mode when it came to romance with the woman he loved. As a youngster Noel was never told he was loved by anyone, and as a younger man he never sought out love. He didn't have any idea what it was like. Sex, yes but love, no.

In retrospect, Noel found that he believed Bear Child could be ded-icated to the idea of achieving a higher educational standard and maybe from that perhaps a higher standard of living. What Noel came to realize was he thought Bear Child was impressed with Noel Two Horses.

Noel had placed himself on a ladder for the young man to admire that evening. He had shared stories of himself with Bear Child, letting him in on his life. He told Bear Child he ran an investigative business from the confines of his mystery bookshop and that he also taught online college-level course work while in the shop. He took pride in his work and wanted to display this as an accomplishment to Bear Child. Well, Noel viewed it as an accomplishment and thought others did, too.

Later, Noel found out some common perceptions held by classmates and even a couple of instructors were that Bear Child was a lazy student and assumed his prior law enforcement experience was an automatic ticket to ride without having to put in the work. What probably stood out most was that Bear Child had an automatic avoidance to accepted theories of clinical psychology. That might be related to his years of policing, thought Noel. Noel remembered conversations with his fellow cops on the job who refused to accept the testimony of psychiatrists who took the witness stand and addressed the state of mind of a dangerous defendant.

Noel Two Horses was an intelligent fellow, but he never thought that soft-spoken Bear Child would ever be thought of or become one of those dangerous defendants. However, there were a few folks in The Chicago Police Department who were laying the groundwork for that very thing to happen.

CHAPTER 5

FEDERAL INVESTIGATORS WERE ABLE TO CONCLUDE THAT THE ANGER management scam worked something like this: The use of cellphones was being monitored by law enforcement agencies working in task force organizations such as FBI, DEA, Homeland Security. The only reliable means of conversing was in person which evaded eavesdropping technology, court-ordered or otherwise. The anger management group provided the three men the opportunity to converse freely during the bar drinking sessions, skillfully orchestrated by someone in that criminal enterprise and in the city of Chicago's hierarchy. One of the three men would engage Bear Child in a conversation while the others talked about their business out of Bear Child's hearing range. Later all three would convene in the men's room to discuss issues without Bear Child being there.

The one question in this case, and it was a very big question, arose because there was only one group member who was not killed or present for interviews by authorities. For a matter of fact, he was not even available. That was Tim Bear Child. Now, because of Bear Child's occupation and professional proficiency with a handgun, he was automatically positioned to the number one fat and juicy suspect category. Could he have been part of a Mexican cartel or maybe even a Ukrainian mob hit man? Hard to say, but as far as the process of elimination went, he became appropriate click-bait.

Bear Child could not be found during the standard course of the Chicago Police Department's local door-knocking campaign because this was the time when he had made his first trip to Arizona. When someone in that very same department's human resources group stumbled upon Bear Child's resignation letter, they linked former officer Tim Bear Child to the same Tim Bear Child of the anger management group. There was not much of an investigative technique involved.

It was required that the investigating Chicago police officers interview the person from human resources who secured the information. Police detective Jim O'Brady and detective Tom Leary left the smokey confines of the drab color of a city unmarked police car, a Ford Taurus four door, and proceeded into the City of Chicago Administration offices for this interview. Karen Rowhouse knew that someone from the police department would be interviewing her at some point that Tuesday, according to her supervisor. When the two officers walked into her office cubicle, she located one more chair for the detectives, and they began. Detective O"Brady seemed to be more occupied with asking her questions about his insurance coverage while Detective Leary stayed on track with questions about Bear Child.

"No," she never knew him, "no," she never met him, "no," she did not handle his employment information personally, and "No, Detective O'Brady, you cannot sell or trade your vacation hours to another city employee nor can you directly purchase additional vacation days."

Continuing, she added, "You detectives may have been given some information that may not be accurate."

Leary responded by asking her, "Is that right?"

"Yes, you see I found Mr. Bear Child's employment information on our department computer system."

"Is that right?" asked Leary again.

"Well, yes, you see I accidentally ran across a copy of his letter of resignation while researching another employee's information."

"Is that right?"

"Yes, Bear Child is an unusual name, and I remember his name popping up in another conversation here in our department."

"No. Is that right?"

"Yes, another conversation about the three men who were killed and who also were city employees."

"Just who did you discuss this with in this other conversation?" asked Leary.

"It was a conversation at lunchtime with others here in our department, and I can't recall with whom. Normally things like murders do not happen to most of our city employees."

"That right?"

"Yes, most of the time we lose employees to cancer, car accidents, and as a result of perpetrator actions, but these are normal for a department the size of ours. Let's just say three employees in this fashion is not normal. It seemed odd."

"Odd, Ms. Rowhouse?" asked Detective Leary.

"Well yes, odd, detective. Out of the ordinary. Another detective was here earlier in the week, and he thought so, too."

"Is that right?"

"Yes, I believe he was a detective, an Agent Twist?"

"I am sorry, Ms. Rowhouse, but he might have been from another unit," suggested Leary. "I am afraid sometimes we overthink our investigations and re-interview folks needlessly."

"Thank you for your time," offered Leary. "We may be in touch again later," warned O'Brady.

Neither Chicago detectives spoke again until they got back into the safe confines of the city's unmarked car. Both lit up cigarettes without opening the car windows and remained in a static position, not starting the car's engine. O'Brady was the first to speak, "What the mother of Jesus and God hell was that? Huh?"

"You know, I was similarly smitten by that," declared Leary.

"Another detective, Agent Twist? Agent? The feds are snooping around?" posed O'Brady .

O'Brady suggested, "Before we mention this upstairs, let's check out Rufus King to see if he knows who the hell this Agent Twist is."

"Yeah, spot on, if Rufus doesn't know, no one knows," stated Leary.

O'Brady just sat behind the wheel and looked at Leary for several long seconds. Before starting the unmarked car and pulling out into traffic, O'Brady advised, "Crack your window, Leary."

CHAPTER 6

RUFUS KING WAS THE OLDEST BUT MOST RELIABLE SOURCE OF STREET information in that part of Chicago. Born sometime in the late 1940's in Chicago, he had a police record just as long as his arm. Petty this and petty that. There was just enough dope dealing to have cost him a four-year term in the joint.

His primary source of information was street intel from his kids and grandchildren. Rufus King had an extended family of fifteen kids and a dozen adult grandchildren. At any given time, someone in his family was doing time in prison or incarcerated in the county jail. During the brief periods that they would be in-between court dates and free to move about, they were dealing or delivering controlled substances on the streets of Chicago or sitting in the offices of sheriff or police departments and sometimes even the offices of the FBI trying to strike up an agreement to lower charges bestowed upon them by the different law enforcement officers of those agencies.

Few people, if any, could directly link Rufus King to police snitching. But between his pot operation and his snitching fees, he netted somewhere around $45,000 per year. Rufus had safe sailing in the pot trade; police folks in Chicago would sometimes turn a blind eye to his commerce. He had very low overhead, and he kept it that way. He never supported any of his children or grandchildren financially, nor did he share the proceeds of their information sales with them. The secrets he sold were harvested by asking his kids and their kids questions like:

"Who is that, What does he have that for, Who fronted that shit to his dumb ass, or Who is he running with?"

Rufus was not afraid to charge high fees to the police he did not know or to act like he was doing a favor to the police he did know when he charged them excessive rates. Rufus would say, "The dope business will go away someday (when it was legalized), but the business of information would always be valuable to those who did not have it."

When he was visited by Det. O'Brady, Rufus was coming out of his house wearing a loud yellow and red Hawaiian shirt, a dark blue pair of slacks and Dollar General store sandals. O'Brady paid him a compliment on his attire and asked him for a few minutes of his time.

"Mr. King, you look great in that Hawaiian shirt today!" yelled O'Brady.

"Well, thank you for noticing, Detective O'Brady!"

O'Brady thought, "Helen Keller would have noticed."

"Tell me, how are you, Detective? What can this old man do for you?"

"I have a problem, Mr. King, and needed to visit with you for a few minutes. I'm glad you are at home."

O'Brady thought that if he had said "I'm glad I caught you," the old S.O.B. would have shit himself.

Rufus would have invited O'Brady to sit on the porch chairs and talk, but he didn't want anyone to realize he was snitching. Instead, the conversation took place in the middle of the street because that was where Rufus met O'Brady after rushing down the steps to cut him off.

Without saying anything more, O'Brady slowly reached into his side suitcoat pocket and removed a small square of white paper. He passed this white square to Rufus, a small notebook page folded in two. Inside was a handwritten question about Agent Twist. Also inside the folded note were three twenty- dollar bills. The written question was "Do the feds have an Agent Twist working here?"

Rufus read the note, handed the notebook paper minus the money back to O'Brady, and made several very dramatic shakes of his head from left to right to indicate "no" to O'Brady; well, actually to those in the neighborhood who may have been watching. This performance normally gave the audience the idea that Rufus King was blowing off the Detective. Later that day Rufus would call O'Brady and provide the information he requested.

The real reason O'Brady wanted to go over to Rufus King's house was because of a very light-skinned teenage-looking girl who hung out at his place. She was some shirttail relative of Rufus'. She had caught O'Brady's eye several months earlier. Since then they had texted each other several times using his burner cellphone number even though O'Brady was twenty years her senior. Just assuming she was much younger was his first mistake. His second mistake was to share obscene texts and obscene cellphone photos with a possible grandchild of Rufus King.

When O'Brady got back into the unmarked car, he told Leary that the old man would call him later. "Meanwhile, let's make sure there is no Detective Twist that we are unaware of in our department or over at the Sheriff's department, ok?" Leary raised his thumb to indicate agreement.

Leary asked, "Was that really worth $60?" Both detectives knew what Leary was hinting at, and it wasn't the Agent Twist inquiry. O'Brady responded with a middle finger of his right hand extended in the air towards Leary, as both laughed.

Since Rufus was aware of Brady's interest in the girl, in his mind O'Brady would have much more money he would have to pay down the road. Two hours later Rufus King had occasion to ask a grandson if he knew of a FBI agent named Twist. The grandson had just walked down the stairs from his sleeping spot in his Grandpa Rufus' attic with the light-skinned girl directly behind him.

"Zip up yo goddamn fly, boy," yelled Rufus. Between grumbles he said, "Somebody think y'all be trying to pee on 'em, fool." After a few more grumbling seconds he added, "Y'all sho'nuff some stupid young bloods."

The grandson walked over to the kitchen sink and began to wash his hands. While he was wiping on pieces of paper towel he had ripped off a roll, he still had his back to Rufus. He playfully winked at the girl and said, "Don't know no FBI Twist, but I do know a Homeland Security motherfucker named Twist," and smiled.

Rufus asked, "What's Homeland Security? Sounds like some Soviet shit or some'n."

"You know, Border Patrol and stuff, old man" answered the grandson. He then smiled again because he recognized that his grandfather was uninformed.

"Y'all gonna be needing Border Patrol, y'all use up all my towel, man," yelled Rufus.

When Rufus called O'Brady later in the day, all he told O'Brady was "Border Patrol." And when O'Brady enlightened Leary as to Agent Twist's identity, all he said was "Border Patrol," thus ending the connection between the FBI and the Chicago police department and widening the linkage blindage. Not being aware of the investigative powers given to Homeland Security by the U.S. Congress when it was created because of the 911 terror attack in New York only moved the federal investigation of the three shooting victims further away from Chicago P.D.'s investigation.

Rufus King would not get the chance to implement his extortion ideas against O'Brady. All of his lucrative plans literally went up in smoke when his house burnt down with him in it a few weeks after O'Brady made his $60 inquiry. The state fire marshal's office determined it was a blaze of unknown origin that engulfed the two-story family structure and caused the death of Mr. Rufus King. People in the immediate neighborhood said it was the competition in the drug trade that caused his demise. Still others (police officers) more familiar to Mr. King claimed, "Snitches get stitches."

CHAPTER 7

BEAR CHILD WAS BUSY ORGANIZING HIS MOVE TO ARIZONA. HE NEEDED to first secure a position in Prescott or attempt to live there on what would be his accumulated retirement fund from the Chicago Police Department. He checked his last printed statement, and it appeared to be somewhere in the neighborhood of sixteen thousand dollars. Not a lot, but it would hold him together when he combined school Pell Grant money that was available to him should he apply to Prescott College for admission. He was still getting his income while he was on administrative leave from the police department, so that amount was factored into his stash. However, that would stop once he submitted his letter of resignation. He knew that, should he decide to stay with the Chicago P.D., his career would be snuffed out by those who did not support him: his sergeant, his union, and whoever was teamed with him as a partner. His assignments would be crap assignments, and that was in the cards unless he decided to become a crap cop like his sergeant and others in his union.

The internet was a useful employment tool for him to scout out positions in the Prescott area, but he still found very few jobs. Bear Child thought maybe he should consider the possibility of school more seriously. He reviewed the types of programs available to him as an undergraduate but also what could be available to him as a Graduate student once he got a bachelor's degree in psychology. He spent a great amount of time researching the idea of obtaining a master's degree in clinical psychology and becoming certified in Equine Assisted Therapy at the same college. Equine therapy was an approach that used horses to enhance the therapy experience for clients needing approaches which were an alternative to talk therapy in an office. Understanding how horses deal with their surroundings and comparing those actions with the patient in an anecdotal way or metaphorically helped the patient process his understanding of his own behavior. Equine assisted therapy was also used by medical doctors who worked with patients with serious physical injuries as well. Riding assisted patients to regain balance and strength. The community where Bear Child grew up had horses. He liked to be around them whenever he could. His horsemanship was one of his strong attributes, and he loved the relationship he had with horses.

Bear Child thought that maybe this would be a cool way to go. His trips to the psychiatrist in Chicago probably fed into this decision. He did get something positive from his therapy sessions at times, and it was not uncommon for those in therapy to relate to the therapist the way young trauma patients who have been burned or are seriously ill relate to their doctor and/or caregivers. They idealized them; they sometimes experienced an urge to mimic them or even follow them into the medical field. His understanding of the field of psychology was limited, but that is what the program was for. It would provide him with a better grasp of psychology, and the idea of providing therapy to those in need of help appealed to him.

The next objective would have to be housing. Unlike his other shot at college, he did not want to live in a dorm, this time with a bunch of younger undergraduates. He would find a mobile home for rent or buy a camper trailer while he was still employed and had a credit rating. That is exactly what he did and soon found shopping for his home to be fun. He located a space for rent that offered electric, water hook ups, and camper toilet disposal. There was WIFI and parking included in his lot rent, so that was not a bad deal.

It was just a matter of a few days, and his letter of acceptance from the school in Prescott was in his mailbox in Chicago. When he read the letter, he really felt good. He found out that he could obtain nineteen academic credits for his life experiences. There had been so many months of feeling depressed and angry, but now in his mind he was beginning to see light at the end of the dark Chicago tunnel. His goal of becoming an equine-assisted therapist could happen faster than he thought. The same day that Bear Child got his letter of acceptance he shopped around for an RV dealer and struck up a good deal on a used camper trailer. The dealer even offered to take his car in trade for an older pickup truck that would safely tow the camper cross-country. His credit score was strong enough, so he went for both the camper and the truck and had the dealership take care of the purchase with a lending institution out of state.

His decision process was quick and decisive, and that may have been because the idea was a viable option. He had been locked into a very bad situation for such a long period of time. The educational path would bring him rewards that would outweigh the work, stress and risk normally associated with a lifestyle change. The academic path seemed to excite him more so now than before. It may have had something to do with him being more mature. When he was younger, he had no idea how bitter his life could become and how quickly he could learn to hate. Bear Child realized he would need to contact Noel Two Horses and consult with him to find out not only how to proceed with his educational plans but also how to properly initiate his assault on the Chicago Police Department. He would need logistical help, investigative services, and legal assistance in Chicago.

Bear Child was pleased with his decision but wanted to scout out the physical aspects of his new home before moving out there. There wasn't any buyer's remorse going on, but he wanted more of what he had recently discovered. Fun, spare time, and traveling by air was entertaining and exciting. He wanted to have lunch with Noel Two Horses again. Later that day Bear Child placed a call to Noel, and the two of them agreed to meet whenever Bear Child could get there. Searching the airline and discount airfare websites was interesting, but Tim Bear Child was not in the mood for saving four or five bucks by using a popular but confusing website. After booking his flight, he found himself becoming more tense which reminded him of his old self, his Chicago self. He wanted to stay positive and to do so, he might be required to stay busy, so he continued to pack his things and plan out his trip back to Arizona.

During his first trip he had rented a car in Arizona. That went well, so he wanted to repeat that by renting at the same place, same agency, same rental terms. Later he could vary his travel plans by driving from Chicago across the great plains and Rocky Mountain routes. There was so much of this country that he had not seen. He witnessed a lot from his two flights but not yet at ground level from a pickup truck windshield.

He intended to bring his laptop on this trip in case he wanted to research some of the local websites like his school. Or maybe the websites of a few behavioral health agencies that might need part-time help, although he had his doubts they would be hiring. He wanted to take time and get to learn a few things about the Prescott area. He sure didn't want to have to settle for something like he did when he joined the police department and had to live in Chicago. He knew he had to put in a change of address and notify his landlord he was leaving. This he remembered from meeting his landlord when he first moved in. His landlord told him he did not want to forward mail if he moved out. As a temporary idea, he thought he would use his parents' address on the reservation and ask them to screen and forward his mail until he got settled in Arizona. This was not a big deal because he could do this on-line. He knew things would come up that he couldn't think of now or remember, but he would cross that bridge when he got there. What Tim Bear Child did not know was that there would be some serious bridges to cross in Arizona.

CHAPTER 8

Sunday, November 15, 2020
Arizona Daily Star
By Curt Prendergast

Feds: Drug-money scheme funneled more than $10M through Arizona bank

A money laundering scheme funneled more than $10 million in drug proceeds through a bank in Arizona, prosecutors say. The flood of money began with drug sales in at least 15 states and ended up in bank accounts in Mexico, according to documents filed in U.S. District Court in Tucson. Prosecutors say the scheme was made possible by a corrupt bank manager in Rio Rico and at least 18 people recruited to open 89 fraudulent bank accounts.

Enrique Monarque Orozco pleaded guilty to helping orchestrate the scheme from January 2017 to April 2019, including by sitting next to the owners of the fraudulent bank accounts as they opened the accounts, handing them the cash to deposit, and telling them where to wire the money according to court documents filed November 2, 2020. Nearly all of those deposits to these "funneled accounts" were less than $10,000, the threshold for alerting federal regulators according to court documents. Prosecutors say the conspiracy was aided by Carlos Vasquez, who was the manager of the Wells Fargo branch in Rio Rico while the alleged money laundering occurred. Vasquez was indicted in September in September 2019 and pleaded not guilty to federal bank fraud charges.

FBI AGENTS AND AGENTS FROM DEA WERE MEETING WITH AGENTS from the Department of Homeland Security in downtown Chicago at the Federal Court House office location the same day that Bear Child landed again in Arizona. The purpose behind the meeting was two-fold; the first item was the exchange of information on the recent murder of three persons in Chicago who appeared to be important within the Mexican cartel system, and the second item on the agenda was the idea of offering Timothy Bear Child a spot in the Witness Protection Program. Should he be found sometime in the near future, Bear Child might be in a position to offer testimony in an ongoing Grand Jury investigation pertaining to the three recently departed cartel honchos and the cartel itself. Nobody but Bear Child would know what the three talked about during the various get-togethers of the therapy group, and that information could be a golden harvest.

While the federal agents were meeting, Chicago Police Detectives O'Brady and Leary were asking around the vicinity of the Chicago station house out of which Bear Child had worked if anyone had heard from Bear Child or if they had seen him. Once it became clear that the flavor of the day was "No," the two now had to visit the District Attorney's office for some advice on making a decision whether to file three charges of murder or just one charge of flight to avoid prosecution on Bear Child. If they got the green flag from the D.A., they could make a run on the department brass at their shop to go for it.

O'Brady said, "It appears to be a rather unknown case, you know a quiet case, but it has the makings of a real career-making case," as he drove the unmarked car to the County Court house to meet with the District Attorney.

"Think about it, Leary, three guys killed by the same guy."

"Serial killer arrested by Chicago's finest," mocked Leary in his attempt at a newspaper headline declaration.

"Hey, think about this, just suppose there are more bodies?" posed O'Brady.

"No shit, there are? Where?" asked Leary.

"No, no, no, just suppose." said O'Brady, excited now by the smell of fame.

After both had a few seconds to think about this possibility, O'Brady had the idea to maybe wait before they hit up the D.A.

"Maybe we should cross-check our data and see if we can't link another body or two to our friend and co-worker, Officer Bear Child. I mean, why go ahead with a charge and have some other copper grab another victim unknown to us as of now and take the collar? You know, down the road. I mean, why share the department awards and possible promotion with some guy or team?" O'Brady went on, "Why stop now, if you catch where I'm going here?"

Leary asked, "You mean, hook up another open shooting to Bear Child?"

"Hell yeah, not any victim, but one that fits his M.O. Approximate the same time as the discovery of the body, ya da, ya da, ya da, you know, 9 mm, victim age about the same etc., etc."

"We could wash him out later before someone gets wind of it. But it would ultimately be up to our Pusshead Indian Bear Child to prove he didn't kill him, too. What do you think?" asked O'Brady.

Leary answered immediately, "Without hesitation, endeavor to persevere."

O"Brady just laughed and Leary joined in saying "Pusshead Indian" as they made a u- turn in heavy traffic.

Leary and O'Brady set out to find another victim that week, not by literally searching in and under the bushes for a corpse, but via the department's computer system. They were able to find two unrelated deaths, both by gunshot, both about the same time period, and both older males. One of the dead males was apparently shot with a large-bore weapon while the other may have been shot with a .38 or a 9 mm.

Leary said, "Tailor made." "Let's visit the Evidence Room, shall we," asked O'Brady as he pushed away from his computer terminal.

"Well played," said Leary as he pushed away from the same desk after looking at what was discovered on the department's computer program.

That afternoon, Det. O'Brady removed one of the three spent 9mm shell casings found at the scene of the drainage ditch murder victim that was attributed to Bear Child and placed it in the evidence package of the victim they had discovered on the software earlier that day. "A simple case of not noting the discovery of the shell casing at the scene in the police report," remarked O'Brady as the two retreated from the evidence room.

"You know, the brass will want to sit on this case awhile because our serial killer is a cop." O'Brady was thinking out loud now, "Suppose we drop our search for the time being and focus on the terrible discovery we made? The brass would appreciate a little more time to polish up our image with the press, don't you think?"

Leary asked, "When should we hit them with it?"

O'Brady decided, "Right now!"

"Wait, wait, wait" Leary pleaded. "If one will work, why wouldn't one more work, too?"

"Are you nuts? Add two more to our body count? What the hell for? No, just one and only one," reasoned O'Brady.

"It was you who said, and I quote, 'Why stop now, if you catch my drift.' Remember that? 'Why let some other copper grab another victim unknown to us as of now and take the collar?' Remember using the vernacular of possible promotions?" cited Leary.

O'Brady gave in saying, "Okay, okay we'll do some more research on possible candidates. But that's it, ok, just research."

After a few seconds Leary spoke up and said, "I didn't mean exceed that of the Saint Valentine's Day massacre."

He paused a few seconds and then continued, "That was inexcusable," pausing again and then saying, "Over the top as it were. No, we will keep it within certain reasonable parameters."

Later he added, "We will harvest only the best candidate or candidates, and at that junction, we will then come together and discuss proceeding with or terminating our quest like any criminal justice professional."

What the two did not realize was that the police administration was going to fast-track the investigation of the three homicide victims in an attempt to apprehend Timothy Bear Child before any more victims were discovered. The brass did not want to leave the residents of the city of Chicago with the impression that a rogue police officer was a serial killer and still roaming the streets of Chicago.

"From here on out the details of the three victims will be sanitized as much as possible while the police identity of Bear Child will be downplayed," decreed the Police Chief. "The only way to do this would be to not investigate the murders but rather focus on the apprehension of Bear Child," explained the Police Public Relations Liaison. "The employment of Bear Child has to be handled in terms of him being an *ex*-cop. Even though he is not on the payroll and not a sworn officer, the public will view him as a cop," responded the Chief of the Detective Service Bureau.

CHAPTER 9

NOEL TWO HORSES WAS BUSY STOCKING HIS MYSTERY BOOKSHOP counter with the current best seller paperback, something titled "Death Smells." When he looked through the shop window, he saw Tim Bear Child crossing the street to get to him. Noel was pleased to see him and welcomed him into the shop. There were no customers at the time, so they were able to have a good conversation.

"Tell me what brings you back to Arizona today. Did you decide to look into going back to school?" asked Noel.

"No," answered Bear Child, as he watched Noel's happy face slump into an expression of concern. "I'm not looking into it, I'm doing it, Noel."

"Oh man! That's great, you will not regret it," exclaimed Noel. "Can I be of any help to you?"

"If you don't mind, I can use all the help I can get," admitted Bear Child.

Pressing on in a more serious tone, Bear Child added, "I also need to hit you up for some professional help in my legal actions against the City of Chicago. I know this type of work can be expensive, but I am ready to pay you for your time and expertise."

"Well, I certainly appreciate your vote of confidence and will do my best to assist you," said Noel.

"I have a retainer form I normally have my clients review, and if they approve of the terms, I will ask them to sign it. We can go into that later, but let me suggest something to you," offered Noel as he waited to see Bear Child's response.

"Your case is unusual, yet it really isn't that much different than what we have been dealing with for years and years. Many years ago, I had the good luck to meet several Bureau of Indian Affairs tribal police officers at a Dept. of Interior BIA police academy in Arizona, when I was working for a CIA contractor. It was called Evergreen Air, but it used to be known as Air America, and it was located at the Evergreen Air Center in Marana. The BIA police academy was there, and so was a State Dept. Diplomatic Service School, sort of an academy for Secret Service-type training used by the Dept. of State to protect embassy folks, American ambassadors, and visiting dignitaries. Among other things, they taught evasive driving for the limo drivers and other agents. They had the running boards attached to the limos, and the instructor would teach how to use the security detail as a shield to protect the diplomat or dignitary."

"There was also an Armed Forces Special Operations Jump School there as well. Sometimes you would hear a rustling-type noise overhead, and when you looked up, there would be maybe a half dozen or so Navy Seals raining down on you with parachutes hovering all over the place."

"What these tribal police cadets were used for after graduation were as uniformed police officers on various reservations. Not normally their own reservation because of the concern about conflict of interest when so many people were related, but for other tribes. Sometimes they were abused by the tribal members where they were assigned. Hell, it goes as far back as Sitting Bull. His death was the direct result of orders from tribal police and Indian Agency officials; it was a tribal police officer who shot and killed him. Native American police have often been used in political or criminal arenas and would often be the scapegoats or pawns. The Department of Interior has broad authority in Indian Country including managing federal relations with tribes, making decisions on federal recognition of tribes, administrating mineral rights on tribal land, educating some Native Americans, and providing police forces. They also run national parks, provide oversight of wildlife and endangered species, and they approve drilling oil and gas and mining. What I am saying is that where there is money, there is corruption, and throwing cops under the bus is normal. Let me get into the situation with this police sergeant and the mall security people. It sounds like the department knew of or had a history of this cop impersonation going on there."

"They did. The sources available to me at the time indicated a long record of complaints from people who saw them use the cop crap on them," said Bear Child, as he felt himself suddenly getting worked up over it again. "I couldn't get verification in documentation form, but someone higher up must know of it happening, maybe even at the station-house level."

Noel said, "Let me look into it, I also have friends at the higher-up level. Now are you officially no longer with the police department back there?"

"No, still on the books but that was another thing I wanted your advice on. I've never resigned from any department, much less one I wanted to sue in court. Should I retain an attorney to do that for me, you know, officially?" Bear Child asked.

"No, you don't have to be a Justice Ginsburg to draft a letter of res-ignation, but you should have an attorney to assist you after you resign," instructed Noel. "A good attorney will notify the city that you are asking for the right to sue because of what the police department did with hid-ing the complaints about the mall security and what you went through during your suspension. Legally it's called a claim, you are filing a claim. Your attorney will explain everything to you. I can suggest one or two attorneys there who would love to handle your claim," offered Noel.

"Why don't you bring me up to speed on your college surprise, and we will go from there. Have you a school or major in mind? Criminal Justice degree, I assume?"

"No, actually I was considering the clinical psychology route. Equine-assisted therapy sounds pretty damn interesting. I love being with and working with horses."

Noel said, "I do, too." Bear Child went on to explain, "I know I will never make another Noel Two Horses, you know, successfully transition from law enforcement to the private sector of criminal investigation work."

Noel explained to Bear Child that transition is a big part of maturing. It's a continuing education for young reservation guys just like transition from the reservation to college and eventually to the Chicago P.D. was for him. "You know, you might want to consider working for me and my partner, Claire Blue Crow, from time to time while you are in school. Your experience could come in handy, and we pay good money for experience."

What Noel had in mind was placing Bear Child into an undercover position as a long-haul trucker. As he explained it to Bear Child, he had been retained by members of two Southwestern tribes to help investigate missing women from their reservations. Noel had the idea to use a long-haul trucker to search for these missing tribal members.

Noel began by telling Bear Child, "If you think about it, long-haul truckers have the profile for the perfect sex offender or kidnapper. They may not have a criminal record, or they may use an alias. Normally, there are no criminal record checks. The only requirement for most is a valid CDL (commercial driver's license). In theory, a sex offender can get a CDL and move throughout the entire United States of America although he is required to register with the sheriff in the county that he resides in. Yet that would not stop him from driving state to state. The only restriction would be if he is on parole or probation and has mandatory weekly or bi-weekly meetings with his agent."

Bear Child interrupted Noel and said, "Yeah, I am familiar with the Missing and Murdered Indigenous Women network (MMIW). For many years now, women and young girls have been missing from reservations in Canada and the United States. Tribes have been very judgmental about it because of the minimal progress in solving the apparent abductions; there appears to be a lack of interest from law enforcement officials."

Noel added, "Well, the truth is that the approach taken by the police has been disconnected, unlike the comprehensive and cooperative approach used by investigators involved in white communities where the various departments talk to each other, compare notes, and share information."

Bear Child said, "There are thousands of missing women, that is scary."

"Do you know what is really scary?" Noel asked. "What is really scary is that the people who we rely on to search are some of the same who are two to four times more likely to abuse their own partners, male cops who physically abuse their wives."

Noel said, "When missing person complaints are filed, sometimes days go by before action is taken. Is that because most departments are primarily male officers? I know a lot of the physical descriptions are wrong, many are filed as white or Latino women."

Bear Child told Noel, "Montana claimed to have an epidemic of missing Indian women according to an article I read."

Noel advised, "Arizona has twenty-two federally recognized tribes, and the Los Angeles Times said it is the epicenter of these kidnappings. My clients are several members of these tribes."

"I could look into getting a CDL or maybe go to a truck driving school. Those schools are short and wouldn't take up a whole semester," offered Bear Child.

"Great, we'll cover the cost for the truck driving course and an hourly wage while you are doing it," pledged Noel. "From what I have researched, they are four, maybe five-week courses. Your Arizona Private Investigator License will be easy enough for you to get."

Bear Child was excited and offered another approach. "Instead of wasting time and money on obtaining a CDL, why not randomly frequent the spots where truckers congregate? You know, truck stops have a lot of female hooker action."

Noel said, "Well, that is why I came up with the truck and trailer idea, but you're right, it wouldn't require a truck and trailer."

Bear Child told Noel that a guy with a laptop could hack the WIFI at truck stops for activity. "I mean, I'm just thinking out loud. " Noel asked Bear Child, "How would you do that? I have never heard of that."

Bear Child explained to Noel, "There are some law enforcement and government agencies that have a small unit that can impersonate a cellphone tower. How can I explain this? Ok, it picks up cellphone conversations and allows the agency officers to listen in is the easiest way to describe it. I have one."

Noel didn't say anything at first but just stood there smiling at Bear Child. When he did come back to Mother Earth, Noel said, "That would not be admissible in court, but it's so cool."

For the rest of the afternoon Tim Bear Child and Noel Two Horses discussed Bear Child's educational plans and his ideas for moving and living in the Prescott area. Noel wanted to invite Bear Child to dinner that evening and to meet Rebecca, the woman who took over his life in Prescott. But it was already early afternoon and to drop a dinner guest on Rebecca this late in the day without warning was a no-no. So instead, Noel told Bear Child he would meet with him in the morning.

CHAPTER 10

October 26, 2019
The Arizona Daily Star
By the Associated Press
Volunteers discover 13 remains hidden in desert
close to resort town Puerto Penasco, in Mexico

TWELVE SKELETONS AND ONE DECOMPOSED BODY WERE FOUND BURIED in a shallow pit in the desert near the Mexican resort town of Puerto Penasco by volunteer workers. Two of the bodies may be women, prosecutors in the northern border state of Sonora said late Thursday.

Tests are being conducted to determine the gender and identity of the bodies. Only one of the bodies was relatively recent; the others were "complete skeletons with clothing," prosecutors said. The bodies were found by a group of women known as the Searchers of Puerto Penasco. The group is made up of relatives of missing people who investigate reports of clandestine burial sites. Because of deficient police investigations, such volunteer groups have been responsible for discovering mass graves and burial pits in many parts of Mexico.

Drug and kidnapping gangs use such pits to dispose of the bodies of victims or rivals.

Puerto Penasco is also known as Rocky Point. It is located on the Gulf of California, also known as the Sea of Cortez. It's about a four-hour drive from Tucson and is popular with tourists. While not as violent as some other parts of Mexico, Puerto Penasco has been known for Sinaloa drug cartel activities and a large-scale shootout between rival cartel gunmen and military forces that occurred there in 2013.

Six weeks later with the investigation of the three murders in Chicago going cold, the intense act of trying to apprehend Officer Timothy Bear Child went into hyper-drive. Detective O'Brady came up with the idea to check with the U.S. Postal Service to see if Bear Child may have filed a change of address with them. The post office complied with the request and furnished his mother and father's home address on their tribal reservation located in upper Wisconsin.

One afternoon the two Chicago P.D. detectives drove to Wisconsin to interview the parents. Upon arriving at the reservation, they detectives drove around for another hour and a half before they got accurate information as to the location of the home. That happened when Leary instinctively ran the plates on a car parked in the drive of a random home. It came back to a person named Lee Tousey. Leary said, "That name sounds like it might be an older man."

"Yeah, from a 1950's black and white TV show," laughed O"Brady.

"Naturally, all this running around gives any perp enough time to flee the home of his parents, not to mention I now have to pee," observed and complained Det. Leary.

"Relax, he is not going to be hiding in a broom closet here like in the city," cautioned O'Brady. "We have the upper hand up here. Just remember one thing, Leary, we don't have any review boards up here. They lie to us up here, we smack the shit out of' em. You afraid of a couple old-ass injuns?" boasted O'Brady. "They ain't going to file any complaints up here."

Ten minutes later both detectives were back in their car, heading away from the reservation and traveling back to Chicago while interrupting each other in mid-sentence. "Did you see the frigg'n muscles on that son of a bitch," asked an excited Leary. "That guy has got to have muscles in his shit, man."

"That dude was huge!" yelled O'Brady.

Leary said, "Matter of fact, I was really hoping you weren't going to become assertive with him like you did."

O'Brady quickly replied, "Slip of the tongue, it was a slip of the tongue! I start many of my sentences off with calling a guy 'chief,' ok. Human nature with this job."

"I'm glad you didn't try to use that on him! He would have broken our necks instead of both our pens," Leary said. "When he poked us in the chest, you know when he poked us in the chest?" "Yeah, yeah" answered O'Brady.

"Well, my frigg'n chest still hurts, he might have broken a bone in there," moaned Leary.

O'Brady declared, "Nothing of this to nobody, understand?"

"Ya got no argument there," agreed Leary.

O'Brady said, "Hang on, I have an idea. I'm going to call the brass and tell them we struck out and ask them to check with the federal bank examiners to see if he moved any of his money out of state."

"Good play," commented Leary thoughtfully, "Good play."

The detectives got back to Chicago in the early morning hours of the following day only to find out that they would not be returning to their home for a meal and hot shower like they had planned. Instead, they were summoned to a meeting with the Chicago Police Department Detective Bureau brass. During the meeting it was established that the department had already connected with the federal authorities. It was disclosed that over twenty thousand dollars had been moved to a new Arizona account for Bear Child and to still another Arizona account in his name only days later. In any normal investigation this information might have had some relative value, but in this particular situation it only offered a possible location for Bear Child. What it did not disclose, however, was that the funds were his retirement account funds that he was requesting from the same department that was investigating him. The funds were transferred from one Arizona bank to another for Bear Child to be eligible for a low-interest credit card from the second bank.

Immediately both detectives wanted to travel to Arizona to charge and apprehend him. The bureau brass flat-out told them, "No, not at this time, not the two of you together, anyway. We still need one of you continue to investigate the shootings here in Chicago, while one of you goes to Prescott, Arizona, to speak with authorities there about our guy, maybe even talk with Bear Child himself."

The Chief of Detectives assigned the job to O"Brady. "Jim, pack your bags and give me a call after you run this past the Prescott shop out there. Let them know we are in a pretty good position to wrap him up for flight to avoid prosecution. And listen, I don't want to hear that you are sunning yourself in an Arizona pool while he is enroute to the Mexican border. It's only a half hour out of Tucson."

No time was wasted getting to Arizona. O'Brady landed in Phoenix Sky Harbor Airport and rented an economy car to get to Prescott. He knew there was a ban on smoking in the rental car, but that didn't apply to him. He booked himself into one of Prescott's cheaper chain motels. He didn't want to leave his new passport in the room in case some illegal wanted to steal it while they made up his bed, so he placed it inside the Bible he found in the nightstand drawer. The reason he even had a passport was because he and his wife had gotten them before they took a three-day, two-night cruise to the Bahamas the previous year.

He was ready to meet the night and immediately hit the Yavapai Apache tribal casino as advertised in his motel room's directory. Chicago's finest drank his fill of happy hour bar rail drinks until he couldn't navigate correctly to the men's room. After almost wetting the tips of his shoes, he returned and left his bartender one dollar in coins on the rail as a handsome tip. He waltzed over to an empty booth and started to read the happy-hour menu that was standing upright on his table. A young waitress addressed him, but before asking for his order she asked him, "Are you a lucky winner tonight?"

Blurry-eyed he replied, "Naw, I never play Indian casinos. I do Vegas. What's your name?" Wanting to say 'Hiawatha,' he drunkenly said, "Highyawater?"

The young waitress dismissed him immediately and said, "We have a special today, our filet of prime rib for only fourteen dollars with your player club card, and that includes the salad bar."

O'Brady replied, "Yeah, skip the salad bar but bring me another whiskey on the rocks, in a tub this time." After the drink and his food,

O'Brady wanted to argue over the cost of his meal because he wasn't a player's club member. Finally, the gaming manager let him know his meal was on the house, but he was no longer welcome in the bar or the casino. As he walked to his car, he was trying to light a cigarette in the strong night wind on top of the hill where the casino was located. The gaming manager had the foresight of calling the Prescott police dispatcher to report him as a possible drunk driver, but he hadn't copied down the plate number on his rental car. Somehow O'Brady made it safely to his motel and into his bed, luck of the Irish.

The next day O'Brady made it over to the Prescott Police Department despite a huge hangover. Upon arrival, he identified himself to the front desk person and asked to speak to the police chief "about a very urgent matter." It was only several minutes later when the desk person buzzed open the wood and steel safety door that separated the public from the police administration and interview rooms. O'Brady was introduced to Sgt. Henry, the shift commander who immediately apologized on behalf of the police chief who was away on 'department business.' At least that is what the NFL game in Glendale, Arizona, would be called this particular day at the police department. Sgt. Henry was a young-looking 40-something police sergeant with short dark hair and graying temples. He had a bit of a beer gut but looked like he could still take guys half his age if push came to shove.

O'Brady said, "No, no, it is me who should apologize, this being a Sunday and all. I mean, the chief would not normally be here anyway, right?" he asked.

Sgt. Henry said, "We have a small staff on weekends, but what can we do for you detective, I'm sorry, I didn't catch your name?"

"O'Brady, Det. Jim O'Brady."

"Ok, Det. O'Brady, how can I be of help to you?"

"You have a serial murderer here," explained O'Brady matter of factly.

"Yeah," laughed Sgt. Henry, "Capt. Crunch, right?"

"No, no wait, let me start over," asked O'Brady.

"You bet, first let me see some identification, ok," demanded Henry.

After O'Brady complied, Henry said, "Sorry, go ahead, I'm all ears."

"We have reason to believe that there is a serial murderer who may be in Prescott. He has already shot and killed three people in Chicago, and we think he has moved here to Prescott," explained O'Brady.

"Where here? Where does he live in Prescott? Do I need to alert our county SWAT team?" inquired Henry very calmly.

"No, not right now, but I want to locate and interview him. Maybe a backup would be all we need," proposed O'Brady.

"Ok, have you got a possible address? We could sit on him first and see what we need. You ok with that?" asked Henry.

After looking at the new address for Bear Child, Sgt. Henry said, "Ok, you have a small trailer park here. Long-term renters and occasional travel trailer bachelors and old maids. Pretty easy to surveil on a good day."

"Sergeant, can you show it to me, and I'll fill you in on our way over there?" asked O'Brady.

"Sure, sure" was the response. "But let me get hold of my first-shift patrol guys and brief them first, ok?"

"Sure, sure" echoed O'Brady .

"We can use the squad room since there are only two guys on today," said Henry.

"Wait, I can't wait to brief your guys in person, that will take too long. He might flee again," O'Brady said in a loud voice. "I was going to brief you on the way over."

"No, you'll brief all three of us together before we go over, alright?" demanded Henry.

"Sure! Why not," said O'Brady as he folded into compliance.

When the other two officers arrived, Henry put O'Brady through the introductions, and O'Brady began the tale of Timothy Bear Child. A half hour went by before one of the officers interrupted and said, "You have a possible witness, not a serial murderer at this point." The other patrol officer chimed in, "And I go to school with him."

A stunned O'Brady said, "Look, Officer, Officer, I'm sorry, what did you say your name is?"

"Randal, Officer Randal" replied the officer.

"Look Officer Randal, I don't give a damn if you're dating him." O'Brady groaned, "He may be a serial killer, everything points to that! I will bet you a hundred bucks he is our guy."

One hour later it was decided that Randal would approach Bear Child's travel trailer while the other three eyeballed him from another car. If Bear Child was in the travel trailer and invited Randal in, the others would drive into the trailer park to be closer and able to hear any disturbance or gun shots in the travel trailer should either occur.

Randal knocked on the door for several minutes before going to the park manager, only to find out that Bear Child was gone and not expected back for several days, perhaps a week.

It was decided that the two patrol officers would go back to work while the sergeant drove O'Brady back to his car where they would plan the next move. Arriving back at the police department, Henry parked next to O'Brady's rental car and said, "I feel bad about this, but it looks like maybe we will have to reschedule. In the meantime, we'll sit on his place periodically until we see signs of life."

"Great, just my luck" said O'Brady . "I will contact the brass and let them know what is up, but thanks for your help, Sgt. ah?"

Sgt. Henry said, "The last name is Henry," leaving the door open for O'Brady to respond, but when he didn't, the Sgt. continued by saying "Look, don't worry, we will be keeping our eyes open for him. You have a safe trip back to Chicago, O'Brady."

The rest of the day went by fast after O'Brady called Chicago only to find out his supervisor was watching some NFL game in Glendale, Arizona. He left a message for him saying he had to change his flight, so he would be at the mercy of the airlines before he could return to Chicago because he had to fly out of Tucson now. He'd file a report as soon as he returned.

He remembered what the Detective Bureau Chief said, "...the Mexican border is only a half hour out of Tucson." O'Brady had decided to study a map of Arizona when he first found out he would be going there. His plan included leaving his smoky rental car in a parking area at the U.S. Mexican border in Nogales, Arizona, and walking across the border into Nogales, Mexico, like some Americans did when they went there for dental work because it was so much cheaper.

O'Brady could not help but think, "All work and no play can make you a pretty dull dude."

CHAPTER 11

The Arizona Daily Star
June 12, 2019
The Associated Press

9 shot dead in 2 gun battles in Sonora

MEXICO CITY- MEXICAN AUTHORITIES SAY NINE PEOPLE WERE KILLED and a child wounded in two gun battles in the northern border state of Sonora. State prosecutors say in a statement Tuesday that the first firefight took place the previous afternoon in Agua Prieta, which lies across the border from Douglas, Arizona. Four men and a woman were found dead in two cars and lying on a street. Some were clad in tactical vests and assault rifles were recovered at the scene.

About two hours later, more gunfire erupted on a highway in nearby Naco. Four men were found shot dead in a car with Arizona license plates. A 12-year-old was wounded by a stray bullet, but his life was not in danger. Police were investigating whether the incidents were linked.

———

The two Prescott police officers were talking with Sgt. Henry at the end of their shift when Officer Randal said, "You know, I appreciate the situation Chicago may have going, but this Det. O'Brady is either ill-informed, or crazy. He wants Tim Bear Child for being a serial killer? Seriously?"

Sgt. Henry said, "Listen, Randal, we can keep an open mind and our eyes open here for a couple of days. That's how long it would take them to send another investigator out to us."

"Well, am I wrong?" asked Randal.

"No, you're not wrong, maybe we should think in terms of person of interest," cautioned Henry, "until we hear from Chicago, anyway. I'll let our chief in on it."

"I talk with Bear Child. He's an ok guy, and something like this could ruin him if he ever applied at another department. How about crapping on a guy's Lunchables while you're at it?"

"Fill me in on this Bear Child," instructed Henry. "What is he doing at the school? You said he is a student, well ok, what is he studying and what is his deal socially? Does he come across as a big time, big-city cop or is he quiet, maybe too quiet?"

"No, He's a normal guy. We're in the same Humanities class. He's shooting for a Psychology bachelors, and I need some Humanities credits for my Criminal Justice bachelors. Huh, I don't know, he wants to work with horses doing therapy, you know, Equine Therapy. I don't know, he's not a loner if that's what you're asking, he jokes around, you know, cop stories, cop jokes," replied Randal.

Henry asked Randal, "So you wouldn't take him home for dinner and introduce him to your wife as a serial killer?"

With a slight grin Randal said, "Depends on what we're having for dinner."

At the end of that week Bear Child had returned to his trailer from his undercover work at a truck stop site in Winslow, Arizona. Using a cellphone tower impersonator, he had been attempting to get a WIFI hack going to pick up any text messaging in the truck parking area, but he was unsuccessful. He saw more solicitation for sex than any important hacking activity. Girls and women of all ages entered the cabs of tractor trailer rigs for the purpose of prostitution. It appeared to follow a pattern of talking with the drivers either outside of their truck cabs or through rolled-down cab windows, and then getting in. The only thing that was surprising was that the women appeared to fit the physical description of Native American or Latino women.

Bear Child thought that if this Winslow crew were the same crew of prostitutes soliciting the truck drivers state-wide, perhaps the physical appearances could be explained. Maybe it was a Native pimp and Native prostitutes? Not one of the women appeared to have been forced in the truck cabs while he watched.

Bear Child thought about suggesting to Noel that maybe using a telephoto lens or even a drone to take individual photos of the women at truck stops in Arizona but possibly also in different states, then showing the photos to relatives, might help in finding some missing women.

Right now, though, Bear Child was tired from his investigation work and wanted to air out his trailer and take a shower. His classes would pick up again the next day, and he was anxious to get back into the classroom. He had picked up his mail on his way into the trailer park and wanted to read the one letter that he received in his absence. The return address on the letter indicated that it was from his lawyer in Phoenix, Arizona. The letter informed him that the insurance company that carried the liability policy for the mall in Chicago where Bear Child was detained and attacked by security guards who represented themselves as "police" did, in fact, want to offer him a monetary settlement quite a bit in excess of their initial offering of $60,000.

The proposed settlement was generous, but his attorney felt that still more would be made available, and perhaps a larger amount should be demanded by Bear Child. His letter was a victory of sorts, but Bear Child knew it was not satisfying enough to him to just get money from the mall's insurance policy. He wanted to hear from the Chicago Police Department about his demand for a letter of recommendation. That would be a vindication from them about his career, and a validation of his honor and service for him personally.

While he waited to hear from the Chicago Police Department, the Chicago Police waited to hear from Det. O'Brady.

At the same time that Bear Child was reading his letter from his attorney, Prescott Police Department Sgt. Henry was in his police chief's office listening to the Chicago Police Detective Bureau Chief's conversation.

"We have not placed any inquiry with the Mexican authorities as of yet, but when the rental car agency contacted us about the recovery of their car on the border in Nogales, Arizona, driven by two Mexican National juveniles, we contacted your state's Department of Public Safety. We have not heard from the Tucson Police Dept. or Pima County or Santa Cruz County Sheriff's Department yet. It has been 72 hours since we have heard from our detective. He went looking for a missing witness or possible person of interest in a serial murder case, and now he is missing. Our next step might be the FBI. Have you guys brought in Bear Child?" asked the Chicago Bureau Chief.

"He was out of town but should be back later today," said Sgt. Henry. "If he shows, we will have him," said the police chief. "We are on it," echoed Henry.

When the call ended, Sgt. Henry and Officer Randal drove over to the trailer park just to do a drive-by quickie check. Bear Child had his truck in the allocated parking space next to his travel trailer. Randal said, "Aw, the hell with it, just pull up and I'll rap on his door like we planned before, ok?" Sgt. Henry pulled the squad car in close. In the event Bear Child wanted to make a run for his truck, he would see he was boxed in. Randal got out of the squad and walked over to the trailer's door. Bear Child opened the door on Randal's second rap and greeted Randal with, "Hey, what's up? How's it going?"

"Nothing, going good, man," Randal told Bear Child. "We got a little problem and needed to speak with you. Ya got a few?"

"I always have a few for one of Prescott's finest first responders and straight A students," replied Bear Child. "You wanna talk inside or in your car?"

"It is kind of important, so you may have to come on in with us, ok," said Randal.

"Wait, it isn't my folks, is it?" questioned Bear Child.

"It's all good, it's about a visit from a Chicago Police Detective O'Brady."

"O'Brady doesn't ring a bell, can you fill me in a little? I'm starting a lawsuit with those guys," Bear Child informed Randal.

"Man, this is uncomfortable, you need to come with us, ok?" demanded Randal.

"Yeah, let's go." Both he and Randal started for the squad car after Bear Child locked up his trailer.

Bear Child laughed saying "Get in the back?" "Yeah, just like on TV," joked Randal, but he opened the back door of the squad car for Bear Child.

The ride to the police station took less than eight minutes total time, and there wasn't a word spoken after Randal introduced Bear Child to his sergeant. Inside the station all three found a place to be seated in the interview room. Bear Child was asked if he would like a coffee, which he accepted right away. Sgt. Henry started it off before the coffee arrived. "Timothy, it's ok if I call you Timothy?"

"Call me Tim, I like that better," replied Bear Child.

"Tim, last week a Chicago Police Department Detective O'Brady came to Prescott looking for you in relationship to a possible serial murder there. Now before we go any further, you are not in trouble, but if you would like, you are not under any obligation to speak with us. I can Mirandize you, but at this point it may not even be required because you are free to get up and walk out any time you please. You ok with that, Tim?"

Bear Child said, "It depends on how bad your coffee is."

CHAPTER 12

The Arizona Daily Star
February 21, 2020
The Associated Press

24 decomposed bodies found in Michoacan

MEXICO CITY-PROSECUTORS IN WESTERN MEXICO SAID THURSDAY that the arrest of a criminal gang led to the discovery of a house that had been used to dispose of 24 bodies. Prosecutors in Michoacan state said decomposed bodies were found in the house in Coene, a township west of the Michoacan state capital of Morelia. Some of the bodies found had been dismembered and buried in the patio of the house, which was under construction.

The Prescott Police Department had little ammo to throw at Bear Child and he knew it. That was not the strategy they were introducing. Sgt. Henry told Bear Child, "We don't know if you did or did not have anything to do with the multiple murders in Chicago. What we are going to focus on is the disappearance of a police detective."

"Did you meet or talk to a Detective O'Brady? Do you know Det. O'Brady?"

"No," responded Bear Child. "I was out of town on the date you say he was here in Prescott. The Chicago P.D. has many dozen detectives, and I don't know an O'Brady."

"Can you tell us where you were? And can anyone confirm that?"

"I was working as a private investigator in Winslow, Arizona, at a Flying J Truck Stop. I returned this morning about 11:00. My employer, Noel Two Horses, will confirm that."

"Tim, who is Noel Two Horses? That name sounds familiar. Is he the one who owns a bookstore in town? I've met him before."

"Will you be willing to talk to Chicago police about Det. O'Brady?"

"Well, like I said before, I'm in the process of suing them, but let me run it past my attorney first, ok? I will not talk to them about my lawsuit but maybe talking to them about their missing detective will be alright. I don't have his phone number on me, but maybe I can retrieve it on my cell phone."

Bear Child called his attorney who cautioned him after several minutes of questions about the missing detective issue. "I think speaking to them for this is a legitimate reason, but if they start harassing you about anything to do with your lawsuit, you stop right there, ok?" Bear Child agreed, "Of course. I'll let you know how it goes."

"If it were up to me, I would refuse to speak with them because, as you know, because of your history with them they are not to be trusted. I would prefer to be in on that call, but I understand."

When Bear Child returned to the interview room, he advised the sergeant that he would speak with the Chicago P.D. about the missing detective. Within minutes Sgt. Henry and Officer Randal had a landline phone plugged in and, unannounced to Bear Child, recorded the call.

"Officer Bear Child, this is Chief of Detectives Lewis, did you meet or speak to Detective O'Brady at all?"

"No, Chief, I did not. I was out of town on the date he apparently was here," replied Bear Child.

"Let me ask you this, Officer Bear Child, will you be available should we send another officer to interview you in person, in the near future?"

"I may be available, but I can't guarantee the dates due to my part time employment" cited Bear Child.

"Well, I guess that is fair enough." "We will be in touch with you shortly."

All three heard the phone receiver slam into its phone cradle in Chicago. Randal looked at the other two and said jokingly, "No good-bye?" while Sgt. Henry followed with, "Or a thank you" and Bear Child dramatically fainted, "Oh My! was it something I said." All three chuckled, but it was Sgt. Henry who said, "Seriously, I would appreciate it if you would make yourself available to Chicago and to us should either one of us need to speak with you further about this. This business being the way it is, someone on the Chicago P.D. or this department, as far as that goes, could and may leak something to the press about this matter, and you may have problems because of it."

Bear Child asked, "Do you think so?" and Sgt. Henry said, "Nothing is confidential, and the press can be predatory. Just keep your own counsel, but please think about what I just said."

CHAPTER 13

RANDAL WAS IN THE PROCESS OF DROPPING OFF BEAR CHILD WHEN TIM asked him to divert his squad car to Noel Two Horses' bookshop. Bear Child was just walking into the bookshop as Noel was getting his jacket on to leave. "Hello, am I catching you at a bad time?" "Of course not, walk with me," offered Noel.

"Sure, which way are we going?" Bear Child inquired.

"We are going to get my car and go to Rebecca's for lunch," answered Noel, "Are you up for it?"

Bear Child said, "Sounds great. I don't know where she is, but let me briefly fill you in on an idea I have."

On the drive over to Rebecca's restaurant, Bear Child told Noel about the thought of somehow photographing the prostitutes who work the various truck stops in parts of Arizona. "It isn't a bad idea, although it will be challenging," said Noel. "Let me park and we can go inside, maybe talk about this later on?"

Noel introduced Bear Child to Rebecca who was already seated in a booth and just ending a cell phone call. "Nice to meet you, Tim, please sit down," said Rebecca. "Old Two Horses here has told me much about you." Bear Child sat and slid over to allow Noel enough room to be seated.

"Pleased to meet you, I didn't know you owned a restaurant," said Bear Child.

"It isn't much, but it has a good menu, and the prices are kind to the wallet," said Rebecca. "Will you guys be talking business, or can anyone join in?"

Noel said, "Nope, no business until later on."

"Good, I wanted to ask Tim, how did you like living in Chicago? Will you be able to transition to Prescott right away? I know that's two questions, but fill me in."

"Well, that's the reason I came to see Noel. I may not be in Prescott long enough to find out about transitioning," Bear Child revealed. "Chicago Police Department sent a detective here. They want to question me about serial murders there. To make things worse, the detective disappeared, and the position they are taking is that it seems like I know something about his disappearance."

"Do you?" Noel asked.

"No, I was in Winslow. I called my attorney before I spoke to them on the phone, I kept it short. I was also questioned by the Prescott Police, and they have the same impression that I have. For some reason, I may be a person of interest in both the serial murders and the disappearance of the Chicago Police Dept. detective. I don't even know who was killed and how I figure into the deaths. I think they are trying to dirty my name because they smell a lawsuit coming."

Noel spoke up, "Well, you have retained us, so let me speak to the police here. I know a few of them, maybe I can get a better picture of what has been going on."

"I was with an Officer Randal and a Sgt. Henry. Sgt. Henry thinks he knows you. Does he?"

"Yes," answered Noel. "We have helped each other out. Straight shooter."

The three ate in silence for a minute or two, each contemplating what was revealed minutes earlier. Soon the booth was filled with small talk about Bear Child.

"How is school going for you, Tim?" asked Rebecca. "Do you miss being back home? When are you planning on visiting your folks? Do you like your trailer park?" These were the type of questions that would be posed to someone who moved into a small community from a large place like Chicago.

When it became apparent that it was time to leave Noel and Rebecca, Bear Child asked about taxi service in the area. Rebecca said, "Do you see that older gal in the corner booth getting up to pay her tab? That is our taxi service."

Bear Child said, "I better catch her before she leaves."

Noel offered him a ride back, but Bear Child responded, "It's good, I'll let you guys talk, you look comfortable together."

When Noel was sure that Bear Child was out of hearing range, he asked Rebecca, "What do you think of him? Or should I ask you about his predicament first?" After several seconds and checking to see if Bear Child and the elderly taxi driver had exited, Rebecca asked, "Predicament? A predicament is locking your keys in the car. Noel, this is not a predicament, this is serial murders and maybe kidnapping and murder of a cop."

Noel held up his right hand to stop her from saying more. "Here's the thing. As soon as he jumped into the car, he wanted to tell me about his idea of photographing prostitutes for our missing women case. He talked about it the whole time, not once mentioning what he told us about the missing detective and the serial murders they want to hang on him. I mean, like when the hell would it come up in our conversation? It's like he's dismissive about it."

"Noel, please call Claire Blue Crow and have him use his Chicago Police Department contacts to screen this. Promise me you will have him follow up on this. We don't know if Tim Bear Child can be trusted or if he is dangerous."

"I'm doing that right now. Can you go ahead and give me a few minutes, and then we can leave, ok?" Noel engaged his phone, and his business partner answered on the first ring. "Wow, that was quick, I'll bet you thought this call was the parents of that jailbait you've been messing around with, huh?"

"Yeah, Noel, how did you know? You should be a detective. Oh wait, you can't be because I'm up here, and you need a real seeing-eye-dog detective?"

Noel said, "You are indeed correct as usual, Ol' Tribal Pervert. How about I fill you in on some stuff that I just now found out about our newest client?"

"Sure, go ahead. It's good to hear your voice, it's been a while," replied Blue Crow.

Noel said, "Are you sitting down? You are not going to believe this."

Noel noticed that as he told Blue Crow more that the phone became deadly quiet. At the end of the tale, Noel had to ask if Blue Crow was still there, "Hello, can you hear me?"

"No shit, that boy don't play around, huh?" was Blue Crow's only response.

"I'm on it. You stay safe and don't take any chances with him, Noel," warned Blue Crow.

CHAPTER 14

BOTH NOEL TWO HORSES AND HIS LADY FRIEND REBECCA WERE QUIET in the car on the way back to his home. As they were pulling into his driveway, Noel asked, "Would you like to talk about it?"

"No, not tonight, but please promise me that you will be careful now that you know what you know," Rebecca cautioned.

"I will, but I only know what he told us. It was shocking, but it's only his side of events right now. I hope to know more tomorrow."

Rebecca said, "Noel, I should chew you out, but I won't. I know you have to deal with all types of people in your business. I also don't know what I would do without you." Rebecca grabbed Noel's chin and turned his head to face her as she gave him a deep kiss. This caught Noel by surprise. When she broke from kissing him, she looked him in the eye before speaking and said, "Let's go to bed and talk in the morning, ok?"

When the two got into the house, Noel asked, "Should I lock both the front door and the back tonight?"

Rebecca paused for a few seconds and asked, "Don't you always?"

Noel laughed at her and said, "I'm just kidding."

Rebecca said, "Yeah, I will lock 'em, I'll let you back in tomorrow morning."

Both slept restlessly. In the morning they tried to avoid talking about Bear Child.

Bear Child woke to the sound of loud knocking on his door. He sat up in his bed, and his first reaction was to look around his small trailer before he realized where he was. He stood up and pulled his pants on while leaning against his bed. Shoeless, he went to the door and almost opened it before asking, "Who is it?" The response he received took the oxygen out of the trailer. A female said, "Mr. Bear Child, I am from FOX News Phoenix, and I would like to get your response to the Chicago Police Department wanting you as a person of interest in the disappearance of one of their police officers. Mr. Bear Child, would you care to give me a statement?"

"No, I have no comment," said Bear Child, while thinking, "Thank God there was no mention of serial killings." The person on the other side of the door said, "Mr. Bear Child, I am the only person here, but by noon I can guarantee you there will be a half dozen news vans here with towers extended. Why not talk to me in a peaceful environment now? Mr. Bear Child, are you a Native American? I mean no offense, sir, but your last name *is* unusual," with emphasis on the 'is.'

Bear Child spoke up again and said, "I have no comment," but he was also thinking, "Does a last name like Bear Child sound white? I'd be better off taking my chances and making a break for it than talking with a sharpie like you."

"We can meet somewhere else before others get here. It doesn't have to be here," said the female on the other side of his door.

Bear Child spoke into the door again and said, "No Comment. Now I'm going to ask you to leave, or I will have to call the police."

"Don't do that, ok? Look, I will be at the Safeway parking lot for the next half hour if you want to talk, ok?" asked the female voice behind the door. "Our news van is white with big letters on the outside."

All Bear Child could think of was, "Oh my God!"

He waited for her to drive away before he finished dressing and quickly brushed his teeth. He grabbed his bag and filled it with clean clothes, his phone charger, laptop, and his recent mail. He made a dash for his truck and passed a white news van going in the opposite direction. The thought struck him that maybe it was her, and maybe she was rethinking her offer. Bear Child stepped on the gas while his phone speed dialed Noel Two Horses. Noel told him to continue into his parking structure behind the St. Gregory Hotel, and he would meet him there.

Noel was just leaning against one of the cement support pillars when Bear Child pulled into the parking structure. He walked up to Bear Child's truck and pointed so Bear Child could unlock the door. "Morning" said Noel.

"Yeah, morning. I guess," said Bear Child.

"Someone has shit in your rice bowl, huh?" asked Noel.

"I guess so. I can't talk with the news, so what do you suggest?"

"Tim, I would suggest you take this real serious right now."

"I do take it serious!" said Bear Child.

"We can leave your truck in here for the time being. You're going to have to give up the trailer," cautioned Noel.

"Not a problem, I didn't leave anything behind that they can copy or that I need. Do I hide out for now, and if so, where?" asked Bear Child.

"I will fill you in shortly. Stay in the truck with me and call your attorney. Let him know what is going on. You could surrender yourself to Prescott P.D. for safekeeping for a while. Or you could disappear and leave me as your contact guy. Talk to him first, but mention my suggestions to him, ok? My guess is Chicago P.D. tipped off Fox News Chicago."

Bear Child said, "I know I didn't. I like your second idea, you know, hide out."

"But you will clear it with your attorney first, right?"

Bear Child said, "Right!"

Noel sat next to Bear Child as he made telephone contact with his attorney. The phone was on speaker mode as he explained what happened. "Noel Two Horses is listening and is seated next to me right now. If you need to speak with him, that's ok."

"That's not necessary, but I think you should have him as your spokesperson. Have him contact the media person and let her know you are not interested in becoming involved in the Detective O'Brady issue at this time, that your wish to be left out of it should be respected, plain and simple," was the advice that the attorney gave.

When the call ended, Noel said, "Ok, we have our plan, so let's roll. In case the media is waiting for your return, I will have my friend, Larry, pick up your trailer with your truck. He'll drive around with it for several hours until I call him."

Bear Child said, "It's locked, but I don't think he needs to get in there."

"No," agreed Noel. "Why don't you and I go inside and have a cup of coffee in the St. Gregory. I'll call Larry and have him meet us there."

Bear Child grabbed his laptop and got out when Noel said, "Let me have your keys to your truck, Tim, Larry is going to need them today."

The dining room of the Saint Gregory Hotel was fresh-smelling and restful for a guy like Bear Child who had been suddenly awakened by a television reporter pounding on his door. He was not at all ashamed to order pancakes and coffee for himself while Noel had just coffee. He told Noel, "I want this Chicago lawsuit over with. I'm convinced that this is all part of the same crap down there. One big pile of it."

The coffee arrived, and both men poured a cup while Noel told Bear Child, "I am sure that the serial murders and the missing detective are not as connected as the Chicago P.D. wants them to be. First of all, I know you were not there when O"Brady went missing. I also recognize that we have little information about this cop, and for all we know, his wife had him killed and his body buried in a desert off the freeway. Did he have a drinking problem? Did he have a marital issue? Has anyone in the past threatened his life?"

"Hey, enjoy your pancakes when they come, I'm going to call Larry right now." In less than a minute Noel was in a conversation instructing Larry to come over to the Saint Gregory Hotel dining room to pick up the keys and Bear Child's truck in the parking structure.

CHAPTER 15

LARRY HAD TAKEN HIS TIME BACKING UP BEAR CHILD'S PICKUP TRUCK to his trailer. He got out of the truck and walked over to the Park Manager's office. When he knocked on the door, he was surprised to see that the manager was a former school classmate of his. She recognized Larry right away, and they spent a minute or so talking about just how well Larry was doing and how many years it had been since they had last chatted. Larry explained why he was there so she would not think an unauthorized person was taking a trailer from the park. When the brief visit was over, she went back inside, and Larry returned to the trailer and truck to finish hitching up.

Larry walked over to the right side of the trailer and removed the wheel chuck and then repeated the process on the left side. He raised the trailer with the mounted jack until it was high enough to drive the trailer hitch ball under it. As he began to lower the trailer onto the truck's ball, he saw a man approach the driveway area. Larry had been told by Noel not to speak to the media about anything regarding what he was doing or where he was going. Larry got down on one knee and began to hook up the safety chains from the trailer onto the truck. The man slowly walked behind him while he was still kneeling. Larry was shot in the back of his head with a handgun that the man had concealed under his shirt. Larry didn't hear the full report of the handgun when it fired, nor did he really feel the full force of the round because the bullet exited so quickly, carrying a large piece of Larry's brain, skull, and hair.

Noel Two Horses and Timothy Bear Child didn't comment on the siren noise that erupted in town as both fire and police reported to the scene. They were deep into a conversation about Bear Child's idea of not going to Jackson Hole, Wyoming, because it was a high-end resort town that more than likely would not have truck stop-type hookers working the ski resort clientele. He suggested instead that he go to the truck stops in the Cheyenne, Wyoming, area.

Noel said, "I don't understand, what's the difference? There are reservations all around the Jackson Hole area."

"That's true that most missing indigenous women disappear around reservations. Many who are in the sex trafficking trade are in locations generating from those places with almost triangular patterns toward highly populated areas like Denver or Cheyenne," explained Bear Child. "Most are tattooed by those responsible for the sex trade positions to prove ownership. Tattooed gals are getting younger and younger and have signs of physical abuse, burn marks, cuts, maybe even fresh bruising and probably would not have the resources needed to hang with the resort guys. You know, car, cash, clothes," reasoned Bear Child.

Noel thoughtfully said, "Let me think about it for a while. In any event, Jackson Hole or Cheyenne, that is where I want to hide you, maybe with Claire Blue Crow."

"Both you and Claire can earn some money up there, and we can patch this stuff together down here with the police departments and the media." As the two of them waited for the waiter to return to the table with the check, the cellphone closest to Noel sounded. The police and fire had responded to the trailer park to find Larry and to secure the scene. The person in charge was Prescott Police Sgt. Henry. The call was being made by a Prescott Fire EMT who knew Larry and Noel Two Horses.

Noel did not want Bear Child anywhere near the trailer, so he took him to his bookshop. Bear Child was instructed to pull up a chair in the Sherlock Holmes parlor and work out an approach to his theory about Cheyenne, Wyoming, until Noel got back from the crime scene. He was also informed that if a customer came in "play it by ear."

Noel approached the crime scene and parked on the shoulder of the road like half of Prescott was doing that day. He approached Sgt. Henry and shook his hand.

Sgt. Henry asked Noel, "Mr. Two Horses, I have to ask you if you have had any contact with Tim Bear Child today or if you know where he is?"

"Yes, and yes. He's in a safe place and may have been with me when this happened."

"We need to speak with him, can you bring him in?"

"Of course, but I need to speak with you before I do that, agreed?"

"Let's go and get into my office for privacy," advised Sgt. Henry as he pointed to his squad car.

Both he and Noel were in the front seat when Noel said, "I haven't seen the body, are you sure it's him?"

"Yes, unfortunately it is Larry. The State Crime Lab has been called because of the media crap."

Noel said, "Look, no offense to you or anyone in your department, but I think we need to call in the FBI. This has the makings of a Chicago Police Dept. screw up or cover up."

Sgt. Henry didn't say anything for a few seconds and just stared out of his squad car's driver's side window. He then turned to face Noel and asked, "What have you got?"

Noel said, "We need a cartridge casing match with those from the Chicago murders, and we need the FBI Lab to do the match, not Chicago P.D. We have a very calm murderer."

"The guy waited in the bushes until he thought Bear Child had returned. He didn't know it was Larry. He was calm, patient, but mistaken."

Sgt. Henry said, "Ok, I agree, I don't want to get in between Chicago P.D. and the media on this one." He continued to talk after he got the squad car door open enough to step out of it. Noel took the cue and did the same. "I am sure my chief will see things my way."

"I have to let my guys look around here and secure the trailer after the state looks at it." Noel knew he meant impound the trailer. Sgt. Henry then said, "Let's bring Bear Child in for a sit-down, ok?"

"Ok, we can be right with you." Noel waited until he saw Sgt. Henry get back into his car and then walked back to his. On the way to his bookshop, he admitted to himself that he hadn't wanted to see Larry's body at the trailer park.

Larry Figueroa had been a friend of Noel's for several years. He used to be a rough-around-the-edges kind of guy, and Noel knew he needed a little help. He didn't mind being Larry's friend and took great care to do for Larry what others did not. He taught Larry how to run his own small business and then to expand it. Larry knew how to pilot a plastic drone, and Noel used him to take undercover photos with it.

Larry was working as a part-time county employee at the time. He was doing a one-man night shift security detail at the Yavapai County Courthouse when Noel first met him. Later, Noel would use Larry on odd investigative jobs. Unfortunately, one evening Larry became so afraid during a surveillance with Noel that he wet his pants and had a noticeable trauma-induced tremor after that. Noel felt guilty about it so got Larry his own security contract for that same county courthouse. In the process he got Larry Limited Liability Corporation (LLC) status with the state for his startup security company and would do Larry's books for him. He even encouraged him to save money for a nicer apartment and motivated Larry to stop smoking. It wasn't all out of guilt; Noel wanted Larry to be able to succeed. Now he felt that he unknowingly made Larry a target for the filth who shot him. He now knew the people who needed killing: they were the ones hunting Bear Child.

CHAPTER 16

SGT. HENRY DOUBLE-PARKED HIS SQUAD CAR ON PRESCOTT'S WHISKEY Row with the four-way flashers on. Parking on Whiskey Row was normally at a premium, but because this was a Friday, it was extremely crowded. Noel parked his car in his spot inside the parking structure at the Saint Gregory Hotel as usual. Henry and Noel met at the front door of his bookshop at the same time. Bear Child looked up from his laptop as the two walked in.

Bear Child paid his respects to Sgt. Henry saying, "Sgt. Henry" and Henry responded with, "Tim."

Bear Child asked, "Are you ok, Noel, I feel really bad, is there anything you need or anything I can do to help?"

"Yes, there is, Tim," said Noel. "I need you to go with Sgt. Henry. You will be in good hands. He needs to ask you some questions. There isn't anything we can do for Larry. I want you safe right now. The shooter thought Larry was you. He'll find out that he made a mistake. I assume you are an important target, and he'll want to finish." With that Bear Child stood up, closed his laptop, and handed it to Noel. He then walked outside with Sgt. Henry, got into the squad car, and was driven to the police station.

Noel had a very unpleasant job to do, call Rebecca and fill her in on Larry's death. Noel was at a loss for words to describe what happened. He felt so weighted down with guilt that he considered not making the call at all. Just as he reached for his cellphone, it went off in his hand. When he looked at the caller information, he somehow recognized her name. His vision was blurry with tears that he didn't know he was crying. Several of his tears had rolled into the hand holding the phone, and it was still ringing. Noel answered saying, "Hi, can I call you back?" Rebecca said in a soft and understanding voice, "Of course you can," and ended the call.

Two Horses walked slowly to the front door of his bookshop and locked it. He dimmed the bookshop lights and found a chair in the Sherlock Holmes parlor, sat down in it, and cried softly until he was cried out. He had lost track of time, and when he stood up, he realized he was exhausted beyond belief. He was too tired to drive safely, so he called the taxi service in town. When the taxi arrived, he unlocked the door of the shop, stepped outside and relocked it, got into the back seat of the cab, and told the driver his address without any of his actions really registering with his brain.

After getting home he couldn't even remember if he tipped the driver or not. Rebecca embraced him when he first walked into the house and told him how sorry she was for him. She suggested that he take a hot shower, and she would join him after his shower. Noel nodded his head yes and walked into the bedroom to get out of his clothes. Just before he began to undress, his phone sounded. It was Sgt. Henry calling him.

"Yes?"

"Noel, this is Henry over at the Prescott P.D."

"Yes, Sergeant Henry?"

"I sent both Officer Randal and Tim Bear Child over to the Marriot for the night."

"Yes, good, thank you."

"I'll have a third shift officer relieve Randal at midnight. Ah, look, this is touchy, but I may have a camera photo of our shooter. No guarantee, but it looks good."

"You have to be aware of this condition, you did not get it from here, understand?"

"Of course, Sergeant."

"We lucked out, the park manager was the source, she had one of those doorbell cameras. Your copy is on its way to you as we speak."

"Thank you, Sergeant."

Just then Noel's doorbell rang. He could hear Rebecca talk to the officer who delivered his copy of the photo. Rebecca walked into the bedroom. "This just arrived for you" she said. "Yes, it may be a photo of our shooter, thank you." Noel opened the large envelope and looked at the grainy image of what appeared to be an adult male with dark hair and mustache. He was wearing a long sleeve shirt and something that looked like a dark leather vest with jeans. The man was passing the doorbell camera in a westerly direction leading to Bear Child's trailer location in the driveway. From the vantage point of the camera, it looked like the vest had an extra layer of material on the back that might be indicative of a large patch.

A leather vest could and often did conceal a handgun. The patch could be a biker patch. Noel planned on soliciting Prescott P.D. for a search of every camera in Prescott starting tomorrow to see if they could salvage any additional shots of this guy as he came into or left Prescott. Larry was killed in the morning hours. This guy must have spent the night before somewhere in Prescot, and maybe had breakfast before he killed Larry. Noel no longer felt exhausted; rather he felt excited that there was a possible lead or evidence that could lead to identifying the shooter.

The next several days were taken up with notifying Larry's family in Tucson of Larry's death and making funeral arrangements. Noel assured Larry's brother that he would handle all mortuary expenses as well as a funeral service, if that is what the brother wanted. Noel knew that Larry did not have a faith that he subscribed to, so he verified that his brother would not object to a cremation. When Noel asked to keep Larry's ashes in an urn on a shelf at the bookshop in the Sherlock Holmes parlor because Larry was part of the agency's team, his brother also agreed to that. Larry only had a small business, and there were no debts or profit to declare. The county would have to be notified that Larry would not be providing security services any longer during the evening hours for the county courthouse. There would not be any additional billable hours due.

Bear Child had agreed to stay at the Marriot for the next few days until arrangements could be made to stay elsewhere. The Prescott Police Chief advised Noel that the FBI had been notified of the murder, and that they would respond to Prescott within 24 hours. During that time period, Noel still had Bear Child's laptop. He intended to sign into it somehow and review any and all information relating to what occurred in Chicago as well as anything to do with Detective O'Brady's mysterious absence.

Noel took the direct route and asked Bear Child for his laptop password. Bear Child provided it without appearing to have any qualms about doing so. What Noel found was that Bear Child did not document anything about any detective from Chicago P.D. on his laptop, but he did have several entries of interest, so Noel called him again, but this time on the phone in his room at The Marriot.

CHAPTER 17

BEAR CHILD WAS BESIDE HIMSELF. HE HAD STOPPED EATING A DAY AGO, he was staying in a motel and could not relax or sleep. He had never felt so depressed about his life. He had called his family back in Wisconsin to let them know what was happening. He felt like he was a total failure and guilty for what happened to Larry. His parents asked him to have faith and to rest; they assured him that all would be well. Several hours had passed, and he was not thinking clearly. He had no idea what was going on in his life. He almost lost his job, he then resigned, he moved out of state, and afterward found out he was suspect in a string of serial murders and the kidnapping or maybe murder of a cop. One of the people who was helping him was just killed by someone who thought the victim was Bear Child. Nobody could mess up his life so badly so quickly.

When the telephone in his room rang, he was not going to answer at first it for fear that it was someone from the media. After the third ring, he was relieved to hear Noel Two Horse's voice. "Tim, this is Noel, I didn't want this call to show up on your cell. I need some information from you."

"Sure, anything, it's good to hear your voice."

"I've been in your laptop like I said I was going to do. Can you tell me who Stover, Shelf, and Terry are?"

Repeating those three names into the telephone to Noel was followed by, "Yeah, those are the three guys who were in my group."

"What group?" asked Noel.

"My anger management group in Chicago. Three old guys who worked for the city."

"How old?"

"I don't know," answered Bear Child.

"Tim, how old are they?"

"I don't know, maybe late '60s, early '70s."

"I think I know who the three were who were killed in the serial murders," said Noel.

"No kidding, why them?" asked Bear Child.

"I don't know why, but ask yourself this, would you be working for the city at age seventy plus? Would anger management be a problem anyway at that age?" reasoned Noel. "We have to find out if they are the victims because that is the link to you."

"Damn. Wow." Bear Child went on to tell Noel about how he had been feeling bad, about his phone calls to his folks, about how messed up his life got. Suddenly feeling ill and dizzy, Bear Child said, "I think I'm going to pass out!"

"Look Tim, fainting is not a sign of weakness, it's just because your body can't cross the finish line right now. Faint later, ok?"

Several hours had gone by, and then the FBI arrived in Prescott. Since Prescott was only a two-hour drive north of Phoenix, Noel figured it would not take days for them to respond. He got a call from Bear Child who said that the FBI contacted him and would like to meet. Noel suggested the Starbucks not too far from the hotel, saying, "It's public and safe."

"Don't be surprised if the FBI book a room or two at your hotel, ok? This is a small town, so remember hotels are not a dime a dozen," warned Noel. A few minutes had passed when Noel's phone let him know Bear Child was calling him. "Noel, they've agreed to meet at Starbucks in fifteen minutes." Noel said, "Ok, see you there in fifteen."

The Starbucks was filled to capacity with agents all wearing vests and jackets with 'FBI' in yellow lettering on the back except for two agents in suits. They sat at tables pulled together to accommodate at least two more people.

Noel sat down after first introducing himself to the two agents. Bear Child appeared at his right shoulder and did the same. At first Noel let the agents open the conversation but soon took control. "If you don't mind me asking, have you spoken with Prescott Police Sgt. Henry?"

The older of the two agents said, "Yes, he is of the same mind I am."

"And what is that?" asked Noel.

"This is our take, Sgt. Henry and I. Of course, we have information from our field office in Chicago that he does not have, information that Chicago Police Department does not have."

"We have been conducting an investigation into one of three men who were killed in Chicago. This was an investigation that was long-term and splintered until the killings. Mr. Bear Child here knew all three and actually came onto our radar when he had weekly meetings with the three at a hotel in Chicago. Our initial target was a Mr. Revotos, a person of special interest relating to the Sinaloa Drug Cartel. We lost our communication with him and his Sinaloa partners for months until we discovered that he was meeting weekly with two others of different cartels, Mr. Fleahs and Mr. Yeret."

"Stover, Shelf and Terry spelled backward? Or something like that?" asked Noel.

"Yep, something like that," laughed the older agent.

"Look, Mr. Bear Child, we know you did not blow these guys away," said the younger agent suddenly to break his silence. Noel got the impression that maybe he was getting frustrated listening to the story. Noel also thought that maybe the younger agent was the Special Agent in Charge of the Chicago investigation.

"We made a mistake, and the Chicago police snowballed it into a personal vendetta."

"What kind of mistake?" asked Bear Child.

"We did not share all of our investigative data and evidence with the police agency that had the bailiwick we were operating in. We short-changed our duty to the Chicago P.D. and to you. For that I personally apologize."

This gave Noel pause to reconsider this agent's position in the Bureau. "Hell, this guy is at least a director," he thought.

"This screw up is on a serious level," the agent continued. "We never told the Chicago police that we were investigating a guy who was high up in an international drug smuggling, sex trafficking cartel. We failed to tell them that the shooter was a hit man with one of the cartels. We assumed maybe we should approach you on the idea of being part of our witness protection program, but they never intended to do the same for you. The opposite was true, they wanted to indict you as being a fleeing felon. They wanted to hunt you down as the shooter, with very little evidence to support this. Now that they are missing a police detective involved in their investigation, they want you arrested and extradited back to Illinois. We're in Prescott today to work on the murder of the young man at your trailer site. We are not here to arrest you."

"I'm glad you responded, because I'm afraid my client is in grave danger right now," said Noel. "He is a part-time investigator of mine. More importantly, he is my client on another matter involving the Chicago P.D. Have you thought that there could be other options open, such as a modified witness protection approach. Right now, his media exposure has proved to be fatal to a friend and employee of mine. We need a media blanket now, without delay," said Noel.

"Absolutely," said the younger agent as he turned to the older man as if ordering the media blanket. "Let's order some coffee, I'll get my crew to the scene, and we can discuss what you know about the Sinaloa Chicago connection."

CHAPTER 18

"WE HAVE NO IDEA WHAT YOU MAY OR MAY NOT HAVE HEARD IN CON-versations with the three men in your anger management group. Can you enlighten us a bit?" Bear Child had thought about this for hours since Noel suggested that the group members may have been the victims of serial murder in Chicago. He started to answer by saying, "To be specific, what would you be interested in?"

"We know that you have a few years in law enforcement with the Chicago Police Department. You are not a stranger to the drug issues and the sex trade in our country, so let's start there," suggested the younger agent. Bear Child responded, "Most of their conversations were between them. I was never privy to any conversations of this type. As a matter of fact, when two began a conversation, the third guy would engage me, you know, 'How is the lawsuit coming? Find an attorney yet? ' That sort of conversation. I didn't really think much about it, but looking back, all of my conversations were with the same guy in English while the two conversed in Spanish. The other thing, when we paid for our drinks, I paid for mine while he paid for the other two guys' drinks, all of the time."

"The guy who engaged you did that to keep you occupied while the two took care of cartel business," offered the younger agent. "That didn't strike you as a bit odd, I mean the two speaking in Spanish all the time?"

"No, when you have dark skin, people speak in a different language if they can, to avoid hearing others call you names and degrade you; I'm used to that. I figured that is what the old guys were up to. You have to understand, I did not care for these guys, they didn't care for me."

"How do you know they didn't care for you?" asked the younger agent. "Well, they referred to me as a 'Fuck'n injun' one day," said Bear Child, "in the men's can when they didn't know I was walking in on them."

"We need to ask you if you are in possession of a handgun, and if it's a 9mm semiautomatic, we would like to examine it. We could get a warrant, but we would rather not after all of this, you understand."

Bear Child told them, "Yes, I have one handgun, and it's a 9mm. Your folks will find it in my truck under the dashboard in a sling holster. You don't need a warrant, you have my permission to examine it."

When the meeting had terminated and Noel and Bear Child walked away, Bear Child said that he felt much better knowing the full score. He advised that he would like to continue his work with Noel if he could, but he needed to avoid the media and stay abreast of the investigations, both the Chicago serial hit and Larry's murder. Noel knew this to be true because he, too, needed to keep moving forward and he, too, needed to be able to help locate the shooter. What he did not say to Bear Child was that he wanted to do all that he could to confront the shooter. "Once we get the stamp of approval from the FBI, I'm going to check in with Claire Blue Crow and bring him up to date on this."

"I could ask him to take you into Tucson to visit and spend a few days with friends of ours, Dr. Mike Kuntzelman and his wife Dani. Mike is a psychiatrist, Dani is an R.N. They run a horse rescue operation in Marana, AZ, near the Tohono O'odham Reservation, Escalante Springs Equine Rescue. They do equine therapy for PTSD Vets, too. Mike helped me out when I was in a bad place and looking at some dark stuff."

"Mike could help you get your feet wet in equine therapy. He is also a Vietnam combat medic. He's not the bleeding heart most people think of when you say psychiatrist, he also is familiar with the criminal culture. He did psychological assessment in jails and in behavioral health crisis environments."

"I think Dani grew up in Tucson's southside, which is primarily Hispanic. She has been around people of color all her life. She, too, has been working on the rough side from time to time as a nurse at the prison in Tucson."

"I appreciate everything you've done for me. After looking at the academic syllabus for the school program, I know going down there would help me tremendously in getting to where I'm going academically. However, I need to do something else, something much more," said Bear Child.

Noel looked at Bear Child who then spoke again. "I need to stop this shooter. He has taken my life from me. I'm not talking about the Chicago killings because we don't know if he did those shootings. Nevertheless, he is still part of the evil who did, though. My privacy is gone, my reputation as a bad person has been added to, there will be no justice until Larry's death is avenged. I want to avenge it." Noel looked down at the pavement and didn't raise his head until Bear Child was finished speaking.

"I, too, want to avenge Larry's death. We don't need permission from the FBI to do that if we are legal in our pursuit."

"Noel, you said 'our' pursuit. Do you mean you and me?" asked Bear Child.

Noel raised his head and looked Bear Child in the eyes. "Yes."

Bear Child and Noel agreed to meet again that evening and talk about the missing indigenous women case that Bear Child started before Larry's murder. Neither of them wanted to leave it hanging. Noel had more work to do, also, as he found out after Bear Child returned to his own room. He got a call from the Prescott Police advising him that the FBI had suggested that Larry's body be released to Noel after it had been examined by the Yavapai County Medical Examiner. The Medical Examiner said he was finished.

In Prescott, the County Medical Examiner performed postmortem examinations in a building that also housed the Yavapai County Sheriff 's Department. It was only a few blocks from a local funeral home that also took care of cremations. Noel called them and asked for a brief meeting to discuss the arrangements for Larry's body. Later that afternoon Noel found himself looking at cremation urns at the funeral home, selecting one to hold what would be left of Larry Figueroa. The funeral home director had dispatched someone to retrieve Larry's body while Noel was still in his office. Noel did not want to be there when Larry's body arrived, so he selected an urn and left.

After leaving a message for Claire Blue Crow on Claire's cellphone, Noel began to unwrap some books that had arrived at his shop. Even if he couldn't take his mind off of the events that had occurred, he still had a business to take care of and did not want his delivery to just sit on the shop floor. His work was soon interrupted by Claire Blue Crow returning his call. "Noel, I'm so sorry to hear about Larry, I know this must be hard on you. Is there anything I can do to help?"

Noel said, "Not really. I've made arrangements with a local funeral home to have him cremated, and his brother is ok with that. This whole place has been turned upside down the last several days."

"I can imagine. I'm going to add to that with some strange news for you reference my call to Chicago."

"Thanks for taking care of that, Claire, I have to fill you in also."

As Noel filled Claire in on the FBI omission of information to the Chicago Police Department, Claire would interrupt at appropriate times to offer Chicago Police interpretations of events.

"There is no doubt about it, they wanted to hang these murders on Bear Child," said Claire.

Noel said, "If all goes well, maybe right now they will just pester him with the disappearance of Detective O'Brady, wherever he might be."

Claire said, "I have to tell you, I was really a little more than concerned Bear Child might have smoked you, and that you were next in line." Claire paused and added, "Glad you and Rebecca are ok."

"And I have to be honest with you, Rebecca was afraid of that, too!" With that, both broke out into laughter.

"So, we are ok with Bear Child, huh?" asked Noel.

"Yep, he is a good cop, or was a good cop, according to the guys up there," Claire said. "Look, about the security folks playing cop at the

Chicago mall, my contact may have a guy who had the same crap happen to him in 2015. So Bear Child was right, Noel. His attorney needs to depose this guy about his deal in 2015. Looking forward to meeting Tim."

Noel told Claire, "Before you meet him and judge for yourself, I have to tell you the kid was falling apart here."

"Shit, I don't blame him," said Claire.

"He has his head and ass wired together now. I'll explain later. He and I are scheduled to meet, so I'll see you when you get here."

Claire ended the call by saying, "Ok, and again I'm glad you're ok."

A few customers came into the bookshop, so Noel decided to call Bear Child and have him taxi over to meet. In just a few minutes the taxi pulled up. Bear Child walked into the shop, looked at the customers, and told Noel that he did not know selling books was so financially lucrative. Remembering what Rebecca advised him about his initial conversation with Timothy Bear Child, Noel chuckled and said, "It's the investigative agency that keeps the bookshop going, and the bookshop that keeps the investigative agency going. Listen, pull up a chair, and we'll talk while my retirement fund is shopping for a good mystery to read;"

Both walked over to the Sherlock Holmes parlor and sat down in the same chairs that they sat in before. Noel was just going to start speaking when his phone cut him short. It was a member of the FBI forensic team. The team member told Noel that his director instructed him to let Noel know that, after close examination, the person in the doorbell video was wearing a vest that had the word "Press" on the back. Additionally, the same person was at Bear Child's trailer door for several minutes earlier in the doorbell video. "It is our general consensus, after review, that the person was probably a female reference gait, size and build." Facial description or hair color was unavailable.

Noel thanked the FBI team member for the information and announced to Bear Child, "We need to look for any CCTV shots of camera vans in Prescot. And we need to follow up on any reports of stolen camera vans or reports of missing camera crew gear, specifically lettered vests." After Noel explained the reason behind the FBI call, Bear Child said, "I'm sorry, Noel, but I have to tell you something."

"Just before I decided to run from that Phoenix TV station person, she asked me to meet her in the Safeway parking lot. She described her station's camera van to me, you know, white with large station call sign lettering on it, like she didn't know they all had large lettering on them. Well, I was in a hurry to get over to you for help, but I saw a white camera van with station lettering going in the opposite direction toward my trailer. I remember thinking she must have figured out I wouldn't be coming after all. But damn it, Noel, that could have been the shooter!"

Noel asked, "Think real hard, Tim, did this van have the antenna boom and everything?" "No, it didn't, now that you mention it," replied Bear Child.

"It was probably a run-of-the-mill van dressed up to look like a reporter's camera van," said Noel. "The videos in town might get us a plate number or a better view of her. Or maybe there is no plate, why display one if you are going to commit a felony?"

In a very deep voice, one that Noel had never heard him use before, Tim Bear Child said, "That bitch needs killing."

CHAPTER 19

THE NEXT SEVERAL DAYS PROGRESSED SLOWER THAN THE LAST TWO FOR Noel Two Horses. He was given Larry Figueroa's ashes inside the funeral urn that he had selected. Larry's brother cleaned out Larry's apartment and gave everything of any value to a local thrift store. Claire Blue Crow had arrived in town, and he and Bear Child met with Noel at the bookshop to discuss the next step forward. During that meeting the subject of the missing indigenous women came up. Noel felt he needed to show some progress in the case for his clients' sake even if he had a hard time focusing on it.

Bear Child had a little more freedom to move about town now that the FBI ordered a blanket on the news coverage of the Chicago serial killings and the relationship to him. When the FBI put pressure on those who own multimillion dollar news organizations and publishing companies, things happen. The FBI forensic people had released Bear Child's truck and trailer. The cops at the Prescott Police Department got together and detailed his camper trailer; it looked almost new. He found a different lot to place it and hooked it up. There had not been any luck with any local videos as far as tracking the plate on the phony camera van, but one morning Sgt. Henry called Noel.

He told Noel that a patrol officer had placed a warning ticket on the windshield of a van matching that description the morning of the shooting while it was parked in the loading zone of a local coffee shop. They had a vehicle identification number (VIN Number) now because the warning was not written for parking in a loading zone, but rather for not displaying a license plate. Plates can be altered, plates can be stolen, VIN Numbers not so easily. The Prescott Police Department, the Arizona Department of Public Safety, the Chicago Police Department, and the FBI were in full swing now.

Noel felt secure in his knowledge of people from time to time, but this he was sure of, no criminal would remember to cover up the VIN Number on a vehicle with a napkin, book, or other object before committing a felony. They just would not consider it. The number is the vehicle's birth to death story. Who bought it, who sold it to whom, and if it were stolen, the number would be on file to assist in locating it. Additionally, the number will describe the vehicle as four door or two door, automatic transmission or standard transmission, etc. This particular number came back to an unusual vehicle, according to Sgt. Henry and the Department of Justice's National Crime Information Center (NCIC) Crime Information Bureau (CIB). This vehicle was a Dodge van, but not an ordinary Dodge van; it was shorter than normal. This type of van, for whatever reason, was ordered and used by the military. This would be a big help in tracking it down.

Noel had no idea why the shorter length of the vehicle would serve military needs. His exposure to military vehicles was extremely limited because he was a United States Marine grunt. That status meant he had very little exposure to riding in military vehicles. In Vietnam he did a hell of a lot of walking.

With an expedited inquiry the VIN produced U.S. Government, auction sale, owner name and address twice, and final owner Juan Jesus Villa of El Paso, Texas. The owner had applied for a salvage title for the vehicle at the same El Paso address. Noel did not know if the focus should be on the address or the fact that the vehicle could be roaming around Arizona. His instinct told him to leave the address tracing to the feds and maybe meet with Sgt. Henry and FBI team members to suggest alerting the Border Patrol to do a visual tracking at the Mexican border. He wanted a notice sent out to Arizona and California agencies for the van. Sometimes wanted vehicles get into traffic accidents, and detaining the vehicle could spell danger for the officer. Gas station videos can also tell direction of travel to and from the crime scene, so requests should be made to review videos. Noel contacted Sgt. Henry, and the meeting was arranged for that afternoon at the police station.

When Claire Blue Crow was introduced to Timothy Bear Child, he thought maybe time had taken a step backward. He was reminded of what it was like to be a younger version of himself, when he was new to law enforcement and was considering making it a lifetime career. A time before coworkers turned on him and lied under oath to sacrifice someone for what they thought was the good of the department. Claire had been a seasoned cop who had worked with Noel on cases prior to joining Noel in his investigative business. He was a member of the Navajo Nation and had been going through a rough divorce at the time. Claire would sometimes go home to his house on the Navajo reservation and stay there until he had put himself back together. This was one of the things he had suggested to Bear Child after a long conversation with him about his Chicago issues. "You were and are a good cop. Just because you are no longer with Chicago P.D. doesn't mean you are not a good cop. You will no longer be a cop only when you say so. Why not go home to your people and wait this out?" Bear Child said, "No, I will go to visit, but not before we get this woman."

The search for the van used by the shooter resulted in several interesting CCTV photos from a merchant on Interstate Highway 17 in Arizona. One photo showed what appeared to be a passenger/driver place a vehicle registration plate back onto the van. Another photo then showed this same person turn and face the service station building. The person was described as female with blonde hair and apparently a smoker according to the CCTV showing her pay cash for cigarettes. "Further review of the images is being made as of this report date. This is Claire Blue Crow back to you, Noel," mimicked Claire like a news reporter.

Noel said, "Better not find your DNA in that van, Blue Crow. Oh, that's right, you guys from the Navajo get around by thumbing."

"At least we don't get carsick like the dudes from Wisconsin tribes," replied Claire.

"Unlike you Navajos, we don't bump and grind on the spare tire when they make us ride in the trunk like you guys," countered Noel.

It was great to have Noel joke around after the dark of Larry's death. Claire didn't want to press his luck and have Noel slip back, so he brought up plans for Bear Child. "Any ideas for Tim yet?"

"I want him to pick his assignment," said Noel. "I thought he should go spend time with Mike Kuntzelman, but he wants to work."

Claire asked, "Why down there?" and Noel explained, "Tim wants to do equine therapy in school here in Prescott."

"Makes sense, I forgot Mike did the horse and PTSD thing."

"No matter what he decides, I'm going to need you to keep an eye on him. The shooter missed her target and got Larry by mistake. She has no idea what he does or doesn't know about Chicago and the cartel. She's not going away."

Claire said, "That's something I've been thinking about, how high up is she in the cartel? Someone put those old Pistoleros in the same anger management group so they could carry on business as usual. How do you arrange that?"

Noel told Claire, "I don't think she put them together, someone in the city government made those arrangements. But I do think maybe she did the serial hits in Chicago for someone who wanted the old guys out of the way."

Claire asked Noel, "Maybe still another cartel?"

Noel just said, "Maybe."

CHAPTER 20

Arizona Daily Star
December 30, 2020
The Associated Press

ALBUQUERQUE- Federal authorities are incorporating the Navajo language in a bid to find leads in cold cases on or near the country's largest Native American reservation. KOAT-TV in Albuquerque reported Thursday that the FBI has begun a new initiative to release posters on decades-old homicides and missing persons cases that are translated into Navajo.

The posters include details of an incident, physical descriptions of victims, photos, and possible age progressions. FBI spokesman Frank Fisher says the agency is hopeful that seeing details in their own language may jog people's memories. He also says the posters can reach people on the Navajo Nation who don't have access to television or the internet.

NOEL AND CLAIRE HAD MET BEAR CHILD FOR COFFEE AT NOEL'S book-shop to discuss going into the truck stops for more intel on the missing women. To this point Bear Child made an interesting statement, "We could be out there for the next twenty years. We don't know if the issue is pimps or serial psychopaths." Noel said that the problem has only increased. Claire didn't say anything because he knew the problem on his reservation had been around for a while.

Bear Child continued, "The feds are now opening field offices to assist, and this may be helpful as soon as the various agencies come to terms with the structure of it. There are programs out there that can provide services. I had information that said those programs can act as a nationwide information clearing house, technology that could expedite case comparison, free forensic services like postmortem odontology, you know, dental record comparison, DNA analyses, etc."

Noel told him, "I thought maybe your ability to hack into cellphone calls might help, but it didn't as much as I wished it could."

"Yeah, it was pretty much designed for use against organized crime organizations."

With that Claire smiled and said, "Like the cartel." Bear Child answered, "Yeah" before thinking about what Claire was saying, but when understanding it, he also smiled. "Yes, the cartel!" he declared.

Noel said, "Wait a minute, where is this piece of technology? The FBI had your camper trailer and your pickup truck and didn't mention finding this gadget. I'm sure they would if the average cop would need a warrant to operate it, don't you think?"

"I have it in a U haul storage in town," answered Bear Child. "They didn't hit me with a search warrant, and I didn't volunteer locations of my belongings or assets. They only focused on my trailer and truck regarding any possible connection to the Chicago serial murders." Noel said, "Good, if we can pick up her trail, we'll use it."

Later that same day Noel heard from Sgt. Henry that the FBI didn't find any additional information about the alleged van owner. It was as if Juan Jesus Villa never lived in El Paso, Texas. This just reinforced Noel's thinking that the shooter didn't have the van in Texas before the killing. Noel believed that the van was still in Arizona somewhere.

When Noel spoke to Rebecca that evening, she challenged him with the idea that male thinking is often narrow. Rebecca asked him over coffee at the kitchen table, "Why do men think that blondes are always white women?"

"Do you remember how some of the missing Indian women are categorized into the Caucasian or Hispanic profile on missing person reports? Well, you may be doing the same with Larry's killer. I mean, you're the investigator, but I'm just suggesting your blonde may actually not be a Caucasian woman."

Noel didn't respond to her right away, but after a while he said, "At the risk of sounding liking I'm stereotyping, being a Hispanic or Latino would align with a Mexican cartel."

Rebecca said, "Ya think?"

Noel laughed and said, "You are a wise woman," and Rebecca repeated, "Ya think?"

The following day Noel ran the idea past Claire and Bear Child using different hypothetical reasoning. "Suppose our gal is not a blonde? Suppose the hair color was to throw us off if we had her on CCTV? Suppose she is Hispanic and a member of a competing cartel? I mean, why not? Maybe we assumed like the various police reporting agencies do when they say that our missing Indian women are Caucasian or Hispanic?"

Claire was the first to throw his hat into the ring saying, "I think Hispanic and the competing cartel theory is a real possible answer. Maybe the FBI has a matching scenario that they are keeping close to their vest?"

Bear Child joined in with, "Why not, they didn't share the original data until I was almost killed. I vote for the Hispanic competing cartel, too. From a business perspective, it makes sense. Eliminate those in control at the same time, the old Pistoleros, and gain immediate control."

Noel said, "Yeah, that might be the assumption we run with until someone comes up with an answer that makes more sense. Let's focus on the van being in Arizona, ok? I'll ask Sgt. Henry to get the FBI to run CCTV all the way south to the border. We have to locate it on CCTV to prove our point. If it went across, maybe the Border Patrol will pick it up on Homeland Security video. Tim, has the FBI given you your pistol yet?"

Bear Child said, "Not yet."

Claire offered, "Seeing it exit off into Phoenix will work for me. There are a lot of cameras in Phoenix. They will pick the van up."

Noel asked Claire "Did you bring your gun?"

Claire said, "Navajo are the Ninja of the desert, my brother from Cheese Headquarters."

Noel said, "Yes, the Navajo women, O'Honorable Sheep Herder with the slop bucket rings on the back of your legs. This is true of the Navajo women but not the men, they are the Soy Sauce of the desert."

With that Claire showed Noel his weapon concealed under his jacket.

"Ok, let me call Sgt. Henry and get the ball rolling," said Noel. "I'll ask him about your weapon's status with the FBI." Bear Child nodded his head yes.

As it turned out, the FBI had already begun to use the CCTV cameras in Phoenix to track any sightings of the van. Noel thought that as long as Sgt. Henry was sharing information about the FBI progress or lack thereof, he would utilize the information without letting the FBI know he continued to be a player in the game. He still wanted and needed to protect his client, Bear Child, but if the truth were known, more importantly he wanted the blonde shooter.

He thanked the good sergeant and brought Bear Child and Claire Blue Crow up to speed. He told Bear Child that his weapon was still in the possession of the FBI. Noel asked Bear Child to retrieve his cellphone hacking machine and give him and Claire a road test. "We'll wait for you here, if that will work for you?" Bear Child agreed and said, "See you in a bit."

When Bear Child left to pick up his device, Noel told Claire, "The feds are still running tests on his weapon, but it's for the Chicago P.D." Claire said out loud, "Damn them, they don't drop it, do they? They sure want him bad!"

"Well, if the FBI lab clears his gun, it goes to help clear him, right?"

Noel said. "And if they clear his weapon, that goes a long way to prove that they've bumbled the investigation. We'll sit it out. In the meantime, we'll get him one to use."

When Bear Child returned, he had two small black metal boxes in his possession. One apparently was the power source and the other the actual device that could hack into cellphone calls by impersonating a cell tower repeater. As Bear Child prepared for his demonstration, he began to orient Noel and Claire on its operation. He finished by telling them that he offered no guarantee it would function properly 100% of the time. This time, though, it worked by relaying a text message being sent to a satellite from a cellphone near the St. Gregory Hotel.

"How do you know?" asked Claire. "Well, the sender said he has been waiting in the bar for half an hour and is dying to try the steak and lobster," said Bear Child. Noel called the St. Gregory to find out the special for the dining room which was confirmed as steak and lobster. Bear Child said, "We did an operation in Chicago. The tech I knew copied the fed's technology and made me one," as he held up the unit for Claire and Noel to see.

"What's the range?" asked Noel. "I would only be guessing," said Bear Child. "Here comes another one." The next one arrived as a cellphone call. It was muffled but still audible enough to understand it. "So that little light on the top of the surface blinks when it is transmitting?" asked Claire. "Yep," answered Bear Child.

CHAPTER 21

IT HAD BEEN DAYS SINCE DET. LEARY HAD GOTTEN ANY INFORMATION on the missing Det. O'Brady. He feared the worst, not for O'Brady, but for himself. He knew he had to get the planted shell casing out of the file of the unconnected shooting victim in Chicago. It was a stupid stunt to pull to increase the body count and make them appear better at their jobs. Now it could cost him his job if it showed up as planned. He had struggled with going into the evidence room and removing the shell casing but did it anyway. A day later both Leary's and O'Brady's desks were sealed with evidence tape and moved to storage in the evidence room. Leary also got called into the Chief of Detective's office. Leary was full of guilt with an upset stomach, thinking he was caught on video going in there and making the switch.

Leary was encouraged to sit down and asked if he would like coffee, which he refused because of his upset stomach and resulting loose stool. He was instructed to remain seated while reviewing a video of himself going into the evidence room and switching out an evidence- tagged shell casing to another file. "No, no," said Leary.

"No?" asked his Chief of Detectives.

"I mean, no, Sir."

"No, Sir?"

"I mean no, I would prefer to not see it. I don't want anyone to see it."

"Not your union representative or even your attorney?"

"Oh God, please, I have a wife."

The Chief was kind but direct. "Most of us do. I want you to have legal assistance here, so it would be better if your attorney saw it. We have a missing cop, maybe a dead cop, and he was in with you on this, wasn't he?"

Leary said, "Yes, but I don't know anything about his whereabouts. Honest to God I don't. Could his wife have killed him?"

"I honestly don't know, but maybe his mom should have," said the Chief Detective.

"Detective Leary, we are getting you some legal help before we go any further here. I am going to ask you to sit outside of my office with your supervisor for now, ok?"

The Chicago Police Department brass knew if Det. Leary intentionally broke the chain of evidence relating to the serial murders of the three Chicago victims, then the case was indeed rapidly going down the drain. The Chief of Detectives used his imaginary white board to process the possible outcome:

1. The FBI purposely failed to share pertinent information with the Chicago Police Department.
2. The lead detective on the case disappeared somewhere between Prescott, Arizona, and Chicago, Illinois.
3. It would actually be to the Chicago Police Department's advantage not to make an arrest in the case.
4. To avoid soiling the case any further, Det. Leary had to be not only fiercely interrogated by Internal Affairs but also by the FBI.
5. The subject of locating Det. O'Brady dead or alive would only darken the Chicago Police Department's reputation.
6. It would be to the Chicago Police Department's advantage to not locate Det. O'Brady.
7. It would be cost efficient to ask Det. Leary to take an early retirement.

There was only one negative reason and six positive reasons when he picked up his phone and ordered Det. Leary's supervisor back into his office. The Chief of Detective's secretary stepped out into the hall and relayed the message.

CHAPTER 22

NOEL HAD BEEN AROUND CARTEL CASES ENOUGH TO KNOW THAT IT MAY not be that difficult to identify the women. Cartel snitches currently doing time in federal facilities could and would provide her identity if the price was right. What Noel did not want to do was let the FBI know he was on to her. Unfortunately, he may have to due to the nature of the request he would have to make to get at that one federal snitch. After waiting around Prescott for almost four days and not hearing anything from Sgt. Henry about the FBI follow up of any CCTV video from the Phoenix area, Noel decided to have Claire escort Bear Child to another possible missing woman sex worker site.

The last few years Claire stayed with Noel and Rebecca whenever he was in Prescott. That way the agency didn't have to pay for a motel for him. Claire didn't mind, he liked Rebecca and Noel's company. In Claire's life, there wasn't much family time, and he missed that. During coffee Noel ran an idea past Claire. "I have been kicking this around and around," admitted Noel. "I think between us we can come up with a snitch."

"Have you anyone in mind?" asked Claire

"No, but that is where you come in," said Noel.

"Oh, really?"

"Yeah, we've done a lot of cases where one Mexican cartel or another played a part, haven't we?" asked Noel.

"Well, now that you mention it, we have," admitted Claire. "Hey, how about that time Boy George shot his little friend while they were inside that Corvette!" exclaimed Claire as he remembered the incident.

"That's exactly what I'm talking about, Claire, we must know someone doing time who knows Mexican Sinaloa Cartel people."

"He's not in prison. Maybe I shouldn't say that because with his history maybe he is, but what about Louie? Louie Louis and his brother knew a few cartel people. Hell, they knew Boy George. I'm sure we must have a contact number for Louie, don't we?" asked Claire.

Noel said, "His probation and parole people must. You know, also the DEA would have a pretty good handle on who's a good gun for hire."

Claire proposed, "Let's make a call and see if they can shed some light on this for us. You know, informal like."

"Yeah, they're always trying to flip someone already in custody," said Noel.

One call made it possible for Noel and Claire to harvest some information from their contact person at DEA. During the fall of the year another tunnel was found under the road on the American side of the Mexican border in Douglas, Arizona. This was the latest discovered in that area of the state rich in Mexican cartel tunnel history. This one was equipped with a small rail system that allowed tons of drugs to get into the U.S. undetected. Noel found out that the end of the tunnel was in the basement of an old boot shop in Douglas. There were several Mexican fellows arrested on the spot but one in particular was already providing information to Noel's DEA contact. The contact said as luck would have it, he had scheduled a visit anyway and would get back to either him or Claire after he talked to the fellow the following day.

Noel met Charles Johnson years earlier while working a very early morning case with DEA agents in southern Wisconsin. Charlie had been left behind to keep an eye on the DEA car as the other agents and Noel performed a raid on a crack house in Racine, Wisconsin. It was hoped that a wanted killer was lurking about somewhere in the basement of the house as an informant's affidavit had spelled out the day prior. When Noel asked about Charlie Johnson, the other agents just said, "He is bad luck," "new," "dangerously new" just to quote a few descriptions.

After coming up empty-handed during the raid, the agents and Noel returned to their car and told Charlie to drive them to a local Pancake House for breakfast.

While enroute to the Pancake House, Charlie interrupted the on-going conversation to find out if they wanted to book the alleged killer into the Racine County Jail first? Apparently, he had been taken into custody by DEA Agent Charlie Johnson and placed into the trunk of the car to make room for the other agents and Noel when they returned from the raid. For a rookie cop to have that much swag impressed Noel. From time to time, Noel and Charlie would compare notes and talk cases, so when Charlie told Noel he would "visit" a possible informant, Noel could rely on the informant becoming a source of information.

How reliable the information is from an informant usually depends on how badly law enforcement's help is wanted. If there isn't much to offer to the informant, he may play his contact. Even if there's a good trade opportunity, the officer still won't know how reliable the information is until it's acted upon. Informants are people, and people lie to cops and their girlfriends. That's what they like to do, whether it's for fun, profit, or out of fear - they like to lie.

Charlie went through the normal procedure of locking his weapon in the available gun locker at the federal correctional facility in Tucson. He was buzzed into the visiting booth that had one table and two stools welded to it. Everything was painted a dull gray, including the floors. The windows in the booth and the door were clean and shiny., though. When the Hispanic inmate was brought into the visiting booth, he was not handcuffed and was wearing a freshly laundered hunter orange jump suit with shower shoes and white socks. Charlie knew ahead of time that the inmate was an English speaker who had been thrown out of the country on at least one occasion.

"I'm DEA Agent Charles Johnson, and I understand you like tunnels. You are in trouble and whatever assistance you can provide me will be appreciated. Let me tell you right now, you will not have to testify to statements made today in court. I am looking for a female who has cartel friends and who likes to shoot people."

CHAPTER 23

"YOU KNOW THAT EXIT ON I-10 AT CASA GRANDE? THE LAST TIME I WAS there I don't remember seeing any CCTV camera," advised Noel.

Claire said, "I suppose Casa Grande can't afford the system. There is a lot of migrant labor there, and it's not as large as Phoenix or Tucson."

"I suppose a van could exit there and not be noticed," said Noel.

"Yeah, but remember this van had TV station lettering on the side of it. That might be eye-catching," cautioned Claire.

"Yeah, it would, but I recall several trailer parks not too far from that exit," said Noel. "If you didn't drive it that far into Casa Grande, how many people would notice it? Let's check it out. Between the three of us we could cover a lot of Casa Grande."

Claire asked, "Why Casa Grande, why not Yuma? If the van didn't go into Phoenix, maybe it turned on I-10 toward California or Yuma?"

"Because Charlie Johnson said there is a gal in Casa Grande who has cartel friends," revealed Noel.

It didn't take much time in getting the operation moving. Casa Grande was south of Phoenix on I-10 a little over three hours driving time from Prescott. Within a half hour Bear Child hit the jackpot. Behind a used car dealer on the main drag sat a white Dodge van with tv station lettering on the driver's side. The passenger side of the van didn't have lettering. When he called Noel, he was told, "Do not approach. We will meet you there in a few minutes."

As Noel got there Claire was already getting out of his car. A man in a polo shirt and jeans was walking toward them. It appeared that he wasn't armed, but Noel did not want to take any chances, so his hand hovered over his gun.

"Greetings, y'all buying one car today, or are all three of y'all buying?" asked the man. "I'm Don. What can I do you young fellows for?" Because Noel was still in his car with the door open watching the man just in case he suddenly turned sour on them, Claire smiled and said, "Well, we are interested in that van. Is she for sale?"

"Oh, ya betcha. We're just getting her ready for sale. Come on with me. Is he with you?"

Claire said, "You mean the old guy in the car? Yeah, he's just slower, that's all." Bear Child chuckled at Claire describing Noel. "What's with the lettering on the side of the van?" asked Claire as Noel joined them.

"The station in Phoenix sold two of these at auction, and the person who bought this one traded it to us. Great shape, low miles, even has air and some goodies inside, take a look."

As Bear Child went to work giving the van the once over to satisfy the man, Claire and Noel talked about getting the van out for a test ride in an attempt to lift some good prints. "Looking the van over without ruining latent fingerprints might be tricky. It would almost have to be done on site, right where she sits," said Noel.

"Might be a waste of time unless we want his prints instead," said Claire.

Noel said, "Better off focusing on the paperwork, finding out if there was a trade. Maybe our guy can give I.D. on our shooter for us."

"Have you the paperwork on this van?" asked Noel. "We would like to check out owner info because we don't want to buy a stolen van. This one was stolen from a station lot in Phoenix." The man started to stutter but gave Noel a description of the customer that could fit anyone out of a hundred women. "About thirty, blonde hair, nice body if you know what I mean?" Noel kept pushing the man, "Get us her driver license photocopy you made and the copy of the sales contract, the sooner the better!" he demanded.

Pointing at Bear Child, Claire said, "Don, the detective here will take down your information, and I will be taking the van into impound immediately. Thank you for your cooperation in this matter. I know you will be ok, you were just operating as a merchant when you got caught up in this fraud. Maybe we can get this sorted out before you lose too much money. I will be leaving my vehicle here for the time being."

"Wait, wait, wait, I think there might have been a mistake. This isn't ours, it is, but it isn't. Aw, we have it here for safekeeping," implored the man called Don.

Noel looked around the dirt lot with no fence and questioned, "Safekeeping?"

"Well, as collateral," explained Don. "She owes money on it."

"A lien?" asked Noel.

"Sort of a lien," said Don.

"Sort of a lien. Ok, Don, you know and we know that, as a dealer, you cannot have a sort of a lien on a stolen vehicle. We want her, not you or the van. Where is she?"

CHAPTER 24

NORMALLY, LARRY WOULD HAVE BEEN THE REMOTE DRONE PILOT. NOEL couldn't bring himself to go into Larry's apartment in Prescott and gather up a drone and drone equipment, but by nightfall Claire and Noel had finished setting up the drone they had purchased in Phoenix. Bear Child stayed in the Food City parking lot in Casa Grande and watched the Cookie Cutter Coffee Shop apartments located above.

The target apartment had three windows above the coffee shop. The shop itself was on the corner of the block directly across from the parking lot where Bear Child was observing from inside his car. Claire had kept Bear Child posted on their progress and, when ready, called him again to let him know they were enroute to his location. When they finally arrived in Casa Grande, Bear Child reported that he had seen nothing of the target, but the lights in the apartment had come on. It could not be known whether the lights were on a timer until they launched the drone with its operational lights covered with black tape. Once drone videos were taken of the woman in her apartment, a little headway was made. But after looking at the video, there appeared to be only partial images taken.

When there was video of the person's back as she walked away from the camera and into the light, not many details were seen. However, when video was taken of the person in partial dress or undress, the viewers could tell that the person was missing her left arm from the el- bow down. It was imperative that the home be broken into and entered to secure a good set of prints from whatever she touched to properly identify her.

The drone was able to show the three viewers that the exterior door at street level exposed an interior stairway leading up to her apartment and had a camera located above the door. A closed drone view of the exterior windows disclosed another camera mounted above the middle window, giving her computer monitor screen a street view below her apartment. Bear Child ventured a guess that there would be at least one more camera, probably in the rear of the building. The three decided to leave the Casa Grande area and gather up additional equipment to monitor her until they could come up with a better plan to capture her fingerprints. In Noel's car at the Food City parking lot, they talked about turning her over to the FBI or taking revenge now. If they had voted immediately, the outcome would have been a landslide to take revenge, but they took the time to discuss the pros and cons.

Noel cautioned, "Suppose she's not our shooter? Getting her prints would fill in some gray areas, like who the hell is she?"

"If we flip her to the FBI, how do we know if they will bring our shooter to justice? They may throw out the van evidence because of our little illegal search," warned Claire.

"Maybe," agreed Bear Child. "But we didn't discover any evidence inside the van that would normally get her convicted of shooting Larry. Short of arson, how would we get her to leave the apartment?"

Noel decided that they had to stay on her like "stink on crap" until they could get a latent print that would aid in identifying her. That would mean tailing her in the event she came out of the apartment while they were gathering equipment to monitor her. Bear Child offered to stay behind or come back early in the morning and watch until the other two got back. "No," said Noel, "I'll take the first watch, Claire will have second watch and you will do the late shift. I'll ask Rebecca to run the surveillance bag to us here in Casa Grande. First, drive around the back and check out the back door. I'm going to the can and will be back in a few." With that he walked across the street to the Veterans of Foreign Wars Post. Bear Child told Claire, "I got it" and hopped into his car to check out the back of the Cookie Cutter Coffee Shop. Bear Child drove into the alley behind the Cookie Cutter and noticed two heavy metal doors but no rear exit leading from the upstairs apartment.

When Noel came back to his car in the parking lot, he had three Styrofoam coffee cups in his possession. Bear Child told Noel what he had told Claire earlier. "There is no outside exit from upstairs, just the two large metal doors for the Cookie Cutter. The upstairs apartment probably has a rear exit to the interior of the coffee shop."

Noel asked, "Did you see a camera back there?"

"Yep, same setup as the front, one camera above the metal doors and one higher up giving a view of the alley," said Bear Child.

Claire asked, "Did you save me any toilet paper at the VFW?"

Noel responded, "When did the Navajo start using toilet paper?"

Bear Child broke out in a very high-pitched laugh, and Claire answered, "When we stopped using your mom's bowling shirt." All three were laughing until a Pinal County Sheriff's car turned into the parking lot.

Claire said, "Oh, oh" but Noel said, "Don't worry, I already called to let them know we would be here working a surveillance. He's just bored and wants to check us out." After the squad car drove through the parking lot, Bear Child said, "I hope the guy in the car lot and this deputy who just drove through aren't on her payroll."

Claire and Noel said in unison, "Me, too."

CHAPTER 25

DURING THE LONG NIGHT IN THE PARKING LOT, NOEL FILLED THE GUYS in on what he found out from his DEA contact. Apparently, the wannabe snitch turned out to be a United States-born citizen who worked for the Sinaloa Cartel digging tunnels. To date, he had constructed four of the numerous tunnels discovered beneath the streets of Douglas, AZ, at the Mexican border. The tunnels that he provided were air conditioned and had small electric-powered rail cars to haul the drugs. His job was to find the locations near the border that would provide cover, easy removal of tunnel material, and more importantly, the labor to dig and provide the material to shore up the tunnel. He was paid a healthy amount of money for his services.

He wanted to get out of the game because the Sinaloa Cartel was in the process of changing control and product. Large amounts of cocaine and marijuana were being replaced with smaller amounts of heroin and deadly fentanyl. The last labor force he provided were executed by the cartel after finishing the tunnel. It was only a matter of time or the wrong leader in control and he, too, would be scraped off the floor of the tunnel and hauled off to a mass grave somewhere.

The snitch felt comfortable with Charlie Johnson, the DEA agent. He told Charlie that there was an American gal who may be the person Noel and crew were interested in. She was Hispanic and grew up in the Yuma area near a small feed lot in Wellton, Arizona. Her dad worked at the feed lot part-time. When she was a little girl, she was with her dad when she got the sleeve of her jacket caught in the machine that conveyed the feed to the cattle, and she lost her hand. She had to have many surgeries. Because of that, she fell behind in school and became bitter about her deformed arm. No prom, no boyfriends, all the stuff a young girl would experience. She grew up with a deformed arm, dark skin, and much older than the other kids in her class. She dropped out of school and started to do her own thing. Older men, drugs and eventually drug sales.

"This might be our gal?" asked Claire.

"The snitch thinks so," said Noel. "He thinks she had the reputation of being a pretty tough woman, according to Charlie Johnson. It was rumored that, as a teenager, she got rid of a couple of cartel bad asses in Eloy."

"Eloy?" asked Bear Child.

"Yeah, Eloy, just a couple miles east of here," explained Noel.

Bear Child asked, "Well, if she made her bones with the cartel, why stick around Casa Grande?"

"Pinal County has a pretty heavy drug corridor, and we are in Pinal County right now," explained Claire. "Maybe she has family or maybe she has the perfect cover here."

"She left her family so we could maybe rule out that first possibility and stick with the second," offered Noel.

"Did Johnson have any ideas about her cover?" asked Claire.

"No, and we don't know if there other Pistoleros nearby," cautioned Noel.

CHAPTER 26

REBECCA DROVE INTO THE PARKING LOT ALMOST AT THE CRACK OF dawn with the surveillance equipment and a large thermos of black coffee. All three climbed out of Noel's car and greeted her as she handed them the bag of equipment and thermos through her driver's side window. She didn't turn off her car's engine as Noel stayed behind to talk with her and left the parking lot a few minutes later when delivery trucks started to arrive at the Food City store area. After some fresh doughnuts from Food City and some hot coffee, Bear Child was sent back to the car lot with a fingerprint kit.

He was able to come to an understanding with Don at the car lot. Then Bear Child used dusting powder and transparent tape to attempt to lift any latent prints on the steering wheel of the van. There were prints, but they were only from the driver's right hand. This was interesting; it could be easily explained away since many drivers use only one hand on the steering wheel. However, the way things were shaking out it appeared that Larry Figueroa may have been shot and killed by a woman with one arm.

The prints that were lifted by Bear Child appeared to be of good quality. They were immediately photographed by Claire and sent by cellphone to Agent Johnson. The bag that had been delivered by Rebecca contained the fingerprint kit, one automobile tracking device, several expensive digital cameras with long distance telephoto lenses, and a hand-printed note that read, "No stink'n nudes!"

As the guys were reading and laughing about the note left for them, a black Ford Mustang with California plates pulled up to the curb in front of the Cookie Cutter Coffee Shop, dropped off the target herself, and drove away. "Well hell's bells, how the hell did we miss that one?" asked Claire with a puzzled look on his face.

"Obviously she has another exit we missed," declared Noel. "Probably in a building next door connected by a common basement hallway."

"Or tunnel," said Bear Child.

"Did either of you notice her arm or hand?" asked Noel.

"Yeah, she looked like she was holding a book in one hand," said Claire. "I saw her close the door on the Mustang with the other hand."

"Gentlemen, we are sucking at this surveillance," declared Noel. "Is she or isn't she handicapped?"

Claire said, "I have an idea, I can go knock on her door and introduce you two to her." Claire made a gesture like he was knocking on a door and said, "'Good morning, Miss, this is Jeffery Dahmer and Ed Gein from Wisconsin. They wanted to thank you for your support.' Then we can stand there and watch to see if her hand or arm falls off."

"Very funny," said Noel.

"I was the one who saw her book hand and her car door closing hand," qualified Claire. "You guys didn't see squat."

Bear Child said, "That's true, but I'm the one who can lift her latent prints off of the doorknob she just touched to get back into her place."

"Well played," said Noel. "Well played."

It was decided that until they heard back from DEA Agent Johnson on the fingerprints, there wasn't any reason for a 24/7 surveillance of the target. They knew where she was located. And the longer they stayed in the Food City parking lot, the sooner she would make them and know she was under surveillance. Without a definite timetable from Agent Johnson, they would be wasting resources there. As a precaution Noel wanted to ask Claire to take Bear Child down to Tucson and check with the Mexican Consulate there to see if this gal had a Consular I.D. Card issued to her. But without a last name, fake or otherwise, this would not be possible. Consular I.D. Cards are issued by foreign governments to provide a method for their citizens to identify themselves. Biometric identity verification techniques including fingerprinting and retinal scan are currently used. Countries like Mexico and Guatemala do comply.

Instead, Noel asked the two to switch off observing the apartment location until sunset. He planned on returning to Prescott and would meet with them in the morning at the bookshop. If he got a positive read from Agent Johnson that the latent prints from her hallway door leading up to her apartment matched those taken from the van, he would tell the FBI about both the discovery of the van used in the shooting that killed Larry and about the shooter. He didn't want to discuss it with Bear Child while in Casa Grande, but he owed him that much, so he elected to propose it to him in the morning in Prescott. He was struck by something Bear Child had said about "not getting justice." If, for whatever reason, the FBI wanted to bury this under the rug, the three of them could always pursue it without them. The FBI buried critical information about the shootings from the Chicago Police Department while the Chicago Police launched a crusade against Bear Child. Police image is important to those in power, and maybe tarnishing a cop's badge is still cheaper than doing the right thing. Noel kept running this over and over in his mind. He felt a tug in his gut when he thought about Larry and being this close to Larry's killer. Noel had driven a short distance toward Prescott when his cellphone rang. After taking the call, Noel contacted Claire to give him the information he received.

"Claire, I'm coming back, Johnson just called and the prints match," reported Noel.

"So, the driver of the van was our gal, huh?" asked Claire.

"Oh yeah. I'm giving the info to the Bureau in about two minutes. When they arrive, we will withdraw, but until that happens, we need to keep an eye on her."

"Look, Noel, we have moved to the roof of the Food City store. Up here we have a better view. The manager gave us the ok. It was Tim's idea," said Claire, giving Bear Child the thumbs up.

"How about the back door on the Cookie Cutter Coffee Shop?" asked Noel.

"Tim has it taped so we can tell if anyone has opened it. We'll check on it until the FBI gets here or until you say otherwise," said Claire.

CHAPTER 27

Arizona Daily Star
Friday, January 29, 2021
By Santiago Billy
The Associated Press

In Guatemala, families say 13 killed in Mexico were migrants

COMITANCILLO, GUATEMALA – IN THIS IMPOVERISHED INDIGENOUS village, families are convinced that 13 of their relatives were among the 19 bullet-ridden, burned bodies found in the northern Mexico border area last week. Mexico has not yet identified the bodies, so it's not clear they were migrants. But people in Comitancillo near Guatemala's border with Mexico, are so sure that they have already put photos of the mainly youthful migrants -10 men and three women -on traditional alters for the dead, surrounded by candles and flowers.

On Saturday, authorities in the northern Mexico state of Tamaulipas found 19 bodies piled in a burnt-out pickup truck on a dirt road across the Rio Grande from Texas. Four bodies were found in the cab and the other 15 were piled in the bed of the truck. All had been shot, but crime scene evidence led investigators to believe they were killed somewhere else. Camargo, the area where the bodies were found, has long been the scene of turf battles between rival drug gangs, and authorities said three rifles were found in the burned pickup truck. If the bodies are identified as the Guatemalan migrants, the killings would revive memories of the 2010 massacre of 72 migrants in the same gang-ridden state.

———————

When the FBI finally arrived in Casa Grande, it was not like Noel had first imagined. The FBI agent in charge walked up to the guys on the roof and told Noel, "We will have to debrief you three assholes. I hope you clowns haven't soiled any of our evidence." With that, Noel took the agent by the arm and walked a few steps away from Bear Child and Claire with the agent in tow. "First of all, it is *our* evidence, and it may not be turned over to you. We might turn it over to the Sheriff of Pinal County, Arizona, if you try to cop an attitude out here."

"All three of us are former police officers, and we are well aware of what's considered the rules of evidence. You see that young muscular fellow there? His name is Tim Bear Child, and the FBI cost him his career and almost his life because of the way you guys handled this case. The FBI did cost me a friend and part-time employee several days ago in Prescott because of the way you've fucked this case up with the Chicago P.D. Sound familiar? You bet your ass it sounds familiar, I can tell by the way your facial expression has changed that you have been briefed and are familiar with this fuck up. Right now I have a good mind to throw your ass off this roof, so don't cop an attitude. Get on your fucking cellphone and get your guys over here. We're leaving, but don't let me hear about you fucking this up, you understand?"

Bear Child and Claire heard the entire conversation, (actually the sermon). They followed Noel's lead and gathered up the equipment to leave the rooftop. As they walked past the agent, each introduced themselves to him, "Tim Bear Child" "Claire Blue Crow" and joined Noel in the parking lot.

Noel said, "Follow me, we're going over to Florence."

Bear Child asked, "What is Florence?"

"It's where the Sheriff's Office is located and the State Prison Complex, the Death House, gas chamber," explained Claire.

Noel added, "It's just for show, I'm sure Snow White will have us followed now to see if we would actually turn things over to the sheriff. See you guys in the sheriff's parking lot."

Upon arrival in Florence, Noel got out of his car to meet the other two when he was approached by a Sheriff's Department Volunteer who asked him if he was Noel Two Horses? Noel acknowledged his inquiry and was told that the FBI had called his department and asked for Noel to call upon his arrival. Noel thanked the Sheriff's Volunteer and called the FBI number given to him. He was surprised to find out that the number was the mobile number for the Assistant Director he had met with in Prescott.

"Hi Noel, sorry to have to put you guys through this after assuring you we would cooperate fully with you. We will be in touch with you shortly after we establish our operation on the target. We think she may be on the run from her Prescott mistake. We are in the process of starting a cellphone link on her and will know more shortly."

"I think you better know she has another way to get out of that building," warned Noel. "There may be a tunnel or passage to an adjoining building."

"Ok, thanks, good to know. We're calling in air assets from out of our Phoenix Office as I speak."

"Thank you for keeping us in the loop," said Noel.

"No, Noel, thank you for keeping us in the loop. Good work. We'll bring you up to date as we go along. We'd like to have her under wraps today, if possible."

"Good hunting," said Noel, and the call was terminated. Noel told the guys about the context of the call and followed up by saying, "She will boogie if she keeps hearing the Bureau chopper overhead. Maybe that is what he wants her to do."

Bear Child added, "Sure, and they could listen in to her plans as she flees if she uses her cellphone."

Claire said, "I am all for hanging around the area for a while. I mean, Tim is paying for it." Noel laughed and said, "That's right, he is."

Bear Child said, "Money well spent."

Noel said, "No, just kidding Tim, this is on me. I want a crack at that bitch who thinks she is a shooter."

Claire said, "I got dibs."

Bear Child said, "You got what?" Noel and Claire just laughed.

Late that afternoon Claire took Bear Child to the prison gift shop located just north of the prison complex in a small wooden shack. before they closed for the day. Denim was special at the prison in Florence; visitors to the prison were not allowed to wear denim because incarcerated prisoners wear denim. He bought Bear Child a used denim jacket that was once issued to an inmate. It was how the prison raised money. Bear Child wore the jacket proudly and joked with Claire about sending him his prison-issued jacket should he be arrested for the three killings in Chicago. Claire said, "Don't send me your underwear man, I'm serious, don't do it."

Noel asked Claire to find accommodations for the night while he disclosed part of his plans. "Tonight, we are going to get some rest and sleep. I have a feeling that we may be hunting down some folks tomorrow, so we will need to be fresh." Noel asked Claire, "What does it look like as far as rooms go?"

Claire told them that Tucson was the best bet because it was closer than Phoenix and that he'd already made the reservations at a chain motel just off the frontage road on I-10. Noel said, "Ok, saddle up, we can take two cars and leave one here."

At dinner that evening at another chain-operated restaurant next door to the motel, Noel explained his entire thought process to the two guys.

"We have one target, and we don't know her. The prints don't tell us who she is, but they tell us she drove the van. We need to know her name. Maybe the Bureau will ID her if they capture her, or maybe not. Tomorrow I'm going to try to kick up some dust with any hospital in the Yuma area that may have treated her for the hand injury years ago. Meantime, Claire, you will be going down to the Mexican Consulate here in Tucson to try and get a lead on her. It's going to be hard without a name to go on, but they may have issued a Consulate ID Card to her as disabled which may have set her apart from others."

"Needle in a haystack," said Claire.

"Well, especially if she is an American citizen like the story said," added Bear Child.

"Yeah, but the word 'especially' is used to single out one person, thing, or situation over all others," explained Noel. Bear Child and Claire looked at each other and back toward Noel for clarity. "We may never ID her, but maybe we can rule out American citizen or phony, fraudulent Mexican ID Card holder. The result could help us sort out that haystack. Suppose she is a Mexican national living here and maybe mixed up in a cartel or heading up a cartel. Remember we were talking about Eloy and the drug corridor here? The foot traffic in this area is transient and from Mexico, illegal immigrants humping drugs for the cartel or else! Her role here could be pivotal, so she could be of high-ranking cartel status. Factor in the California plates on the car that dropped her off the other day. The Sinaloa Cartel has roots in Mexico but its fingers in California and here."

For Noel, the rest of the evening was spent in the shower, then calling Prescott and speaking with Rebecca. Bear Child and Claire showered and fell asleep watching television. Their clothes were getting ratty-looking, so all three would be buying new clothes after breakfast. The Tucson Mall was not that far away. They were men and would not be shopping for a wedding, so it would not consume a lot of time.

During breakfast Claire told Bear Child about shopping for clothes with an old client arrested for murder named Louie Louis, a former Mexican cartel member and confirmed kleptomaniac. "Because I had to spend a lot of time with this little dude, I did some research on people who steal, people who were real kleptomaniacs. Not just part-time shop-lifters but real kleptomaniacs," said Claire. "Kleptomania is an impulse disorder. Most kleptomaniacs are women, and the cause of kleptomania is unknown, just an irresistible urge to steal." He told a story about a therapist who worked with those who had impulse disorders and used Equine Therapy to help them recognize triggers that caused problems for them. A short period of time transpired waiting for Claire to finish his story before Claire said, "Get it? Equine therapy and trigger? You know, Roy Rodgers and Trigger, his horse Trigger? Get it?"

Bear Child said, "Before my time." Noel said, "Mine, too." "Come on!" complained Claire.

Before leaving to go into Tucson to shop for fresh clothes, Noel wanted both Bear Child and Claire to know that he might leave the mall area after shopping to head back to Casa Grande just to keep an eye on the FBI operation. "I think there is enough evidence with the matching fingerprints to get a search warrant. I have this idea we're missing something," he said. "She has to have some sort of ID to function today, either Mexican Consulate ID Card or American credit cards, driver's license, checkbook, or whatever. Unless it's all fake, then it wouldn't make any difference what she has."

"Well, one thing is for sure," said Claire. "She has a history, everyone has a history. Whoever treated her for her hand injury when she was a kid needed her name, it's on file somewhere. I've been in that area and sure, there's a hospital in Yuma, but suppose they couldn't do the hand surgery there, and they had to fly her to Phoenix. That air ambulance service would have records."

"Yeah, you're right, instead of doing a Mexican Consulate record search today, hit the phone from your motel room after we get some clean clothes," Noel said. "I'll let you know what's going on with our FBI. I'd like to be there if the feds get a search warrant."

CHAPTER 28

NOEL CALLED CLAIRE LATER THAT MORNING TO LET HIM KNOW THAT the FBI was going to use the aircraft to surveil the woman in Casa Grande after all. He and the agent in charge talked about the chance of spooking her with the aircraft and having her run. The FBI agent said, "We don't want to have a chase in the desert, but if our plan works, we can maybe nail her as she walks out." Noel asked him, "How about a search warrant based upon the matching prints we have?" The agent told Noel, "We have that in the works right now, just waiting for it to come through. It's been six hours so far. Look, Mr. Two Horses, we know we screwed up with the Chicago P.D. situation by not sharing the info on the shootings, now we have the shooting in Prescott that is probably the same organized cartel, and your friend paid the cost. I think we are on solid ground for a federal Judge to sign off on it any minute now."

"Oh, I agree, and call me Noel, ok?" said Noel after feeling a little better about his relationship with the agent in charge. "Maybe this might be a good time to get the sheriff's people and the police department here ready to contain the area if that call comes through?" The Sheriff's Department and the Arizona Department of Public Safety had placed units at all entrances to Casa Grande while the police department joined the federal cars in the Food City parking lot. When the warrant call came through, the agent in charge and his team moved down to ground level to enter the target's apartment with the police department officers on scene.

Noel was asked to remain outside until the apartment was secured and the agent in charge sent word for him. To their surprise, neither the front door nor the apartment door was locked so the entry into the apartment was uneventful. When Noel couldn't hear any voices other than the guys breaching the apartment, he knew she had evaded them. He hoped the apartment would reveal a lot of information once the FBI forensic team arrived on scene.

When the agent in charge returned to the sidewalk area where Noel was, he said, "She must have used the old tunnel connecting the house over here," pointing across the street and next door to the store where the FBI were located. "Our guys are still inside the house and tunnel, and it is old, old, old. Probably goes back into prohibition days." Noel said, "Damn, she probably parked next to me." "Or me," added the agent.

It would be a few hours before the FBI forensic team would get on scene, and that meant another three or four hours before Noel could be allowed into the apartment. Noel asked the agent if he would humor him and have the Bureau do a record search on any air ambulance service in the Maricopa, Arizona or Yuma, Arizona area that may have been involved in a medivac to a Phoenix hospital from the Yuma area back in the day when the target was a juvenile or adolescent. "This is a shot in the dark, but they may have her name recorded somewhere, someone had to cover the cost of that medivac flight. I know it would be a lot of Bureau manhours, but it would reveal pure gold in terms of information if we could nail it." "Noel, not a problem, we have been ordered to assist you, and this would be a step in the right direction."

Noel called Claire and instructed him to cancel the phone record search, explaining why. He told Claire to head back to Casa Grande and filled him in on the missing woman and the old passage under the street. "As soon as they let us in, we may have some work to do here, and if not, well, we'll know soon enough." Claire was a pretty good tracker and if there were any tracks, shoe prints, or anything that might be tied to the woman, he just might find it. Noel had respect for the FBI forensic folks, but sometimes even they missed things. The Bureau was interested in pursuing any leads that might provide a location for her, and they might appreciate additional help.

Throughout the day small pieces of information were provided to Noel. The apartment did not reveal her name, nor did the available U.S. Mail provide any information. All of the gas bills, water bills, and apartment history came back to several different men with Mexican names. There was a Father Jesus, of course, and a Poncho Villa Jr. just to name two. The same was true of the house across the street that shared the same tunnel. Latent prints other than hers were the only ones found until late afternoon. Then a clear set of prints revealed that one of the people in the apartment recently was a fugitive from American justice, an important fugitive and member of the Sinaloa Cartel. These prints were on the bathroom wall about waist level above the bathtub and one partial print on the commode handle.

Federal agents canvassed the neighborhood asking about the woman and her habits. According to several people she was seldom seen during the day, so when Noel and his team spotted her leaving the car with the California plates two days earlier, it was a rare occasion.

Late that night, Noel and his guys were given the green light to enter the apartment and the passage or tunnel under the street. After putting on booties and protective suits, Bear Child and Noel went into the apartment while Claire went into the tunnel. There was not a lot to see in the apartment. All of her clothes had been bagged and removed for forensic examination, and the rest of the apartment was void of any television equipment, phones, computers, laptops, or printers. The contents of the refrigerator and freezer were removed, leaving a spotless kitchen and pantry. Tracking down the source of the groceries would help in possibly establishing ID, while electronics might assist in establishing habits, likes, dislikes etc.

Noel thought that Claire may have found something when he reappeared after inspecting the tunnel. Claire showed Noel and Bear Child a cellphone photograph he captured of what appeared to be the print of the edge of a sports shoe on a cement floor. Noel and Claire shared it with the FBI forensic team and told them that the woman may have been wearing sport or jogging shoes and advised that this information should be made known to other agency team members as it could help ID her.

Claire also said that the passage ended in the furnace room located in the basement of the house. The target probably exited the house through the rear door at ground level.

Noel decided to have the guys return to Prescott and called Rebecca to let her know he was coming home. While traveling back on the interstate, Noel got a call informing him that an FBI tech was able to retrieve an old Arizona Republic Newspaper story about a young Hispanic girl caught in an ambush between U.S. Border Patrol Agents and Mexican drug smugglers. Apparently, the young girl suffered extensive injuries to her hand and arm and was the subject of a series of newspaper articles about her treatment and rehab. What became the focus of the tech was that she was airlifted to available emergency care by a Border Patrol aircraft according to the old article. The FBI tech was in the process of trying to assemble the available articles and would reach Noel the following business day. Noel felt that this might be progress after all.

When Noel arrived back in Prescott, he first stopped at his mystery bookshop at the Saint Gregory Hotel to check for voicemail messages on his shop's phone system. When he got home, Rebecca met him at the door and told him she had a hot supper in the kitchen. Noel could smell the aroma of a great hotdish in the oven and commented on it. "I'm hoping you will join me? I know it's late, but I stopped at the bookshop to check for messages." Rebecca told Noel, "Don't worry about that, and yes, I'm going to eat, too."

After Noel freshened up in the upstairs bathroom, he came back down to see the kitchen table had been set for two and even had fresh flowers in a mason jar in the center. He told Rebecca that he had missed her and thanked her again for making the drive to Casa Grande to bring him needed equipment.

Rebecca said, "I'm glad it was helpful. I hope you were able to put it to good use." Noel mumbled under his breath, "Oh, hell yeah, damn good nude photos." Rebecca grabbed his ear and asked him, "What did you say?" Noel laughed and said, "Nothing, nothing!" Rebecca rubbed the top of his head, "That is what I thought you said."

As Rebecca sat down, too, she asked Noel to bring her up to date.

The two of them enjoyed the meal of fresh bread and hot baked casserole. Rebecca listened carefully as Noel described the woman who killed Larry. When Noel was finished speaking Rebecca said, "Noel, the child who was shot years ago may be a different person from the child who had her hand and arm damaged in the feedlot years ago. Do you think that the FBI tech may have landed on the right woman?" Noel said he didn't know, but he knew that stories change. "My information originally came from a guy who wanted to snitch because he was in lockup. This latest information is coming from a reliable source. I think my gut tells me to go with what is reliable and available. Maybe the tech can deliver a name for us after mining old news articles."

Before they finished their meal Claire's vehicle pulled into the yard. Claire joined them in the kitchen, and all three ate and talked. After Claire had a chance to eat some of the casserole, Noel told him about the phone message from the FBI tech. They talked about the chances of that child being the target they were pursuing.

Noel asked him, "What do you think of Tim Bear Child now that you have spent some time with him?" Claire said after a short pause in the conversation, "Tim is a sharp guy; he has also shown some degree of anger with this gal in Casa Grande and the damn Chicago Police. I noticed his anger climb while we were in Casa Grande. We were on the roof of that grocery store when he said something about getting his shot at the gal. Not a shot, but *his* shot. He was no longer a young fella when he spoke, but a pissed-off warrior."

It was Rebecca who spoke in response to Claire's observation, not Noel, and she said, "Look, I met a young guy at my restaurant who was starting school here after all the crap they made him go through in Chicago, and it cost him his career anyway. He came off as a guy full of anger but willing to play by the rules and still got pissed on when the FBI interviewed him by phone here in Prescott. When they killed Larry thinking Larry was him, that uncorked a lot of hate in him." Noel added, "We have seen him grow old by the years here in front of us. Larry's death hurt him, too. I think we are traveling with an angry, wounded bear."

CHAPTER 29

WHEN NOEL OPENED HIS BOOKSHOP THE FOLLOWING MORNING, HE found a short note printed on the Hotel Saint Gregory letterhead taped to his front door. It instructed him to contact the management office upon his return. Noel had entered into a lease agreement with the hotel. He had the feeling that the note was about his shop not being open as stipulated in the lease. At times he had to close the bookshop to travel or to work an extended case. When Noel had advance notice, he would normally contact one of his two part-time people. They were both his students at the local college and full-time single moms who shared a house near the bookshop. After unlocking the front door and entering the bookshop, Noel threw the notice into the waste bin. There weren't any new phone messages, so Noel went to the wall that contained the hidden door built into it. That door opened into the hall where the public restroom was located, and he unlocked that door. He no sooner did that when a delivery driver entered the shop with a carton of books for Noel. The delivery man and Noel exchanged small talk about shipping costs. Noel didn't want to burden the guy with complaints about something he had no control over, so Noel just agreed with everything said. When the delivery man left the shop, Noel opened the book shipment and started to place each book on the table after visually checking for obvious scratches or printing errors on the covers and full-page count. When he was finished with that, he took a jackknife out of his pocket, opened it, and cut along the tape holding the box together, folded the box and placed it next to his checkout counter. Throughout the morning and early afternoon, the bookshop had several customers but only one had made a purchase.

One man introduced himself as a hotel guest and asked Noel, "Are there any magazines here?" Noel explained to him, "The store is a mystery bookstore, we don't carry magazines."

The man became angry and told Noel, "I spend a lot of money at this hotel, and I just may not stay here in the future," declaring this as he tried to poke at Noel's chest with his pointed finger. Noel immediately blocked this action and softly said, "I don't care where you elect to sleep, screw, or shoot yourself." The man said, "I insist upon talking to the management," and that is when Noel retrieved the note from the waste bin to give him, pointing out the address on the letterhead. The man threw the note to the floor and abruptly left the shop. Noel expected another note on his door in the near future.

The reason Noel opened his mystery bookstore in the first place was to be able to research and sell books in a peaceful setting. Noel was not born into an academic environment, but he understood the value of reading. In his often-violent life he knew about people who were being victimized. He also knew about the people who abused others and turned them into victims. Noel felt strongly that when those stories were told or written they needed to be as factual as could be. Noel wanted readers to be able to believe in the accuracy of stories of crime, fictional or otherwise. The readers needed to see what life was like in the part of the world that they themselves may never have experienced. Only then could they understand how a victim reacts to an injustice perpetrated by an unjust actor. An unjust system rarely affects those who do not live in that part of reality.

Just then the phone call came in from the FBI tech who had discovered an old Arizona Republic newspaper article. The tech told Noel a little bit about his research findings but said he was going to send Noel the information via the internet, and Noel could develop his own conclusions. Noel thanked the tech, recorded his telephone contact number, and assured him he would download the information as instructed. Within minutes Noel was able to bring up the news article about a young girl who had been shot in the arm and had to be airlifted to Phoenix for surgery. One night in November, 1983, a young Mexican girl in the company of other unarmed migrants in the area at the Mexican border in Yuma, Arizona, was struck by agents of the Yuma Sector of the U.S. Border Patrol as they returned small arms fire coming from a group of Mexican smugglers. The girl was airlifted to a hospital for surgery to save her injured hand. The various articles did not reveal the victim's name because of her age. As Noel downloaded additional articles, it became apparent that the young girl's hand could not be saved and had to be amputated. A number of charitable organizations became involved in financially assisting with the cost of her medical expenses. One of the organizations had a director who was a young minister that Noel knew and who could possibly provide additional information to the injured child's story.

Noel looked through all of his saved business cards. Before the internet and smart phones, most people had to rely on business cards and a desk rolodex to retrieve telephone numbers of people that were important to them. Noel had a system; friends with business cards were kept on one side of his desk, business associates sometimes were honored to be included, while others occupied the other side of his desk in a stack reserved for sales or company cards. The young minister was on the correct side of the desk, and Noel was hoping he still had the same number. When Noel called a man answered and identified himself right away. "Hello, Pastor Phillips speaking."

"John, Pastor John Phillips, this is Noel Two Horses, how are you?"

"The famous Mr. Two Horses! Good to hear your voice. I'm fine."

"John, I have a favor to ask you. Can you reach into the attic of your memory and educate a few of my male friends that I'm playing poker with here today as to the name of the little Mexican girl who was shot in the hand by the Border Patrol years ago?"

"Noel, you never cease to amaze me, poker at this time of day?" asked the minister.

"Ok, you got me. I needed her name, but I know you can't provide that. Privacy, confidentiality, honor among thieves, and all that church stuff," complained Noel.

"No, actually we never knew her name. Her grandfather and mother were killed that night in the shooting by the smugglers, and we never got a name. We nicknamed her Rosarita, after the refried beans can label," revealed the minister. "Today that would be considered so disrespectful. You know, a Border Patrol agent lost his job over the shooting. Sad thing, his family was in my congregation."

"What was his name?" asked Noel.

"I remember the family name," said the minister, deep in thought, "but wait, his name was Roberto, Roberto Crow. The family was out of El Paso. He lost his job because of the shooting and his family because of his drinking that followed."

Noel said, "Wow" and asked, "Is he still around?"

"He is, in fact," replied the minister. "He works maintenance at the casino here in Yuma, the Quechan Tribal Casino. Where every hand is a winner!"

"Same ol' John, you haven't changed at all," said Noel. "Give you a call when I get to town."

"Kind of figured you would be coming."

"Yeah?" asked Noel. "Yeah," said the minister.

Noel thought about the information he had just gotten from his friend, Pastor Phillips. There were things that didn't add up. Why didn't the news coverage about the little girl being shot years ago disclose anything about her grandfather and her mother being killed? The report covered smugglers exchanging fire with the Border Patrol, and for some reason a Border Patrol agent lost his job. Noel didn't want to waste time checking out a false lead, but this was an unusual twist that needed to be cleaned up. He also needed a name for this child so she could be found before anyone ruled her out as the shooter. The former Border Patrol agent had to be interviewed about that incident. Claire would have to remain in Prescott to keep an eye on Bear Child. The shooter was still free to try and get Bear Child again. It was obvious that the people behind the Chicago shootings didn't know if Bear Child knew more than he should have or not. The safe option was to kill him and end the debate.

CHAPTER 30

When Claire joined Noel at the bookshop, Noel filled him in on the information he got from his friend in Yuma. Claire was ok with staying in Prescott and keeping Bear Child under wraps. Claire asked if Bear Child was ok with the plan. Noel said, "I'll tell him to take care of the bookshop with you, but no separate shifts. I can get there and make it back by tomorrow night. Try not to have too much fun while I'm gone."

Noel grabbed some extra operational cash out of a hollow fireplace log in the bookshop's Sherlock Holmes living room and blew Claire a goodbye kiss as he was leaving. After retrieving his car from the hotel parking structure, Noel stopped at home to grab some travel items and his overnight bag. He called Rebecca at her restaurant to let her know where he would be. She warned him to be careful and to hurry back. Noel was on the I-17 heading toward Phoenix and from there I-10 toward California before he was relaxed enough to listen to his favorite group and relax even more. As he was enjoying The Mavericks, he almost forgot about losing Larry. Ashamed by that, he reacted by violently turning off the music.

When Noel arrived in Yuma, he drove to the Cocopah Tribal Casino and Hotel just off the interstate. He was able to register and get inside his room to freshen up. While there he debated calling the Quechan Tribal Casino to ask to speak with Housekeeping about Roberto. The housekeeping supervisor would be able to tell Noel that Roberto would or would not be working today, but knowing he would forewarn Roberto about the call, Noel did not place it.

He thought that he'd drive over to the Quechan Casino, have an early dinner, and try to locate Roberto. He parked his car and walked across the parking lot while being on the lookout for any possible housekeeping people who might be outside for a break. Looking for a dark-skinned male employee in a Native casino wasn't tricky. However, identifying him by his name might spook him. For years the Native casinos have always had employees wear name badges, and Noel hoped the same was holding true of this casino.

Noel helped himself to a seat in a corner booth in the restaurant where he could observe staff coming and going. He then pocketed a cardboard drink coaster. The casino had a very good restaurant, and Noel was pleased to find out that they had an excellent ribeye steak and salad special. When the waiter took his order, Noel ordered it rare and asked for ranch dressing on the side for his salad. Rebecca had been at him to eat healthy, and he did try to do that on and off. He struck up small talk with the waiter but avoided asking the waiter if he knew Roberto and if Roberto was working. Noel finished his meal and put it on a card with a healthy tip. He asked the waiter to have the bar help get him a Jack Daniels and water with an olive in it and bring it to the bank of slot machines near the men's room closest to the restaurant. Noel walked over to a bank of slot machines near the men's room that he had described, sat down at a penny machine, and started to play a penny machine for about five minutes before his drink arrived. Noel tipped the server a 5-dollar bill and played until his drink was finished. Noel slowly rose from the machine and walked into the men's room. As he went to the sink area, he took numerous paper towels dispensed from an automatic machine and walked into a toilet stall. Noel dropped the drink coaster into the toilet, and the paper towels followed seconds later. The toilet immediately began to back up and overflow. Noel left the restroom to sit back down at his slot machine. A bar server approached him to see if he wanted to order another drink. Noel did and asked the server if she could report a 'water on the floor in the men's room' issue to the casino housekeeping department.

As Noel played his slot machine and drank his Jack and water, he kept looking for the housekeeping person to respond to the men's room. A man in his late 40's, maybe early 50's, arrived minutes later and set up a plastic cone to keep men out of the restroom while he worked. Noel waited several minutes and walked into the closed restroom. The clogged toilet had been cleared in minutes but while the man was finishing mopping, he turned around and saw Noel looking at him. He asked, "Mr. Two Horses, I presume?" Noel laughed and said, "Yes, I'm sorry about the mess. I thought I was being clever, but I see Pastor John tipped my hand." The man told Noel, "Yeah, he does that. What can I do for you?"

Noel said, "I know what happened years ago was difficult for you, and it might be hard to talk about, but I need to find out the name of that little girl who was shot in the hand on the border years ago." The man stopped mopping, said he would be going outside on a break in 20 minutes, and if Noel wanted to talk, he would be near the main entrance. When the two of them met, the man told Noel "First of all, she was not on the border. She and her family were several miles south of the border when the shooting started."

"We were not where we were supposed to be when someone on my side shot her. One of the guys I was with opened up, and the rest of us did, too. Someone yelled 'incoming!' We were taking it, and we kept pouring it on."

Noel asked, "Roberto, were there any rounds fired from the group of migrants?" Roberto Crow looked up at the night sky and said, "Hell no. There was an investigation if you want to call it that, but no bodies were found, no spent ammo cases were found, because the location under review was on the U.S. side of the border. All B.S."

"But you had her airlifted," said Noel. "There had to be coordination for that flight, right?" Roberto told Noel, "Oh, there was coordination, but only after she was driven across to our side of the border."

"What about her grandfather and her mom?" asked Noel.

"Back in the day, loose lips sink ships and jobs, huh?" said Roberto.

"Her family was just chalked up to migrant death in the desert?" asked Noel.

"Yeah, but that didn't satisfy me. But it cost me my job when I pushed it. I was disposable back then. Not anymore, I am not disposable. What else do you need, Mr. Two Horses?"

CHAPTER 31

THE NEXT MORNING THE TWO MEN HAD BREAKFAST AT THE COCOPAH Tribal Casino and Hotel where Noel was staying. Before meeting Roberto, Noel had placed five hundred dollars cash in a hotel envelope that he had taken from the desk drawer in his room. After greeting Roberto when he came into the restaurant, both sat down and ordered from the menu. The waiter poured coffee into their cups, then Noel reached into his back pants pocket and produced the envelope with the cash in it. He handed it to Roberto and told him, "Here is an information reward." Roberto took the offered envelope but just stared at it and then looked at Noel.

Noel said, "I would like you to take it." Roberto kept looking at Noel who added, "My client would like you to take it, too. Roberto, Pastor John's program will also get a donation from my client."

Roberto asked, "If I keep it, will I have to testify?"

Noel looked Roberto in the eye and said, "Only if you want to testify." Roberto took the envelope and pushed it into his pocket.

"I'm curious, how did you get the last name Crow? Are you Native?" asked Noel.

"From my dad's side, Pueblo out of New Mexico," said Roberto. "My mom was Mexican. That's how I made it through the Spanish course in the Border Patrol Academy." Noel laughed and said, "Yeah, Spanish was hard for many of the guys I knew back in the day. You flunk Spanish, you flunk the academy."

Roberto asked, "Were you Border Patrol?" "No, but my friends were," answered Noel.

Roberto took a sip of his coffee and said, "There are a few who should have flunked out of the academy, but I used to think there was no God. Two that were with me that night died of cancer and the third guy died from a case of direct lead poisoning, so I know now that there is a God." Noel asked, "What kind of lead poisoning?" and Roberto answered, "9mm lead poisoning." Noel said, "Yeah that's the worst kind." Just then the waiter brought the breakfast that they ordered and after serving it, asked if there was anything else he could provide. Noel thanked him, and he left the table area.

Noel asked Roberto, "How did he get poisoned?" Roberto replied, "Still an unsolved open case. Apparently, he had just gone home from his shift when someone popped him as he got out of his car. The agency, FBI, and local police never found a clue. It happened a dozen years after the little girl got shot, but I think it was retaliation for her injuries and the murder of her family members."

"What was the agent's name?" asked Noel, and when Roberto told him, Noel's response was a blunt, "Families don't forget."

Roberto told Noel, "You know, I always figured it was the girl's family. She never spoke to anyone all the while she was in the U.S. She went back to Mexico to live, and one year at Christmas time she sent a clay impression of her hand, her healthy hand, to the pilot who flew her that night. She had painted it green for Christmas and addressed it to the 'angel pilot.' The pilot didn't work out of our sector, so our supervisor gave it to me because I was there that night. When they gave me the boot, it was the only thing in my locker that I kept."

As they were leaving the restaurant, Noel asked Roberto if he could get his phone number if he need to contact him again. Roberto dug into his wallet and handed him a business card. On it was his name and a P.O. Box address listing him as a private investigator. Roberto said, "I am a good investigator. This was my last week at the casino, I'm trying to make it out here."

Noel told Roberto, "Don't give up, the good ones don't give up, Roberto."

"No, I gave up once before, and I'm done with giving up. I've been doing some public defender investigation work for Yuma County, but the county budget is pretty thin right now."

Noel laughed and told Roberto, "It is always thin, I know because it was thin when I was doing it here in Yuma years ago. I don't suppose you ever learned her name, did you?"

Roberto smiled at Noel's persistence and said, "She wrote her name on the wrapping paper, you know where the return address would go, and it was in her kid's handwriting, it was Alita Lopez."

"Look, Roberto, I could use you here in Yuma. I'll fill you in later today by phone before I head back to Prescott." Roberto quickly said, "Thank you, Mr. Two Horses," but Noel interrupted him to let him know his friends call him Noel.

Noel planned on returning to his room to pack up his stuff and to place a call to his old friend, Pastor John, but first he wanted to take a cup of coffee with him. Once in his room he opened the plastic lid on his coffee cup and smelled the aroma. Then he called his friend to socialize and to thank him for the connection to Roberto.

"You are most welcome, Noel. He's a good guy, isn't he?" asked Pastor John. "Yes," answered Noel. "Hey, are you going to be available for a few minutes today, John?"

"Unfortunately, I have a funeral today, and I'm running late as usual. I'm sorry, Noel."

"Well, I'm going to be sending you a special donation from one of my clients. His last name is Bear Child, Tim Bear Child, and he is a special person. Thanks again, John," said Noel.

"Travel safe, Noel" said Pastor John.

Noel could not help but think how lucky he was to have friends who were good people. He thought that Pastor John was right about Roberto; he, too, thought Roberto was a good guy. Noel was impressed with him. As he enjoyed his coffee, he kept thinking about how hard it must have been for Roberto to lose his career and his family because some asswipe cop wanted to throw him under the bus. The three who were involved with Roberto that night might have had their just desserts after all, cancer and lead poisoning. Little Alita Lopez thought the rescue pilot was a good guy and sent him a child's Christmas gift of her handprint in clay. Without missing a beat, Noel threw the coffee cup into the wastebasket and grabbed his overnight bag while calling Roberto's phone number. Noel walked out of the hotel knowing the credit card he left on file would be used for billing his stay. When Roberto answered his phone, Noel was getting into his car and instructing Roberto to find the clay handprint and meet with him as soon as possible.

CHAPTER 32

CLAIRE BLUE CROW'S CELLPHONE CHIRPED TWICE BEFORE HE LOOKED at the screen with hopes that the call was from Sylvia. Every time his phone went off, Claire hoped it was Sylvia calling him. Claire had been divorced from his wife of 12 years for almost the same length of time he was married to her. It all started out innocently enough. Sylvia was a young nurse on the Navajo Reservation Claire met when he stopped on the road to help her with a flat tire. Claire noticed her old GMC pickup truck on the side of the road as he approached the bottom of a large hill. At first the outline of the truck looked like it had been abandoned, but as he got closer, he saw someone kneeling near the rear tire on the side closest to the ditch. Claire stopped his car behind her and got out to see if she was ill or had truck problems. As he walked toward her, she got to her feet, brushing off her jeans, and acknowledged Claire's "Hello" with her own "Hello."

"Tire trouble, huh?" asked Claire.

"Oh yeah, my grandpa's truck, old tires," she explained.

"Does your grandpa have a spare?"

"Yeah, probably as old as this tire."

Claire stuck his hand out to her and said, "I'm Claire Blue Crow."

She accepted Claire's hand and said, "Sylvia Horn."

As Claire began to retrieve the spare tire, Sylvia said to him, "I'm afraid I don't have any money on me to pay you." Claire responded with a smile and a shrug and said, "Not necessary. A gentleman always helps a lady." In an attempt to put Sylvia at ease he said, "I was a cop up here years ago, and I did a lot of this."

Sylvia asked, "What do you do now?"

"Oh, I'm still a cop but in Chicago now," said Claire.

It didn't take that long to change the tire on the old truck, and just before leaving Sylvia thanked Claire and offered to buy him a beer the next time they met. One thing led to another, and before too long, they had a relationship going and got serious. They married and Sylvia moved to Chicago for a while, but the metropolitan pace of Chicago became too much for her. Claire was never home, and it seemed like he was always working when they should have been together. When she left Claire, he resorted to working and drinking. During the summer he would go back to his reservation, but she never wanted to meet him. She stopped talking to him entirely and filed for a divorce. Claire never let on to anyone that he had a broken heart.

Some days he would daydream that they would be together, but as time went on, he knew it wouldn't happen. One time a fellow cop remarked to him, "Chief, you know you are the only divorced cop I ever met who doesn't bad-mouth his ex." Claire replied, "I am not a chief, and she does not deserve to be bad-mouthed." Claire eventually regained control of his drinking and left Chicago. He went to work for the L.A. Police Department in California, but that, too, came to an end. Years later he admitted that he wanted to work for a large police department so he could get lost within the population of sworn officers. Claire never said much about working in the L.A.P.D., and Noel never pushed him about it. He sometimes thought Claire got tired of it all.

This call was from Noel. Noel told Claire about finding and speaking to Roberto Crow and more importantly, that he may have a name for the target if she was the shooter. He also provided an explanation for the shooting of the little girl that night near the Mexican Border. "If she is our shooter, we will at least know if she is still a Mexican national living in Arizona. This is important because that may put a priority on the investigation by the Bureau, especially if she is a Mexican cartel assassin. Roberto gave me a clay impression of that little girl's hand. We may be able to match some points of similarity that can help us ascertain if she is the shooter by comparing to the latent prints we have from the shooter's apartment in Casa Grande and the latent prints from the van. If that hand impression was made by some other little Mexican girl a dozen years ago, we are back to square one. I don't think we have a damn thing to lose, so I photographed the hand impression with my phone and sent the photos to the FBI team for comparison. We're not trying to prosecute her based upon the hand impression from twelve years ago, we are only trying to identify her, so we have some leeway here. Oh, before I forget, the little girl's name was Alita Lopez."

This was turning out to be the longest day that Noel had spent on the road in a long time. He was convinced that, based upon the speed this investigation was moving, he would hear from the FBI before he got back to Prescott. But the clock kept turning with the miles he drove. Soon he was pulling into Prescott and still no response from the Bureau.

When Noel got back, he drove directly to his parking spot in the parking structure at the Hotel Saint Gregory. At the front door of his mystery bookshop, he was glad to see that it was open for business and that both Bear Child and Claire were inside. He greeted them and advised that he still hadn't heard anything from the FBI team. Claire looked at Bear Child and back at Noel and said, "The FBI called here and said we have a match or similarity on at least a dozen points on the hand impression and the latent prints. I assumed, I mean *we* assumed you heard." Noel said in exhaustion, "No, no idea. Of course they would call here! Hell, we now have a name for our shooter; watch out Alita Lopez, we are coming!"

"Dinner is on me, let's lock up, and I'll have Rebecca meet us in the dining room. Tim, I hope you don't mind, but we're going to send Roberto a bonus on top of what we already paid him."

"Why, what did we pay him?" asked Bear Child as they turned off the lights. Claire laughed and said, "Don't worry, it will all be recoverable when Chicago P.D. squares things with you." "Hey that reminds me," said Bear Child. "My attorney said they want to settle out of court!" Noel advised as he was locking the door, "Drinks are on you!"

Rebecca showed up at the dining room of the hotel as the guys were looking at the menu and finishing their second round of drinks. All four of them had a great dinner and enjoyed each other's company. When it was time to leave, Claire caught Noel's attention as Bear Child was talking with Rebecca and asked, "Do you want me to check on him later tonight? That's what we have been doing."

Noel asked, "Do you mean you and Officer Randal from Prescott P.D.?" Claire nodded. "Yeah, go ahead," said Noel, and Claire responded, "Ok, good."

When Rebecca and Noel returned to the house, both checked the doors and turned in. Rebecca told Noel, "I'm really glad you got some positive information to run with. I was worried about it once you told me she did a Houdini on you guys down in Casa Grande." Noel asked Rebecca, "Have you ever doubted me?" There was absolutely no pause before she said, "Hell, yeah!"

Noel said, "You know that hurts. I'm hurt."

Rebecca warned him, "You will be hurt if you don't come over here."

CHAPTER 33

NOEL WAS PRETTY ACTIVE WHENEVER HE WAS IN PRESCOTT. HE HAD A mystery bookshop to run, he taught college level Criminal Justice courses online as well as ground classes, and he ran a private investigative business. A private investigative business that was doing criminal defense work for criminal defense attorneys. Lately, however, he was doing criminal investigative work to capture a criminal who killed a friend of his. He and two other guys were doing the work that criminal justice professionals should be doing. Between the three of them they had extensive experience in finding and capturing people, so that they could be held accountable in a court of law. After Larry was killed, the three of them went all out to track down the killer. The resources of the FBI were brought into play, but the FBI was being used pretty much as a backup since the shooting. Noel had entertained the idea that maybe the FBI knew who the shooter was but was not sharing the information with them. It was nothing more than a gut feeling, but it was there just the same. If the shooter was a cartel shooter, maybe the FBI couldn't lay a finger on her.

Noel mused. If she had been on the street for such a long period of time, maybe she had played both sides of the street? Maybe killing the three in Chicago was alright with the FBI, and they didn't press too hard in capturing her? Maybe that is why they didn't share the information with the Chicago Police Department? Maybe her going after Bear Child but killing Larry by mistake was totally out of their control? The flip side of that theory was that they didn't have any information on the assassin, nor did they know have a name until Noel and crew discovered she was a female shooter named Alita Lopez. Noel was in the business long enough to know that an all-out hunt for her would be needed if she was a cartel shooter.

To try to execute Bear Child could only mean one thing: if the three killed in Chicago were Mexican cartel, she was, too. There couldn't be any other explanation. The next twenty-four hours would tell if the FBI was trying to confirm the information that they received. It would have been damned hard to fabricate the latent print information discovered by the private investigators.

While Noel was busy in his bookshop, three men in slacks and dress shirts minus the ties entered his shop and identified themselves as FBI Agents out of the Tucson Office. Noel invited them to take a seat as he locked the front door to his shop. He asked them if they had a chance to grab coffee since leaving Tucson, and they responded they did, but it was gasoline station coffee. Noel called the hotel dining room and ordered two carafes of hotel coffee plus the normal cream and sugar with instructions to bring it in via the back hallway. Once the order arrived, the agents and Noel sat down for a briefing on what Noel would soon learn was an international manhunt for Alita Lopez and elements of the Sinaloa Cartel protecting her in Arizona.

As the information was being revealed to Noel, one of the FBI agents asked for the location of Claire Blue Crow and Tim Bear Child. He apparently had affidavits in his possession that they needed to sign as photographers of the latent prints from Casa Grande, Arizona, which had been submitted to the FBI. Noel excused himself to call the two and ask them to come to the bookshop.

He walked into the back hallway and called Claire. When Claire answered, Noel said, "Look, I have three FBI Agents here in the bookshop that look like the cast from the Book of Mormon. They need you and Bear Child here to sign affidavits. Call Tim and let him know, ok?" Claire agreed to do that and told Noel to give him fifteen minutes.

Claire and Bear Child arrived together. Noel unlocked the door to let them in and locked it again when they entered the shop. While Claire introduced himself and Bear Child to the agents, he also checked out the carafes for coffee, poured himself a cup, and sat down.

The lead agent introduced himself as Special Agent O'Brady. He said "Don't worry, I'm no relation to your missing Chicago police detective O'Brady. We have several items to discuss with you this morning. First, let's get the affidavits signed, ok?" After Claire and Bear Child signed several affidavits, they became the property of the FBI. "We have forensic proof of more than one woman living in the apartment above the Cookie Cutter Coffee House in Casa Grande. Forensic examination of the various articles of clothing provided two different sets of DNA. Additionally, we positively have established fingerprint identity of one of those females as the same person provided to us by you via your Yuma associate. The second person in that apartment carries all of the DNA identifiers of a female. We are looking for two females. One of those females, A.K.A. Alita Lopez, is a known enforcer for the Sinaloa Cartel, according to our information from the Mexican government."

Noel and Claire nodded acknowledgement to these comments while Bear Child sat silent. Agent O'Brady continued, "We believe she flew into Chicago from Phoenix under the name of Leticia Lopez. During a period of several weeks in Chicago, she executed the three older Mexican cartel lieutenants. We can only assume she attempted to locate Tim Bear Child while she was there, but failing at that, she returned to Arizona." Noel asked, "Was she sent to Chicago because the Sinaloa Cartel is reorganizing?"

"We don't know, but our intel makes it appear very possible that may be the case. As you may or may not know, there are Mexican cartels fighting each other for turf. Nothing new, but the fighting has spilled over into the major border cities. Decapitations and hanging of the headless corpses over the railings on highway overpasses is now the new rage down there. Mass graves to hide murdered alleged informants and to keep others from informing. Shock killings to scare others who might want to cooperate with other cartels."

Bear Child spoke up, "We used a drone to look inside the apartment down there in Casa Grande, and we only saw one female within viewer range. I'm thinking out loud right now, but I wonder if the other gal is a cartel shooter, too?" One of the agents answered, "We don't think so, and that's based upon forensic inspection of clothing. There appeared to be two different- sized wardrobes, and only one size had GSR, gun-shot residue."

Agent O'Brady thanked everyone for cooperating and asked Noel for the little kid's hand impression received from Roberto Crow. Noel went behind the front desk, retrieved a small green disk, and handed it to the agent closest to him. The agent looked at the green disk and said, "This looks like the peanut butter cookies my four-year-old daughter makes. They aren't green, but they look the same." One of the other agents encouraged him by saying, "Taste it."

After the agents left the bookshop, the three of them had a chance to sit down and finish what was left of the coffee. Noel looked at the guys and said, "I don't think they're leveling with us, what do you guys think?" Claire said, "I may be wrong, but I think there had to be more than latent prints from one hand in that apartment, just saying." Bear Child chimed in with, "If the other gal was the shopper for the two of them, that would explain the shooter not being seen by local people. But the shopper's prints sure as hell would show up."

Noel said, "Ok, they don't want to give us a name so we won't get in their way while they are trying to locate her, I get that. What I don't understand is why they think we would give up now?" He went on processing, "If I were going to keep my lover hidden or unseen, I would become a Notary Public and notarize her car titles if they were cars that were going to be traded in or sold. I would also notarize paperwork needed to survive today, like credit cards, debit cards, bank accounts, passports, driver licenses. I say let's check out the Arizona Secretary of State Office for a name that would match that address in Casa Grande."

Bear Child said, "I wish we could get a flight manifest, a list of people from that flight the shooter took to Chicago when she blew up those old guys. There might be a name on that manifest that would match a name from the Arizona Secretary of State information."

"Who picked her up at that gravel car lot in Casa Grande after she traded in that van?" asked Noel. "Maybe we need to visit our car salesman, Don, again."

CHAPTER 34

BECAUSE CLAIRE WAS SOMEWHAT KNOWLEDGEABLE ABOUT THE OPERation of the Arizona Secretary of State Office, he was assigned to conduct a computer search of Notary Publics. Meanwhile Bear Child indoctrinated himself with the airline industry by being introduced to a former Border Patrol Agent who became a U.S. Air Marshall, like many of them did because the career path on the Border Patrol was somewhat limited. Noel made the call, and Bear Child took it from there. Noel decided to drive back down to Casa Grande and interview Don, the car salesman.

In a matter of a few hours Bear Child had the information he was looking for by eliminating the male names on the flights between Phoenix to Chicago during the time period around the three shootings and the return flight back to Phoenix for Leticia Lopez. It was unknown whether the two women had flown together because the second name still hadn't been identified.

South of Phoenix, down in Casa Grande, Noel was putting the heat on the car salesman named Don which Don didn't appear to appreciate. "I don't want to talk with you. You aren't a cop anymore, the FBI told me that."

"They told you that you didn't have to talk with me?" asked Noel.

"No, they said you're no longer a policeman, I said I don't have to talk with you." Noel grabbed Don by the collar. He kept turning the material tighter and tighter on his shirt until Don offered to tell Noel what he wanted to know. The person who picked up the shooter was the same person who met her at the car lot several minutes after she pulled into the lot.

Don said, "I don't know how tall she is because she was behind the wheel of the car and never got out of the car. She has dark hair and maybe 135, 140 lb., I think."

"Long hair, short hair?" asked Noel.

"Short, short, yes, short", said Don.

"Glasses, Don, does she wear glasses?" asked Noel.

"No, no" answered Don. "I see her in town. a lot, I saw her yesterday, I don't know her name, honest."

Noel tightened the shirt material, and Don cried out, "Ouch, Oh man!"

"Don, you see her in town a lot, but you don't know if she is short, tall, has a wooden leg and is missing a foot on the other leg? Come on, Don, you and I are going for a ride, and you may not be coming back!" yelled Noel.

"Wait, wait! Ok, ok!" gasped Don. "I know where she might live."

"You better be correct, Don," warned Noel, "because I know where she lives, too. Have you seen her since we last visited you?"

"Yes, at my wife's salon where she works."

"Who works there, her or your wife?"

"My wife, my wife works there."

"You're positive, Don?"

"Yes, I know where my wife works," said Don. When he realized what he said, he corrected himself, "I mean yes, after you last visited me, I saw her there."

"Ok, Don, you are going to call your wife and find out if this lady has any upcoming appointments," instructed Noel.

"Oh God! No, please leave her alone!" cried Don.

"Who Don, who should I leave alone?" asked Noel.

"My wife!"

Noel assured, "Of course, Don, I have no beef with her. You have to tell me what kind of vehicle this gal drives."

Don told Noel, "I don't know."

Noel repeated his demand, "No, Don, you don't understand, you have to tell me what she drives, or I will not be able to keep your wife out of this."

"Ok, ok, black Mustang, a black Mustang convertible."

Noel released the pressure on Don's shirt. Before he walked out, he picked up the tipped office chair and then took several hundred dollars out of his pocket for Don. This was helpful information, even though getting it was tough going.

Going into Casa Grande to do a quick drive-through for the black Mustang convertible, Noel called Claire. "Hey, it looks like maybe our gal's roomie may not have left the area."

"Our boy Don said he saw her in Casa Grande after we last visited him. When pressed, he said he saw her yesterday. Get this, Claire, she drives a black Mustang convertible."

Claire asked, "Are we heading back there?"

Noel said, "I am doing a drive-by as we speak. I don't know, maybe we should because she is not aware we know about the black Mustang convertible," reasoned Noel.

"I'm all for it," declared Claire.

"I am, too, maybe we can get into the Casa Grande Police for some help?" said Noel.

"I'm glad you called," said Claire. "The State gave me some information."

"Public Notary holders?" asked Noel.

"Yep," answered Claire. "Are you coming back today?"

"Give me another hour, and I'll head back to Prescott," reported Noel. "How about Tim, are you planning on sitting on him at random times tonight? Tomorrow he can be with us so we can eyeball him here."

Claire said, "Yep, Randall and I are switching off doing it. I'll call and let him know Tim will be with us tomorrow."

Noel said, "Ok, see you in a few hours."

When Noel got back to Prescott, Rebecca and Claire were in the kitchen with Bear Child. Noel said, "I'm glad everyone is here." Rebecca smiled and said, "Yes, I invited Tim for dinner with us. We're having pasta and meatballs from the restaurant, we had a ton leftover. Remind me never to have that as a blue plate special again."

During the meal, Bear Child admitted he was swamped, totally overwhelmed with information on female passengers from Phoenix to Chicago during the time frame the killings took place in Chicago. "The Air Marshall fixed you up, huh?" joked Noel. Claire produced six Arizona driver license photos of people who held a valid State of Arizona Notary Public office in or near Casa Grande. Two of the six were men, so those two photos were not displayed at the dinner table.

Rebecca said, "That is a lot of notaries for such a small town. But maybe not, you didn't say anything about real estate sales, title companies, law offices. No wait, attorneys don't have to have Notary Publics, they do it themselves."

Claire said, "I thought so, too, but now that you mention it, there are several banks and two church offices there that have Notary Publics."

Noel said, "Ok, 135 maybe 140 lbs., short dark hair."

Claire shuffled the photos and produced a photo of a woman with short dark hair. Her Arizona license listed her height at 5' 6' and her weight at 125 lbs. Claire said, "Ok, she lied about her weight. She uses the name Beverly Tanny. She's the only one who doesn't work in a bank or a church office, I've checked."

Noel suggested, "Let's begin by running that name past the FBI and see if we can get a reaction from them. We don't have to tell them how we got it."

Rebecca asked, "If you get a reaction, what will that tell you?"

"Maybe they know more than what they're telling us. They have a history of playing things close to the chest. Ask the Chicago P.D."

Rebecca said to Noel, "Ok, you guys are the trained investigators, but I think maybe they don't know anything about her except this, you find her, you find the shooter. I also think that you may be going down a blind alley with the Notary thing."

Rebecca added, "You know the Mexican folks get into the spirits and saints. Just suppose this other woman is a fortune teller person. I mean, why not?"

Rebecca started to think out loud saying, "If Larry's murderer is cartel, why not go all in and say she has a fortune teller like old-school Mexican folks believe in, or a female lover."

Claire said, "I am going to say it even if I might regret it, I thought of a female lover first thing." Bear Child agreed, "Me, too." Rebecca told the two, "There is nothing wrong with suspecting she has a female lover, live-in or not."

Noel said, "I still like my Notary idea. Let's check security cameras down there for the black Mustang convertible, maybe we can get more intel that way. A shot of a plate number California or Arizona, maybe a shot of the driver?"

Rebecca joked, "A mug shot."

Noel said, "Yeah, a mug shot."

Bear Child said, "Signed confession."

Claire said, "A recording of her in the confessional in a Catholic church."

"Without knowing the year of the Black Mustang convertible, let's check in with all the local Ford dealers for any black Mustang convertibles, it did look relatively new. A hit there isn't too much to ask for, is it?"

Rebecca said thoughtfully, "Ok, do you suppose the car salesman's wife would know about her girlfriend? I mean, women do chat in salons."

Noel said, "It's very possible she may know, maybe Don can help me with that."

That evening while they were getting ready for bed, Rebecca asked Noel, "Noel, I hope I'm not coming across like Little Miss Know-it-all when you guys discuss your cases. You don't think so, do you?" Noel took her in his arms and told her she was his biggest asset, and her ideas were good. Noel also told her he valued her judgment and welcomed her thoughts. Rebecca gave Noel a very long kiss, and he steered her towards the bed. Both of them became eager in their lovemaking. Satisfaction bonded them that evening, and both were happy in the arms of the other. It was true, Noel did find her to be one of the most, if not the most, intelligent people he ever met. He realized she was the one who helped him deal with the death of his friend Larry at the hands of the woman they were chasing.

CHAPTER 35

THE NEXT MORNING NOEL WENT TO HIS BOOKSHOP AND STARTED TO make telephone calls while waiting for the guys to arrive. The first call was to a part-time employee for backup help while he was gone, but he struck out. So he placed another call and this time was successful when his other part-time person agreed to keep the bookshop open during his absence. She needed about four hours of lead-in time because of her kids. Noel paid a good wage and an even better wage when he contacted them on short notice.

Bear Child and Claire showed up at the bookshop within minutes of each other. Noel had coffee for them and several hundred dollars in cash for gas, meals, and essential expenses. Noel told them to head down to Casa Grande, travel in separate vehicles, and be careful. He told them he would remain behind making a few Ford dealer calls and would join them when his part-time person arrived. He wanted to call the FBI agents working with them just to bring them up to date on the Ford dealer idea based upon the information he had gotten from Don the car salesman. Deep down he was hoping they would set out some video cameras or stage a few phony D.U.I. checkpoints or roadblocks looking for the black Mustang convertible.

Noel made himself busy while waiting for his back-up to arrive and take over the bookshop. He called the area's Ford dealerships after doing an internet search for all of them. He swept the floor when he couldn't find anything else to do. With his back to the front door while he was sweeping, he heard it open. Thinking to himself that it was about time, he turned, expecting to see his part-timer. But instead, there stood Louie Louis. Louie was wearing off- white slacks with expensive leather loafers and a pink polo shirt. He looked tanned, and his hair was recently style and curled.

"Mr. Two Horses, I heard you have been trying to reach out to me. How are you, my friend and savior?" asked Louie.

Noel admitted to Louie, "Well, I've seen better days, but Louie, it's so good to see you! Please come in and have a seat. You are heaven sent, Louie!"

Louie said, "Oh, please, Noel, stop, you are making me blush."

"Can I get you anything, Louie? My part-time employee should be here any minute, why don't we have lunch next door, and I can fill you in as we eat?"

Within the next few minutes Noel's employee arrived, and after going over a few instructions with her, he was ushering Louie Louis out the bookshop door and into the dining room of the Hotel Saint Gregory. As they were being seated, Noel noticed that Louie kept looking over his shoulder as if he was expecting someone to appear. "Is everything ok, Louie, would you like to sit where you can see the door?" asked Noel.

"Yes, if you don't mind trading seats with me, Noel, that would be fine, thank you."

"Not a problem, but now you have to tell me what's going on, some-one looking for you?"

Louie stated the obvious, "Very observant of you. Yes, I do have a little issue and that is one reason I am here; the other reason, of course, is you were looking for me. As you know, Noel, there are people who do not view me as an honest man, unlike you and Mr. Blue Crow. How is he, by the way? There is a misunderstanding with the authorities as we speak."

"You mean a warrant for your arrest, Louie?" asked Noel.

"There! That is exactly what I mean," said Louie. "Who else would know the awful telltale crisis signs? I am sure it can be sorted out, but it is a rather fatal issue."

"Murder, Louie, you are looking at another murder beef?" said Noel in disbelief.

"Accidental death," corrected Louie.

"Ok, keep your eyes peeled, but tell me about it accurately, Louie," warned Noel.

Louie explained by saying, "Oh, where do I begin? Let's see, ok, I was at a hotel pool just south of California with a few friends when someone had served liquor purchased from an unreliable source. This isn't unusual because they do it at Mexican resorts from time to time. Well, long story short, a man became ill and apparently passed away because of it, the unreliable liquor."

"Apparently passed away, Louie?" questioned Noel. "Is he dead or not?"

"Yes, he is dead, herein lies the problem, Noel," said Louie matter-of-factly.

"Louie, who was this unfortunate person?"

"Which one?" asked Louie.

"There was more than one death?"

Louie said, "Well, yes, there were two, two casualties. Newlyweds, it was their wedding. The open bar was my gift. I have to tell you, the bride did not look that new. The groom had several miles on him as well."

"Louie, they have charged you with murdering two people?" asked Noel.

"Well, they haven't charged me specifically, not legally. Wait, you think the police are after me?" Louie then started to laugh at Noel, "Oh no, I am not officially being charged with murder. I mean yes, two people died, but the police are not involved."

Noel looked at Louie and said, "Louie, who is after you if not the police?"

"Some of my former friends," explained Louie.

"The cartel?"

"Not all of them, just a few hotheads," said Louie. "I purchased the booze not knowing it was spiked. I was simply being a good guest by serving it. Right now I need to be hidden, protected, safeguarded, or whatever. Where is our waiter?"

Noel tried to take it all in but realized Louie was becoming un-wrapped and right now needed reassurance and calming. "Yeah, the service here is slow today, ok, here he comes." I know you haven't looked at the menu, but I would recommend the beef tips, they're great, Louie. How about some white wine? I know I could use a drink."

After they ordered, Noel told Louie, "You asked about Claire Blue Crow earlier, he is doing great. He's assisting us with this new case. That's the reason I tried to reach you, we need your help. You know, Louie, we'll help you, but let me ask about your issues after lunch, ok?" Louie said, "Oh terrific, I knew you would! You guys are great, just great!"

"You are special to us, and we respect your judgment," fibbed Noel. "Can I impose on you and your memory, and in exchange, I will use whatever resources I have to help you clear up this current issue or issues, ok?"

Louie said, "Shoot. Or maybe I should have used a different verb. Agreed, I agree to it."

Noel chuckled and said, "I laugh about it, but it isn't funny, is it?"

"What isn't funny, my issue or your case?"

"Either," said Noel. "But let me ask you to use your memory and assist us with any information you may have on a late twenty, early thirty-something Mexican gal who only has one hand and might be a cartel assassin."

"Let me ask you, Noel, why are you interested?"

"She is the suspect in three Chicago shootings of older Mexican cartel gentlemen. She also shot and killed Larry Figueroa."

Startled, Louie asked, "Your Larry? Oh my God. I'm so sorry, I was of course only thinking about myself when I made the inquiry about why you wanted information about her. Of course, I will help in any way I can. I remember a young woman with one hand, I personally never met her, but I know of whom you speak. Poor Larry."

"Louie, you have to be made aware that it was a case of mistaken identity, the shooter thought Larry was my client. It was an attempted cartel hit."

Louie said, "I am so sorry to hear that he is gone, and in such an awful way."

"Louie, I need your help in locating her."

CHAPTER 36

The Arizona Daily Star
Tucson man gets federal prison term for firearms smuggling
The Associated Press

A TUCSON MAN HAS BEEN SENTENCED TO 6 ½ YEARS IN FEDERAL PRISON for smuggling firearms and ammunition into Mexico. Prosecutors said 31-year-old Ruben Arnulfo Chavarin also was fined more than $10,000.

On 14 occasions between December 2010 and February 2011, prosecutors said Chavarin purchased eight firearms and over 21,000 rounds of ammunition in Tucson. They said he provided the firearms and more than 12,5000 rounds of ammunition to co-conspirators to be smuggled out of the U.S. and into Mexico. In February 2011, authorities said Chavarin attempted to personally smuggle 8,700 rounds into Mexico but was arrested at the Port of Entry in Douglas, Arizona.

Subsequent investigation revealed that shortly before his arrest, Chavarin had ordered 16 AK-47 style rifles and 10,000 rounds of ammunition, which he also intended to smuggle into Mexico. While under indictment foe seven weapons trafficking offenses, Chavarin fled to Mexico. He remained a fugitive for nine years until his arrest in 2020.

Apparently, Louie had been hiding out more or less at resorts and high-end hotels in California and Phoenix. His only family member, a brother, was killed by a cartel associate, and Louie was left with his brother's assets after everything cleared probate. Louie's brother had been warehousing drugs for a Mexican cartel in the many porn theaters that he owned. To state it bluntly, Louie was sitting on a shitload of cash. Both Louie and his brother had cartel ties before his brother's murder. It was a murder that first introduced Louie to Noel Two Horses and Claire Blue Crow. Working on behalf of Louie, the two former cops were able to get Louie out of a murder charge. Louie had a problem with stealing, and he never did give up his underworld connections in the southwest. Noel debriefed Louie on what he knew of a one-handed cartel shooter as the day wore on, and soon both he and Louie decided to call it a day. Noel had decided to have Bear Child get a room at a Phoenix casino, and that way Louie and Bear Child would be safe for the night if Claire was there with them to safeguard them.

Louie had excused himself from the table to use the restroom, or to "void" as Louie said, and that is when Noel contacted Claire to instruct him and Bear Child of his plan. When Louie returned to the table, Noel asked him "Do you have any objection to spending the night in Phoenix at a casino with Claire and Tim Bear Child?"

"Of course not. To be honest, I was not looking forward to spending a night here in Prescott. Nice to visit but, well, kind of small and too slow."

"Great, have you a bag with you?"

Louie said, "I do indeed, my bags are in my car."

"Louie, I can drive you there if you like," offered Noel.

"Don't be silly, just give me Claire's cell number, and I am off."

As the two traded cell numbers, the dining room bill arrived. Louie grabbed it and told Noel, "I insist, my treat, and my thanks again, Noel, for all you have done."

Noel followed Louie into the parking structure at the Hotel Saint Gregory and watched him get into a bright yellow convertible with a rental car sticker on the rear bumper. Noel gave Louie a few minutes head start and then got into his own car to follow. Noel's instinct had told him that Louie's behavior would give him away and sure enough, hiding but driving a bright yellow convertible instead of renting a dull business sedan would highlight Louie's presence. At least in a casino parking lot nobody would pay that much attention to it. Noel called Claire again and this time told him more about Louie and his recent exploits. He also told him that he would join them at the casino, but for the time being he didn't want Louie to know he followed him and would be there too.

Noel wanted to be sure Louie did not already have a tail on him. Claire told Noel what casino they would be at, and Noel said, "See you at the main bar at 10:00 P.M." Claire followed up with, "Noel, promise me I won't have to babysit Louie 24/7 again?" "Of course not, that is what Bear Child will be doing," and they both laughed very deep belly laughs.

While heading south to Phoenix, Noel made another call, this time to Rebecca. Rebecca wished him good luck in finding the shooter and instructed him to tell Louie hello. Noel said he missed her and wished he could get a few more days at home with her. Rebecca said, "Yeah, me, too." Noel said, "We both knew that when I went to med school, I would come out a great brain surgeon, and I would be called away a lot." Rebecca said, "Is that why you never went to med school?" and Noel said, "Yeah."

Rebecca said, "Well, ya gotta make some trade-offs, huh? Listen Noel, I want you to be safe, ok?" Noel, wanting to change the subject, asked, "Hey, what has a two-inch nob and hangs down?" Rebecca said, "I don't know, what has a two-inch nob and hangs down?" Noel answered, "A bat. Now, what has a nine-inch nob and hangs up?" Rebecca said, "I don't know, what has a nine-inch nob and hangs up?" Just then she heard a "click" and the line went dead.

Even though Rebecca had a smile on her face and loved Noel, there were days that she wanted to beat him with a shovel. This stunned Noel at first when he heard her say this because he thought she would have provided him more dignity the last few minutes on earth. Death by shovel seemed a bit rough. He pictured going into the Medical Examiners on a stretcher with the trademark, "True Value" imprinted across his rear or better yet, "Stanley" imprinted on his forehead.

CHAPTER 37

NOEL MET CLAIRE IN THE MAIN BAR OF THE PHOENIX CASINO AT EX-actly 10:00 p.m. He asked Claire if Louie had settled in yet. Claire replied, "Oh yeah, he and Bear Child are bonding right now. Room service brought them mixed drinks, and Louie is happy."

"Speaking of mixed drinks, what are you having?" asked Claire.

"Already ordered for us," said Noel. "I really don't know if Louie is going to be a help or a problem, but I think we should use his contacts right now."

"I agree" said Claire, "It's actually good to see the little guy."

"Yeah, he sure is noticeable, he's driving a yellow convertible. No one followed him from Prescott, for what that is worth."

Noel tried to fill Claire in on what Louie had told him about the wedding drinks and the death of the bride and groom. "Apparently, they were all cartel connected in some way or another. I assured him we would help him. Right now things are crazy as hell in Mexico with the cartels at war with one another down there. I'm not so sure someone poisoned those folks on purpose, but Louie is taking the fall for it. Maybe we'll see our shooter because the cartel will be using her again."

Noel asked Claire, "Were you able to get us a room near the other guys' room?"

"Right next door to them," said Claire. "As a matter of fact, I'm headed up there now; here's your key card."

"Good, thank you. I'm going to have another drink in peace and hit a slot machine or two. See you up there later."

"I have a question," said Claire. "With all of this going on with Louie, and Bear Child still being a target, how are we going to provide 24/7 safety for both of them?"

Noel answered, "I don't know, but I may have help in Yuma. Roberto has a valid State of Arizona P.I. license. Maybe we could use him and eventually get him on our agency license." Claire said, "Give him a call, and have him come over here tomorrow."

"I'll do that."

"Second question," said Claire. "How are we going to pay for all of this?"

Noel looked at Claire and said, "Timothy Bear Child is in settlement talks with the Chicago P.D. as we speak." Both Claire and Noel began their low belly laughs again.

Meanwhile, Louie and Bear Child were drinking and talking in the suite that Claire had reserved for them. Bear Child had explained his problem in detail to Louie, and Louie kept asking him questions about the FBI and the Chicago shootings. When the last room service waiter showed up at the door with another round of drinks and BBQ chicken wings, Louie greeted him and tipped him very generously, not on the room tab but in cash.

"I think I will drink this and call it an evening. Timothy, I would join you in the chicken wings, but to be honest, they are too, I don't know, maybe too common of a meal for those of us who know cuisine. You have a good night on the sofa and don't let Claire tell you he is entitled to it. Remember who is the employer and who is the employee. Good night," and with that Louie took his drink into the bedroom and closed the door. Bear Child told Louie, "Good night," knowing the casino hotel would be providing a list of calls made from the bedroom phone line that night.

Noel ordered another Jack Daniels and water. When it arrived, he left a tip and took his drink with him. In just a matter of a few minutes he found what looked like a promising dollar machine and sat down to win some serious money. Noel had noticed that many of the new slot machines in the casino had an Asian theme. He did not know much about the new technology, but he wondered if the software in his machine was Chinese software? While he was hashing that over, he hit a jackpot that was paying over $2,100 before taxes. Noel decided right there that he did not care if it was Chinese software.

Noel had time to order another drink while he was waiting for the floor guys to bring him his check and to clear his slot machine digital system. When they arrived, he patiently waited while they counted out the $2,100 into his hand. Noel tipped both of them and finished his drink. On the way up to the room he was sharing with Claire, he wished everything would be that easy. Using his key card to enter the room, he softly said, "Darlin, I'm home."

At breakfast in the morning, he surprised Louie by joining the men at the table. "Good morning, Louie. How did you sleep?" asked Noel. Even before Louie could answer, he added, "Louie, nobody followed you here, but please turn in the yellow convertible and get another car, ok?"

Louie was a little slack in the jaw but said, "I slept fine. You surprised me by following me, Noel. Thank you for checking that out for me. I think."

"All part of the service, Louie, but getting rid of the yellow car would help us maintain our low profile," said Noel. "I have some more information to share with you and Tim."

Bear Child looked up at Noel and waited for more while Louie said, "Pray tell. Something good, I hope."

Noel said, "50/50." After the waiter took everyone's order, Noel said, "The good is we are having another associate join us here later today. His name is Roberto Crow, a Pueblo from New Mexico. Former Border Patrol, and now he has a P.I. business in Yuma. He'll be providing security for Louie when we're on the street. The not so good is we need to talk about service fees for Louie and Tim." Noel continued, "I know that we hate to talk about money right now, but we need to obtain a commitment from you guys."

Louie said, 'Not a problem, I brought some cash with me, guys. Let me know how much you need."

Bear Child said, "I didn't, but if my I.O.U. is good, I'm good, too."

Noel cleared his throat and said, "Are you guys $10,000 apiece good?"

Louie laughed and said, "Without a doubt," and Bear Child said, "Hell, yeah."

Noel said, "In that case, breakfast is on Claire and me."

After the meal was served and the waiter left the area, Noel continued, "The reason I asked Roberto to join us was actually two-fold. He had met our shooter when she was little. Second, having been with the Border Patrol he is bi-lingual, and that may come in handy while he is providing services for Louie, should the occasion arise. Now with Tim being with Claire and me, we will have his services covered in that department."

Claire suggested that he and Bear Child do a drive through Casa Grande while Noel and Louie stayed behind until checkout time to meet up with Roberto, "unless you guys would rather go to position 'B' in Tucson and meet Roberto there?"

"Position 'B?'" asked Louie.

"Yeah, that is a Tucson resort, Louie. We didn't want you to have to suffer."

Louie sounded excited when he added, "Yes! Well-played."

Noel laughed and said, "Ok, Tucson it is. See you two there, and I will let Roberto know the location."

CHAPTER 38

As Bear Child and Louie were getting their things together to check out of the casino hotel room, Louie asked Bear Child, "Can I speak frankly to you?"

"Sure, what is it?"

"Tim, I was surprised you didn't speak up when you had the chance."

"What do you mean, Louie, I'm not following?"

"Your $10,000, my $10,000. You are paying what I am expected to pay, yet you work your tail off for them and are satisfied with a casino hotel room? They are charging you expenses and a contract rate. All I am saying is get your monies' worth, Tim Bear Child. Both Noel Two Horses and Claire Blue Crow are great guys, but they are businessmen. That is all I am saying."

"You have to forgive me, Louie," said Bear Child. "But I grew up in a house that did not have running water until sometime is the early '70's. Louie, that meant that we did not have an indoor toilet until the early '70's. I didn't go to a restaurant until I was in college. I don't care what they are charging me or that I eat hotdogs while we work."

"Louie, we'll go to your resort because that's a good idea as far as hiding you goes, and if you want to eat expensive food while you're there, that is fine too. That doesn't affect me, what affects me is we are getting closer to the shooter, I can feel it."

"Tim, you are missing my point!" pleaded Louie. "If you let them charge you what they want to charge you without negotiating, you will be going through the rest of your young life being led by others. I have been around awhile, just follow my lead. Now you and I should move on because Noel wants me to get a different car before we go."

"Louie, you didn't negotiate with them when Noel said $10,000, you agreed to $10,000. You are changing your car because Noel said to change your car. You didn't negotiate with him about the car," reasoned Bear Child.

"Tim, you didn't pick up on the subtle nuances between Noel and me during that exchange, did you? I didn't think so," explained Louie to a now stunned Bear Child. "The operative word here, Tim, is subtle."

Bear Child said, "Yes, of course. Subtle. I think I have much to learn, Louie. I appreciate you taking me under your wing, so to speak."

Louie boasted, "That is my pleasure."

Bear Child said, "Did you know that after our stay at the Tucson resort, you, Roberto, and I will be taking my camper trailer to Claire's reservation to hide out for a spell? Claire will meet us there, I guess," added Bear Child.

Louie was beginning to get pale. Bear Child thought he would push it in a bit further, knowing Louie hated living on the Navajo Reservation at Claire's place. "Have you ever been there, Louie?"

"Oh my God yes! I was living the life of a caveman on that reservation!"

"I mean no offense, Tim. Have you ever lived on a reservation? What am I saying, of course you have! Oh my God, I am so sorry! I can't live there! Please don't say anything to Claire, promise me you won't mention this to Claire?"

Bear Child said, "Of course not, Louie, you have my word. I will be subtle as you instruct."

While waiting in line to check out, Bear Child said, "Louie, I think you have to be open-minded about this reservation thing. Not all reservations are alike."

"Claire has an outhouse!" screamed Louie. There was an immediate silence in the otherwise busy lobby.

Bear Child whispered, "Louie, my camper has an indoor toilet," and added, "but you will have to share it with Roberto and me."

"Oh my God no, no, no!" cried Louie. "I cannot use an outhouse! There are animals in that outhouse!"

Bear Child whispered again to Louie, "Louie, why don't we negotiate this with Noel and Claire?"

Roberto Crow did not join Noel and Louie at the Prospectors Golf Resort in Tucson until late in the evening. Claire and Bear Child had arrived hours earlier and reported that there was no sign of any black Ford Mustang convertible in or around Casa Grande, Arizona. Both of them were enjoying the sights around the golf resort pool before dinner while Noel offered assurances that he would only hide Louie on the Navajo Reservation again as a last resort. He stated that he and Roberto would partner up at the golf resort until this cartel wedding thing could be sorted out in Louie's favor.

Without Louie's knowledge, Noel had briefed Roberto by cellphone as the private investigator drove to Tucson from Yuma that evening. He warned Roberto about Louie's kleptomania and his prior association with a Mexican cartel. Noel let Roberto know that Louie had also driven cartel cash cars into Mexico with money from drug sales. One trip was interrupted when a body was accidentally discovered inside the trunk of the car Louie was driving at the time. Noel cautioned Roberto that Louie was in possession of a lot of cash right now. He was warned that Louie might be doing the cash cars again, or he may have his own money now that his brother's assets had been turned over to him via probate.

Noel combined the $10,000 commitment Louie made for protection with $2,000 of the cash won at the casino in Phoenix the night before and offered it to Roberto for his services to Louie. Roberto agreed to the terms like Noel thought he might.

After dinner Louie suggested that all four of them retire to the main bar and enjoy a few more drinks. Noel, Claire, and Bear Child had ordered the steak special for dinner while Louie had pecked away at an expensive fish dish. Louie was the only one of the four who wanted to have more liquor in him after the "few after dinner drinks" at the table. Claire and Bear Child poured Louie into bed before Roberto arrived. Noel had left instructions at the front desk for Roberto to have dinner when he arrived, charge it to his room, and the four of them would meet him for breakfast at 9:30 A.M.

The next morning, Noel checked with the front desk by room phone to see if Roberto had arrived. After confirming that, Noel showered and headed to breakfast as planned. All five guys arrived in the dining room at about the same time. Louie was introduced as "our client Louie Louis," and Claire was introduced as "my partner, Claire Blue Crow,." while Tim Bear Child was introduced as "our client and business associate." Louie was mumble-mouthed and nursing a tomato juice with a lemon slice in it, but he did manage to say, "A splendid good morning to you, Roberto."

After breakfast Noel asked to Louie to meet him in the lobby where he was advised that he would need to get the $10,000 retainer. Louie agreed, and while at Louie's new rental car, Noel asked Louie directly, "Is this your money or more cartel cash car money?"

Louie responded by saying, "Oh good heavens no, this is my money, I mean my brother's money from probate, so I guess it is mine. It's good. Will $10,000 be enough, Noel?" Louie reached into a white leather gym bag with a gold zipper, extracted several large stacks of one-hundred-dollar bills, and began to hand them to Noel.

"This is fine for now, but you know as well as we do, Louie, that the cost of this can be very expensive. The longer we provide safety and security for you at resorts like this, the costs increase. Are you sure you won't reconsider more economical accommodations?"

Louie just said, "No, no, no," and handed Noel another stack of bills.

CHAPTER 39

NOEL TWO HORSES HAD DONE MANY THINGS IN HIS LIFE, AND HE HAD come to believe strongly in never spreading his guys too thin. Noel learned that while in South Vietnam as a Marine squad leader during the war. Better to borrow guys from other squads even if they were new in country. To be outgunned in the jungle or crossing a rice paddy is a tough way to go. Noel knew people who could keep a secret and who knew how to fight. He knew Phil Cloud, Larry Bird, and John McCall to name a few, former cops who worked with Noel from time to time back in the day. Some were Tucson Police Department retired cops, and some were Bureau of Indian Affairs (BIA) retired cops. Awhile back Noel had to ask a few of these guys to help him find a woman on the border, and after combing some Phoenix, AZ, drop houses, they ended up shooting it out with an armed group of young guys who actually made a living robbing and kidnapping folks who were trying to cross into the U.S. They had connections to a North Korean bad guy who liked to move fentanyl into the U.S. via Mexico. These young guys made the mistake of kidnapping the granddaughter of a retired cop friend of Noel's. Of course, they didn't know she had friends who knew how to survive a shootout and to hunt down people.

Noel knew they were bored silly with retirement. He also knew that asking them to join in this latest adventure would be better than to squander his assets if the current shooter were to reappear out of the blue with Mexican muscle while Louie and Bear Child were being guarded round the clock. Noel reasoned that even though Bear Child was an ex-cop, he may not be able to use him to kill or contain the shooter. Tim could be placed in legal jeopardy should the shooter die by gunshot while the Chicago P.D. were still investigating Bear Child as a serial killer. He had to stay clean.

Noel placed a call to Rebecca and asked her to line up the guys in Tucson for a meeting at the Tucson Zoo the following day at noon. Rebecca was busy but was able to reach the men. She reported back to Noel later in the day that the noon meeting at the zoo was on.

Noel checked in by phone with the FBI agent in charge of the Tucson office to let him know that he was in their area and to find out if there were any additional updates on the possible location of the shooter. He was surprised to learn that the FBI had a possible I.D. on the roommate of the shooter. She was a Jessie Valdez with no known alias from the Eloy area of Southern Arizona. Twenty-seven years of age, dark hair, brown eyes, approximately 5"6," 130 lbs., last known address Bakersfield, California. There was no additional information available at this time. Noel didn't press the agent too much as to what the FBI was doing to follow up on her. He knew that the drug corridor the shooter kept open and running was north of the border in Pinal County, Arizona. That is where Valdez was last seen and where she and the shooter shared an apartment. To Noel it seemed only logical that the shooter and her roommate would not desert it for too long a period. Noel's plan was to cross reference this information with Louie in the event Louie would know of Valdez or her family.

Noel's day was speeding by, and soon it would be time to join some of his old friends at the zoo for a brief meeting. Noel drove into a submarine sandwich shop and picked up a variety of sub specials for his friends.

As Noel was pulling into a parking spot at the zoo, three of his old friends were walking in front of his car. Noel sounded his horn and laughed as the three of them jumped and glared back at him behind the wheel. Within minutes the four of them found a shady spot with a long bench and concrete table much like a chest or checkerboard. The table had concrete stools stationed so the players would face the board and each other. By the time the guys seated themselves, Noel had already made his greeting with each of them. Two wanted to talk about physical or medical issues while one of them asked Noel about his private investigative business.

Noel was halfway into the reason he needed help from this bunch of former cops when one of them asked Noel if he was going to share the food in his bag with them. Noel asked the guys to forgive him and began to hand out the subs. By the time the guys broke up, they were familiar with the possibility that Noel may actually call upon them to assist him on short notice should push come to shove in Pinal County. Noel asked each to clean and load the personal weapon they had and to travel in one car. "Bring extra ammo, water, and prescribed meds with you." He gave each a few hundred dollars to seal the deal. Noel said to all of them, "This is on- call money" and added, "Should I call you up, each of you are entitled to combat pay plus a box of Depends disposables." John McCall said, "If I'm asleep, call again."

Noel had to make hotel reservations for his guys if the shooter somehow or another showed herself again, and Noel was positive she would. Her responsibility for the drug corridor ran from the Mexican border north to the area around Gila Bend, Arizona. She was not going to abandon that much real estate. He thought that her skill as a cartel assassin was only part- time, and unless she demanded massive amounts of money for a kill, she had to either be a major player in the cartel or a key to the success of the drug corridor. Noel was convinced that she would not, could not stay away from her turf. Because now there may be a lead in the roommates' FBI identification, Noel felt that if they focused on her, she would eventually lead them to the shooter.

Several days elapsed while Louie was at the golf resort in Tucson without much going on. His telephone activity was monitored because of his prior history of communicating with cartel members without anyone being aware of it. Louie appeared to be right at home, basking in good food, booze, and playtime. Occasionally Roberto would escort Louie to an up-scale store at Tucson Mall, and Louie would return with something he did not buy. Shirts, socks, or underwear felt better when he wore it after it was stolen. Maybe it was just the little electrical charge he got during the actual theft. In Louie's case it was almost as if he were entitled to it.

One evening Noel had a very brief visit with Louie by phone. Noel had already returned to Prescott when he told Louie, "Remember, Louie, you have to be very selective when it comes to telling people about things. You are in hiding for a reason, please don't make our job of protecting you harder by letting things slip."

Noel did this because he wanted to see if Louie was aware that they were monitoring his phone activity at the golf resort. Noel told the guys to not monitor him for a few days to see if he took advantage of it. He thought Louie's sense of entitlement may also apply to phone liberty. Sure enough, within 24 hours Louie had placed a call to a party in Sells, Arizona, from his golf resort room at 10:30 p.m.

Sells, Arizona, is the largest community on the Tohono O'odham tribal reservation located on the Mexican border. The call from Louie's room lasted twenty minutes. Bear Child reported this to Noel when he called him. Noel instructed Bear Child to have Claire speak with Louie about the call. That evening at dinner, Claire told Louie to stick around because he needed to talk to him in private. After dinner he and Louie moved into the bar to chat. Seated in a booth next to each other so they could see the front door, Claire asked Louie about the call. Surprisingly, Louie told Claire that he contacted an old friend who apparently still worked as the liaison between the cartel and the local border enforcement people in the Sells area. Claire did not know if Louie was referring to the U.S. Border Patrol or tribal police. At this point it wasn't important to know this because Louie was getting the ball moving in locating the shooter.

Louie said, "Tell Noel that I have been able to sort out most of the wedding fiasco mess." He then interrupted his story to order another drink for himself and Claire. "I was not the person responsible for the bad liquor at the wedding. Now that they know that, I am relatively safe."

Claire asked, "They, meaning the cartel people?"

Louie laughed and said, "Oh my! Yes Claire, the cartel people, you are so kind."

"Well, Louie, you have to admit they are vengeful folks," said Claire as he accepted his drink from the server. "What is 'relatively' compared to 'actually' being safe, Louie?"

Louie took a sip of his drink and said, "As it turns out, I will have to wait a bit in order for the word to get out there that I am an ok chap."

"How long, Louie?"

"Well, it may be awhile because the booze was tampered with on purpose by another cartel family member to get rid of both bride and groom. Messy stuff, families," observed Louie.

Louie went on to say almost as a second thought, "Your shooter is back. She was in Mexico waiting for the FBI to clear out of Casa Grande."

Claire asked, "Louie, do you know where we can find her? I don't know if that is something you would know or not?"

"Or not, Claire," Louie said. "Let's order another one and talk about something else."

Both ordered another drink, and Claire complimented Louie. "Nice socks, I couldn't see them before, but those are cool." Louie looked down at the crossed leg that now exposed his right ankle and his stolen striped sock and said, "Well, thank you. Yes, I like the color."

Claire wanted additional information from Louie and was using the soft approach before resorting to applying pressure to get it. He tried to reason with Louie, but with Louie that had often proved to be impossible. Louie was not known for his logic. Claire said, "I guess I don't understand, Louie, but why would it take days to make your situation safer than it was yesterday?"

Louie said, "It just works that way, Claire. Now before you ask who told me this, let me say this, my contacts go back years, as you know." Claire interrupted him saying, "These are the same people who hunted you in the past, and you believe them?"

Louie took a sip of his drink and said, "Well, this is how it works. If I am sufficiently annoyed, I will wait and contact them with a premeditated insult. Something that might cast aspersions as to our relationship. Let me give you an example: I wait, build up suspense, and finally call them and tell them I am simply astounded by the fact that they believe I would want to kill them. Of course, they cannot defend this position, so they tell me they do not, or they no longer want that."

Claire asked, "Build up suspense? Is that what you just said, build up suspense?"

Louie answered, "Yes, I find waiting seems to build up the suspense. Normal people would use the term anxiety, but with a theater background I prefer the term suspense."

Claire now became upset with Louie and said, "Louie, neither you nor your family had a theater background, your brother owned a string of porn theaters!"

"And, let me remind you, they killed your brother."

"Whatever!" replied Louie. After a long pause Louie said, "My brother did not use the same contacts in the cartel arena that I have."

Claire took a sip of his mixed drink while he calmed down. After another pause in the conversation, he said, "I'm sorry, Louie, you're right. Your brother was connected to a different set of players."

"Oh Claire, I'm sorry, too," said Louie. "I can get you some more information if you wait awhile. It is the least I can do for you guys. Give me another day or so, ok? But right now I have to show you the neatest pair of bamboo undershorts I picked up today while shopping with Roberto Crow. He is really a nice man. Speaking of him, here he is right now." Claire looked at the front entrance to the bar, and there stood Roberto, motioning to Louie to wrap it up by looking at his wristwatch. Louie started to slide out of the booth while saying repeatedly "Coming, coming, coming."

All Claire could do was look at the two of them and wonder how the hell did Roberto get Louie to answer his demands? Claire made a mental note to speak to him about it. Roberto would take Louie to his room, turn him over to Bear Child for the night, and sleep next door to the two in the event something should happen. If what Louie shared with him was true, the security for Louie would be ending soon. This might be worth celebrating because it would mean more manpower available to focus on the shooter.

Claire's night would wrap up by calling Noel in Prescott and telling him about his conversation with Louie. Claire ordered another drink and took out his cellphone to make that call.

CHAPTER 40

THE SUN HAD BEEN UP FOR SEVERAL HOURS ON THE AMERICAN SIDE OF the border near Sells, Arizona. Mama coyote had hunted all night with nothing to show for it. There wasn't even as much as a morsel of food, when out of the kindness of the desert and several murdering Mexican cartel members, she stumbled across a rich find. She was chewing on one of the largest phalanges of the human body, a middle metacarpal - a human finger bone she found at the base of a desert shrub.

The motherload was just several inches below the surface as she soon discovered. The shallow grave site produced thirteen bodies in all, but only after a tourist's female pug dog picked up where the coyote left off and only after that tourist notified authorities. The tourist insisted that the police 911 operator "do something before Chloe eats another Mexican."

Within two short months Mexican and State of Arizona forensic team evidence pointed to Chicago Police Department Detective James O'Brady as one of the victims. Dental records from Illinois eventually confirmed those forensics.

The Chicago Police Department was again swamping the Prescott, Arizona, Police Department with calls, and Timothy Bear Child was back upon their radar. Bear Child's lawsuit was settled out of court months earlier, so the rest was just getting Bear Child to sit down for another interview. Bear Child consented to it but only if the questions asked were focused upon the discovery of O'Brady's body and only the discovery of his body. Bear Child was not traveling with the tourist and her dog when they discovered his body in the mass grave. He did not know her or her dog, but more importantly, he never met anyone in the mass grave including O'Brady.

During those two months that it took from the time of discovery of O'Brady's body to the dental record confirmation, the hunt to locate the murderer of Larry Figueroa by Noel Two Horses and his bunch was at an impasse. Now the focus on O'Brady's reappearance would consume them so that they could protect Bear Child from both the shooter and Chicago P.D. Noel had given his Tucson friends the order to stand down until further notice. Roberto had to return to Yuma but told Noel not to forget him should the need arise. However, Louie's intel still repeated that she was back in the Casa Grande area. Noel continued with the daily and eventually weekly drive-by surveillances, but during those 60 plus days they failed to produce any fruit, except maybe one item. The local utility company was starting to do work on the street near the shooters' old apartment, and that gave Noel an idea.

Bear Child's classes would be picking up again soon, and Noel was booked to teach several online classes soon as well. The only available player on the team was Claire, but that meant he and Louie would be paired up again, which would be hard on Claire. Apparently, Louie fell in line with Roberto because as Louie put it, "Roberto reminds so much of my brother. Punctual, no messing around kind of guy when he was younger. I will never forgive those who wanted to hurt him." That is what Claire and Noel were counting on, and they did not want that to change.

One afternoon Claire called Noel and told him that Louie had made another call to his cartel associate to find out if it was safe to come out of hiding. Sometime during the call, the guy told Louie that the shooter was now in L.A. for some family member's funeral. Noel hated to ask Claire the obvious, but this had become routine at this point. "Did Louie tell this guy where he was?" Claire responded with a resounding "No! It turns out the heat is still on Louie." Noel advised that he would fill the FBI in on the L.A. funeral information, and both of them agreed to go from there. With the discovery of O'Brady's body in the mass grave, things were spinning for a while. But Noel soon came to the understanding that he and his group were still functioning as before, although with better insight into the shooter's movements because of Louie's unmonitored phone calls to his people. At some point, if Louie could stay healthy and in one piece, maybe the shooter's exact location would be revealed.

Noel didn't know if keeping Louie safe in Prescott or Tucson was going to be a mistake because of lack of manpower. He posed a question to Claire that might solve the problem. "How do you feel about taking Louie on a cruise with Rebecca if I can talk her into it?"

"What kind of cruise?" asked Claire.

"A cruise on the sea, a sea cruise." Noel added, "A cruise where the last place on earth the Mexican Cartel would look for Louie. A Mexico cruise."

Claire immediately said, "That is a hell of an idea! Yes, let's do it."

"I know I promised you that you would never have to be stuck with Louie again, but if I can talk Rebecca into going along, that is one person who would support you with keeping his profile low and safe."

Claire continued to be excited about the plan. "Let me help sell her on the idea. I'll go down to her restaurant and run it past her. Just researching it with her will be fun."

Noel said, "The fun part is that Louie is going to pay for it!" Both Noel and Claire gave a low evil belly laugh.

After the lunch hour Claire called Noel and told him that it was a go. "There wasn't much of a sales job, she was ready to roll," said Clair. "But we are taking one of her gals along to add cover for Louie. I don't know her, but Rebecca said she will fit right in." Noel smelled one of Rebecca's matchmaker deals in the works.

Louie had to be extracted from the Tucson golf resort after it became apparent that the shooter was not going to materialize as quickly as first thought. The group had to move the operation back to Prescott and, of course, Louie was becoming restless there. Claire and Noel had put him in the Yavapai Apache Casino Hotel in Prescott while Claire and Bear Child kept an eye on him.

Noel called Louie and left a message for him to return the call as soon as he got back to his room. Later in the afternoon Louie called Noel and apologized for missing his call. "I was in the gift shop here and doing a little shopping." Knowing Louie liked to acquire things without paying for them, Noel asked "Oh, ok, what did you get?"

"Just a few trinkets."

"No clothing?" teased Noel, trying to stay on Louie's good side.

"Well, maybe a few items of clothing. I couldn't resist."

"Louie, I have a great idea, reserve a table for four this evening at your hotel, say around 6:00 p.m.?" Noel was hoping Louie would agree.

"Oh yes! A party sounds like fun. Not that I am complaining, Noel, but after all I am going through, a party sounds like so much fun right now."

"Well, Louie, let's enjoy it then, see you at 6:00."

Noel called Claire back and told him to get Rebecca and Bear Child over to the casino hotel for dinner by 6:00 p.m. "Let both of them know we have to sell the cruise idea to Louie," instructed Noel. Meeting at 6:00 p.m. would give him a few hours to restock a few books, check into his online course program, and be able to chat with a few students as required by the college before he would have to leave for the casino hotel.

Noel found a parking spot in the lot on the bluff upon which the casino and hotel were built. Finding Louie and the rest of his party in the dining room was fairly easy. It was a slow night, and there were several tables open. Louie was dressed in blazer and slacks. He appeared to be enjoying himself and insisted upon picking up the check. Noel told him, "We will fight over it after dinner, ok?" and Louie agreed.

The group had a few cocktails before ordering, and all agreed on the hotel seafood dish. This provided Noel with an excellent segue into his idea. He began by telling everyone how much he enjoyed seafood, and it gave him an idea he wanted to run past Louie. Knowing how much Louie enjoyed his own counsel, Noel added, "Louie, be honest now, but give this a minute to ferment. Don't hold back if you disagree; I honor your mature insight into things of this nature." Louie raised his wine glass signaling for Noel to begin.

"Louie, your safety is paramount in our current operation. Things seemed to have come to a standstill in our other operation. Wouldn't you agree, Timothy?" signaling Tim Bear Child to pile onto the B.S. he was laying down to Louie.

Taking his cue, Bear Child said, "Exactly, ah, like we talked about today, ah, earlier. I think it is time to move on, don't you, Noel?"

"Absolutely," answered Noel. "Louie, you know the border with Mexico is an especially crazy place right now. People being beheaded, mass murders, cartels after each other, drive-by shootings, and now mass graves on both sides of the border, crazy."

Rebecca jumped in, "It would be so much better for people if there was a protected place to go, you know, like a safe little island." Louie had been nodding his head in agreement and joined the discussion when Rebecca said the word 'island.' "Oh, that would be so cool, an island," said Louie as he was eating it all up. "And fun, too," added Claire. Louie agreed and said, "It would be."

"That is exactly my point!" declared Noel. "I was thinking the same thing, but in terms of a safe cruise - fun, dining, a cruise with people you didn't have to worry about." Rebecca added, "You dine at the captain's table on a cruise." Claire threw out a tidbit, "Free drinks on a cruise." Louie asked out loud but to no one in particular, "Captain's table, huh?" Looking back on it later, Noel became convinced that his component was the one that sealed the deal when he said, "Each cruise ship has its own shopping mall of sorts."

Louie was obviously sold. "Louie, how do you feel about hiding for a while on a cruise?" Without hesitation Louie said, "I have given this idea some thought. It does not take me long to provide an analysis to a problem when one is needed. I think you have a few things that need to be worked out, but I can help you do that later. I would say that idea of yours, rough as it is right now, would work out well. Let's do it, shall we?"

"Everybody but me," Noel said. "I'll stay here to remain on top of information. You and I will get together, Louie, to plan, but I'm so glad you like the idea. I think you have become more sophisticated as time goes by, Louie, I don't know how you do it." "Great minds think alike, huh, Noel?" offered Louie. "Absolutely, Louie, drink up."

It should be noted that none of the group had ever done a complete background on Louie. It wasn't known whether Louie had any training past high school or even if he made it to graduation. He once said his high school friends used to make fun of his name Louie Louis because it reminded them of the song by the recording group called The Kingsmen titled "Louie Louie."

As the evening meal ended with dessert for some and another drink for others, Noel pulled Louie to the side and expanded on the Mexican cruise idea. "Last place they would look? I love that!" said Louie.

CHAPTER 41

The Arizona Daily Star
Wednesday. April 7, 2021
By Rafael Caranza
The Arizona Republic

A HEAD-ON COLLISION INVOLVING TWO BUSES CARRYING WORKERS AT a gold mine killed 16 people and injured 14 others south of Arizona-Mexico border. The crash happened at 3:36 a.m. Tuesday near the entrance to the Noche Buena mine, about two hours driving distance south of the Lukeville port of entry, along Federal Highway 2, according to the Sonora Attorney General's office. The mine used the two buses to shuttle workers, it said in the news release. Images from the crash site showed that the two buses had crashed head-on, obstructing the two-lane road.

All of the 16 passengers traveling in the smaller of the two buses died on the scene, while the 14 traveling on the larger bus were transported to nearby Caborca, the Attorney General's Office said. Forensic staff was tasked with inspecting the two buses following the crash. They identified the individuals killed and injured. Everyone involved in the crash is from Mexico, they added. Crash survivors were hospitalized with major bruises and fractures.

The Noche Buena gold mine is owned and operated by the British-Mexican firm Fresnillo plc. The company did not respond to a request for comment. It has operated the gold mine since 2012, according to the company's website.

Noel had no idea when the shooter would reappear, if ever. Looking back on it, he realized how foolish his idea was to have Arizona notaries checked out. Of all the organized crime organizations in the world, why would a Mexican drug cartel require legitimate notary service? Strong arm, fraud, lies, and murder were their trademark.

Now Louie had an associate in the Sinaloa Cartel that told him the shooter was back in the Casa Grande area. Where exactly was the big question. The most Noel could do right now was drive-by surveillance with the hopes she would be spotted, or her friend's black Mustang convertible would be seen. Noel conferred with the FBI about possible residence utility checks for new services, gas, electric, water meter accounts, and the U.S. Mail Service. Years ago, mail carriers knew everyone in town. Noel had even considered asking the FBI to go into online retailers for anything new, including but not limited to, furniture, towels, clothes, bank cards, bank statements, and credit reporting agencies for anyone who might be a new owner or renter in Casa Grande, Arizona.

His idea was that, if she did go back into a community after the FBI ran her out, it meant she would need to replace clothes, mercantile goods, furniture etc. That would be a monster task to check out and a bad idea to run past the FBI. Tempting but none the less bad. Although, a good hacker could get into Amazon Prime, thought Noel.

Noel was from a culture that did not get everything replaced with a new item. The economics of lower-income folks often meant waiting for more affordable options or going without. Some folks had fallback plans, and that was extended family. In families of color, you always had aunts, uncles, cousins. Male family friends that you accepted as uncle, female family friends that you accepted as grandma or auntie. Hostile Native American tribes would even house themselves with other tribes to avoid attack by white military units who, after seeing the size of the enemy encampment, reconsidered attacking it. Noel thought to himself, "God only knows who could be helping her. Mexican Americans, illegal Mexicans, Mexican Cartel Mexicans, Native American tribal members, etc. etc."

It wasn't until the media picked up on the mass grave story that

Chicago Police Department Detective O'Brady and the Chicago serial killings came alive again. The news slant was that a police detective was buried in a mass grave after disappearing while investigating suspected serial killer Timothy Bear Child. This new wave of gaslighting could set off some serious psychological trouble for Bear Child, but, more importantly, it could get him killed should the shooter surface now. Noel suspected the cartel would order her back into service to finish the job she was assigned. No reflection upon Bear Child, but this might be a good thing; it could flush her out into the open.

Noel was operating under the illusion that Bear Child was not yet aware of the media attention, but he could not have been more wrong. Even aboard cruise ships there is CNN, and that is what Bear Child was watching as he called Noel.

"So with all of this stuff going on again, you think I have nothing to be concerned about?" asked Bear Child.

"Well, you do, but not right now," explained Noel. "You are at sea for the next week."

"Ok, but after this week what will we do?"

"I am working on that as we speak," said Noel. "I've seen an ad for a large horse trailer and combination living compartment,"

"You mean a show trailer," corrected Bear Child.

Noel said, "Yeah, show trailer, I was going to talk you into buying that and a horse or two and move to Mike and Dani's place outside of Tucson for a few weeks. We'll talk when you guys get back here to Prescott."

"Ok, I'll think about it," agreed Bear Child.

"Good, now enjoy the cruise on Louie's dime, ok?"

When the cruise was over and the flight from San Diego landed at the Prescott airport, all five people, Louie, Bear Child, Claire, Rebecca, and her lady friend were physically drained and just wanted to rest. Louie was installed again at the Yavapai Apache Casino Hotel. Noel insisted that Bear Child not return to his camper trailer located in the RV park where Larry was killed for fear that the shooter would surface there again. Instead, Bear Child and Claire were placed into the casino hotel too.

In the morning at breakfast Rebecca was animated about her cruise and about the interchange between her friend and Claire. "Love abounds?" joked Noel.

Rebecca smiled and said, "No, but you know Claire has been alone for years, and he really liked her company. I think they may have spent the last night together."

Noel took a long sip of his coffee and asked, "Any porn photos?"

Rebecca grabbed and pinched Noel's earlobe and said, "You think you're funny? I don't think you're funny. Is this funny?" she asked, while applying more pressure to his earlobe.

Noel responded with a long painful, "Noooo."

After rubbing his earlobe Noel said, "Seriously, I will have a long talk with that heathen hostile about sleeping around with white women." Rebecca surprised Noel when she grabbed him by the crotch and whispered, "If you do, I will cut this off with a garden spade."

"Not another word! I swear!" promised Noel.

CHAPTER 42

Arizona Daily Star
Sunday, June 6, 2021
Opinion Column by Tim Steller

Much blood, few solutions

Political violence in Mexico becomes ever more appalling

WHEN MEXICO'S VOTERS CAST BALLOTS SUNDAY, 36 CANDIDATES WILL be missing. They were killed during the campaign in a wave of electoral violence. Either there's been an alarming wave of attacks on candidates by people attempting to remove them from the democratic arena, or murder in Mexico is just so common now that naturally three dozen candidates would be killed in the course of election campaigns playing out across the country. Violence and threats of it are "intrinsic" to Mexican politics, said Michael Lettieri, a senior fellow for human rights at the University of California-San Diego's Center for US-Mexican Studies. "The thing that is old is the practice of violence and the impunity around it, but there are new factors that make the violence useful," he said.

Among those factors is there is now true political competition in many localities. Criminal and private interests can gain legitimacy and greater access by winning local control through elections. Elections aren't so much a source of solutions to violence, but more a focal point of violence as power relationships are re-sorted and private and criminal interests seek to maintain their edge.

**It should be noted that on June 9, 2021, PBS station KUAT-TV in Tucson, Arizona reported that a University of Arizona researcher estimate 90 Mexican candidates were killed nationwide in Mexico.

————————

As Claire, Bear Child, and Louie were being seated with Noel in the dining room of the casino hotel in Prescott, Noel made the decision to put it all out there, something that he seldom did. The four of them ordered, and Noel waited until the server had vanished before he began. "I think that right now the things that are going on in Mexico may take the heat off of us for a while. I've been staying up to date on the news there, and I believe many of the situations are directly related to the cartel shake up we may be having on this side of the border." Everyone at the table looked at Noel, and he knew he had each person's attention, even Louie who looked like he had been up all night drinking.

"Look, without going into detail, our shooter works for the cartel in this area of the border. She may be busy down south right now. With the recent television coverage about O'Brady, I was on edge about Tim being targeted by her again here in Prescott." The dining room waiter interrupted Noel with a courtesy coffee pour, and when he left the table area, Claire interrupted before Noel could speak again.

"I agree, I think she is going to try again. Sorry, Tim, but I'm worried, too."

"We all are," said Louie, finally waking up enough to be part of the conversation. "I have an idea, why not let me send Timothy overseas? My treat, he will be safe there."

Noel explained, "Thank you, Louie, but that is why I wanted to talk with you, well, ask everyone's opinion, actually. I have an idea he may be safe for a while, but I don't want him to be her target, period. I'd like to go back to my original plan. Tim, I know you can disappear over at Mike and Dani's place, and if you miss a few weeks of school, that may be the only thing you risk. I found a four-horse show trailer, and the living area inside the trailer is great. Shower, kitchen, bed, and living room-type area. It even has a small tack room for saddles mostly. My idea was to sell you on this and have you pick up a horse or two for the duration to do your horse whisperer thing while we hunt her down."

Bear Child wanted to be heard, so he said, "Ok, look, I'm fine with the idea. I know I would have to get a fifth-wheel hitch installed on my truck, and I'm ok with that, I'm ok with the whole plan, but I would like to help get her. I don't know how, but I'm available."

Noel waited until the breakfast was served, and everyone was starting to eat before he continued, "I was thinking we use your camper right where it is, just like you are still living there. We get a timer for the interior lights, maybe set up a camera across the road to see who comes and goes."

"Do we share this with the local gendarmes?" asked Claire.

Noel said, "Sure, but we ask for total secrecy. No leaks."

Claire cautioned, "They may not want us to do this because of liability issues, you know, placing the park manager in a dangerous position again. I mean, I'm not against it. Installing a timer light isn't putting anyone in the line of fire."

"You are right, let's do it," said Louie, "although I think Tim and I should go to Europe."

"Thank you for the generous offer, Louie," said Bear Child. "I'm not just being polite, I mean it, I value your friendship."

Louie faked wiping a tear from his cheek and said, "You have to stop, you are the one in peril but work to protect me. I love you, brother!"

Claire faked choking on his food, and Noel announced, "Ok, we're gone."

Bear Child asked Noel, "What should I call Mike Kuntzelman? Dr. Kuntzelman?"

Noel smiled and said, "He answers to Mike. But address him however you think is right. He's a good guy, you'll like him."

Bear Child spent the day working out some of the details of Noel's plan. He looked at the horse trailer Noel had found which was nice and caught his attention. He struck what he thought was a good deal on the purchase price and set off to look at saddles. After googling a feedstore address in Prescott, he found a nice used saddle for sale there. When he sat on it, he knew it was for him. Grabbing a new halter and lead rope, he found himself looking for a nice headstall, reins, and a bit. More than anything else, he found himself relaxing and enjoying his day.

After grabbing a lunch at a chain burger joint, he paged through a horse sale newspaper he had taken from the stand at the feed store. He located a few horses he was interested in meeting. Bear Child did not think in terms of looking at a strange horse to buy but rather meeting the horse. He did not believe in breaking a horse to ride; his process was to teach a horse. He had learned this from his uncles. Breaking meant literally just that, to break the horse's spirit.

Bear Child called the first ad he found. When he got there, he knew he would not need to call any other horse advertiser. There was an animal in a round pen that was already saddled and standing there. Bear Child estimated the horse to be a teenager, thirteen to maybe fourteen years of age. Well- mannered and not about to roll onto his back while unattended, as great as that would feel to a horse who just came out of a stall that he may have been in for weeks. With a saddle on his back, rolling right now would probably destroy the saddle horn or saddle. Bear Child liked him.

Bear Child was greeted by the horse when he walked up to the round pen. The animal slowly came over to him and smelled him before coming any further. Bear Child took his time crawling into the round pen while talking to the horse and walked to him so there was four inches between their two faces. He stroked the horse's cheek with one hand very slowly while gently blowing his breath toward the horse's nostrils. Without removing that hand, he let his other hand follow the full length of the horse to the rear end. A horse also feels with the senses the Creator has given them in their hair, much like a human when something out of place makes the hair on the neck stand up. These are early warning signs that the Creator has given us all because of the danger out there.

Bear Child knew that horses hear, taste, and see like other animals, but they have better hearing and much better long-distance vision. Close viewing is a problem for a horse because his eyes are on the side of his skull instead of in the front. The animal must adjust his head's distance to the object to look at things in focus. Sometimes horses are bitten by snakes as they move their head closer to see what that strange thing is. However, he can rotate his eyes a bit to see things to his rear. This at times creates problems because the perception for a horse is sped up, so a person back there appears to be walking fast when in fact they are walking at a normal pace. It is sort of funny until a horse kicks because he was frightened.

Bear Child slowly began to loosen the cinch and remove the saddle and saddle pad. If the horse was the type who did not like being saddled by a rough handler, he would balk or move away during the process. A seller would conceal this by having the horse saddled prior to the arrival of the unsuspecting buyer. Bear Child resaddled the horse, and the animal stood patiently while he did so. Bear Child wanted this horse for several reasons. One was that he was not a young colt, he was old enough to have the silliness of youth gone from him and would not do something dangerous out of the blue like a younger horse might. Bear Child looked and felt inside the mouth of the horse and noted one tooth had developed a hook-type growth on it. That needed care, but it could be floated or filed down before it caused the horse nutritional issues. He slowly lifted each hoof to inspect it and stretched each leg to check for stiffness or discomfort. The horse had new shoes indicating it had recently been shod by someone who knew what they were doing. The seller claimed that the horse was up to date on all of his shots, and Bear Child was satisfied. There was really no foolproof way to know that a horse was sound until he could actually get on the trail with him.

The second reason he wanted the horse was he found out the animal had a trail companion of approximately the same age who was also for sale at a lower price. Bear Child bought both horses after he gave the second one a quick once-over, and the deal closed with the understanding that they would be picked up within a few days. He felt very pleased with himself and was actually looking forward to something exciting and worthwhile again.

CHAPTER 43

LOUIE HAD LIVED A VERY COMFORTABLE LIFE ON THE SEA AND ENJOYED it, at one point even giving thought to another cruise in the near future. One day on the ship he busied himself by collecting as much printed information on various cruises available. Because of his problem with taking things that he did not purchase, he also gathered numerus silver-plated things. Louie's personal bag was stuffed with stolen salt and pepper shakers and napkin holders, but knowing he had to pass customs on the way back into the California home port, he began to mail things to himself at each port of call. One would think that perhaps Louie's collection of printed material was to keep his other collection from clanging when he walked off the ship from port of call to port of call.

This type of activity by Louie did not come as a surprise to anyone associated with him. It was almost expected that if something caught his eye, he thought it was intended for him. He fooled none, especially Claire who would make snide comments to Louie as he passed him in the passageway of the ship with his bag. "Cash for clunkers, Louie?" asked Claire. "Whatever are you referring to, landlubber?" joked Louie in response. "Now gangway before I have you walk the plank. Besides, it is all for the local economy."

Claire would just keep the info to himself and hope upon hope that Louie would not be caught and sent to await court in a Mexican jail. Of course, this would never happen as Louie had a strange connection to his guiding angel who seemed to always smile down on him. One evening while Louie was entertaining himself in the main lounge, Claire took a significant amount of bounty from Louie's bag and tossed it into a plastic bag for the kitchen porter to pick up. The next day, Louie was beside himself, and when asked why he said, "I have been robbed on this vessel. All of my charitable collection has been pilfered during the night by some actor or actors."

Claire asked, "So the local economy has been slighted?"

Louie said, "Unfortunately I will not be sharing anything with them today, after all. I will have to remain on board and look into this sad state of affairs, this so-called safe passage in Mexican waters."

Claire looked at Louie and said, "Carry on."

Louie mocked Claire by saying, "I will attempt to do so, but my trust has been shaken."

"Shivered your timbers?" asked Claire

"I would not jest, Claire Blue Crow, this is serious!"

Claire offered, "How about if I look into this, Louie?"

"Well, that is different. Once again, thank you," said Louie, taking the bait.

Claire said again, "Carry on."

Noel was still in the process of doing on and off surveillance of the community in Casa Grande. A portion of his technique was old-school while another part of him leaned toward technology. While in Casa Grande he would launch drones, calling them 'Watch Dog sorties.' The small drone could cover a lot of area during a fifteen-minute flight.

Luck plays a role in each day of an investigator's life. Being in the right place at the right time is nothing more than luck, similar to hitting a penny slot machine jackpot on the right day while on the right slot machine. One day Noel picked up a black Mustang convertible parked near a row of mailboxes at the entrance to a mobile home park in Casa Grande. Noel was familiar with many mobile home park requirements. Some parks required the homeowner to be 55 years old or older. It was not a stretch to assume people could fake age and appearance if they wanted to conceal themselves. It would be easy to hide there if the staff who mattered were paid to look the other way. Noel brought the drone down to a level several feet above the ground in an attempt to get a license plate number off of the Mustang without being seen.

When he thought he got the plate number, he did a very quick maneuver and positioned the drone higher to cover the car's exit with hopes he could follow it. As it turned out, the driver was apparently checking the boxes for mail. She returned to the Mustang and drove into the park straight to a home with a carport like the other homes had. When she parked, Noel's view of her was obstructed. However, she quickly left the car and went into the home. Noel had gotten lucky.

Noel recalled his drone and downloaded his video onto a thumb drive after he reviewed it. He was not a techie but had learned how to send a video to the FBI. By doing that he knew he would soon have information on that car and the home. Before Noel got back to Prescott, he was advised that he had struck gold in Casa Grande. The FBI was interested in the driver of the Mustang and the occupant(s) of the home. They politely told Noel to stay away from the area. Noel expected no less from the FBI, but by warning him they let the cat out of the bag. There would not be any more cooperation from the feds.

Because the FBI made the shooter flee earlier from Casa Grande, Noel expected this operation to be more refined. The mobile home park was a relatively wide-open space, but the home under suspicion was at the corner of a cul-de-sac located behind the park office building and equipment yard. The small backyard of the home supported an eight-foot-high chain link fence. Outside of the fence were several acres of open desert that ran up to the interstate. Noel assumed that there would be no escape tunnels in the park, but a short one leading to the open desert was very possible. Noel had made up his mind that he would conduct his Watch Dog drone flights from the desert location out of view of the home and the FBI.

The following day Noel discovered that the other two homes in the cul-de-sac facing the shooter's home were occupied by what appeared to be cartel bad guys, young Mexican males who would check in from the carport of their house with a spotting scope aimed at the windows of the shooter's house. With two houses, Noel calculated that maybe they had six cartel bad guys for each twenty-four-hour shift, but he was just estimating their strength. He knew from the Casa Grande circus that the next act would be with armed support.

CHAPTER 44

NOEL HAD BEEN IN CASA GRANDE DURING A SURVEILLANCE WHEN HE saw street repairs going on near the shooter's old apartment. That germinated an idea to use an industrial roll-off dumpster near the mobile home park to get his men closer to the fight, should shots be fired. Not hiding behind the dumpster but instead inside.

The way he sold the idea to his guys in Tucson was described as aboveboard and direct. He would lease a roll-off dumpster with a canvas cover. Inside the dumpster would be three beanbag chairs for the guys to ride in and three small stepstools they could fire from over the height of the dumpster walls. There would be a small port-a-potty for the guys to use. The thickness of the dumpster's steel walls would protect the men, and the idea of a shot ricocheting around inside the dumpster like a Waring Blender was minimal if the shooter did not get the upper hand by being a story above the dumpster and shooting down into it. Noel told the guys that the mobile homes were not two-story homes. He figured he would have the dumpster delivered as soon as he could, and when it arrived, he would personally flush the shooter out by paying a call on her.

There was no doubt that the FBI had cut his guys out of the picture, and this irritated him. Maybe too much. The correct way to approach this would be to enlist the cooperation of the FBI before he risked the life of any of his friends. Yet, in Noel's mind, one of his friends was already killed, and this was of little importance to the FBI. They covered up the three killings in Chicago which allowed the Chicago Police Department to bring the hammer down on one of their own, an innocent man. He thought, "We found the shooter in Casa Grande, and the FBI scared her away. We ID'd her through an old juvenile fingerprint that matched those partial prints taken from a van used in Larry's killing. And now we locate her again, and they tell us to stay away? No, it isn't going to end like that."

Time wasn't on his side. He needed to get his guys in place, so he phoned John McCall to round up Larry Bird and Phil Cloud and head up to Casa Grande. Noel got hold of Roberto Crow and instructed him to meet in Casa Grande, also. Travel time for Roberto would be about four hours, so that was Noel's window. Instructions were given to the dumpster company to get ready to move the leased roll-off on Noel's order. Now it would be just a matter of getting Claire and Bear Child in place.

That afternoon Claire, Bear Child, and Noel were with the guys from Tucson and gathered around the dumpster located at the contractor's yard where Noel had leased it. This huge roll-off was at least 8 feet wide, 8 feet tall, and 22 feet long. The beanbag chairs, porta-potty and a cooler of bottled water was placed inside, and the guys walked into the dumpster through the hinged doors at the rear. When they were inside, the truck driver went to work and placed the thick canvas tarp over the entire top. He told the guys to "hang on" because he was going to move the dumpster onto his truck. Once it was winched up, he waited for Noel to give him the go-ahead to drive to and drop it off at the shooter's cul-de-sac. Noel's instructions were specific. It was to be dropped at the mouth of the cul-de-sac so the guys could get a clear view of both the cartel bad guys' places and the shooter's place. The drive to the cul-de-sac in the mobile home park would be approximately fifteen minutes from their present location over a bumpy road with a few turns. Noel would have cellphone contact with the guys inside, and as soon as Roberto arrived, they would begin the journey.

Roberto called Noel, letting him know he was just minutes away. Noel told the guys inside the dumpster, "Get ready to roll," and all three of them sat down on their beanbag chairs for the ride. Ten minutes later

Roberto arrived, and Noel gave the command to the roll- off truck to go ahead.

John McCall explained to no one in general, "I missed breakfast and lunch," as he unwrapped a sandwich from a paper bag he had brought along. Larry Bird struggled to get to his feet but somehow made it over to the porta-potty to urinate. When he was finished, he zipped up his pants and was able to keep his balance and make it back to his bean bag chair. After watching Larry Bird, Phil Cloud then got the subliminal stimuli to want to urinate also. Phil lost his balance getting up from the beanbag chair and almost ran the full length of the dumpster before smashing into the opposite end while it was moving down the road. When he stood up, he made it to the porta-Potty and began to "void his bladder" as the story was told later. Just as he began to enjoy the feeling of relieving himself, the truck suddenly slowed to make a turn, and again Phil lost his balance and went down on one knee and then onto his back.

It was later described by some who were inside that dumpster as "Like a baby boy getting his diaper changed but you forget to cover him, and he pees straight up into the air." As the urine shot toward the dumpster's tarp and fell onto the floor, a fine mist of pee sprayed onto John McCall's unwrapped and partially eaten grilled Havarti cheese and turkey sandwich. Phil Cloud attempted to apologize to McCall as he clumsily worked his way over to John, who was seated on his beanbag chair. Unfortunately, he lurched and stood with his wet crotch in John's face. John immediately instructed Phil to "Get your old ass the hell away from me! Nasty son of a bitch!" John threw his sandwich down, made a fist with his right hand, and started to rub his soiled knuckles against the short-sleeve Hawaiian shirt that he was wearing.

Cloud's pool of urine picked up velocity as it raced on the floor of the dumpster to Larry Bird's seated position. Larry spotted the mass moving at a vicious speed toward him and started to tap dance with his feet to avoid the pee. He could not gain enough balance to avoid falling into it as he tried to stand and escape. John McCall yelled, "Holy shit! Am I the only sane one in this fuck'n dumpster?" Looking at Phil Cloud,

McCall said, "You frolic in it, and Bird goes swimming in it? Pick that fool up and help him get back."

Phil crab-walked with his wet pants over to Larry Bird who was still lying in the urine and helped him get back to his beanbag chair. Without realizing how foolish it appeared, he offered his handkerchief to Bird. McCall's cellphone chimed, and when he answered it with, "Now what?" Noel instructed him to "Get a grip on it, we're pulling in now. Lock and load." McCall acknowledged the call by saying, "Ok, we're ready!"

The entire convoy came to rest at the mouth of the mobile home park where a marked sheriff's unit would not allow them entry. Noel asked the young deputy, "What's happening?" and the deputy stated, "The FBI and our department are conducting a search at this time. You're going to have to have that dumpster truck back out and turn around."

It was obvious that the FBI had moved on the shooter and her bad guys. Noel wanted to tell his guys in the dumpster what was happening, but before he could walk over to them, automatic weapon fire started to sound nearby. He and the deputy looked at each other briefly before the deputy ran to his car radio, and Noel ran to the truck to tell the driver to back out and block the road. Noel stood on the running boards of the cab of the truck. He told the truck driver, "Drop it and leave, get away from the park." The dumpster drop made a loud noise and popped the guys in the dumpster into the air. When they fell back onto their beanbag chairs, the seams split, shooting Styrofoam pellets everywhere inside the dumpster. The sudden jolt hurt the tail bones of all three guys, but they had weapons at the ready and were looking out of the top of the dumpster from underneath the tarp while they stood on their stepstools. More shooting erupted as Noel, Claire, and Bear Child moved behind the car they traveled in.

Roberto crawled in a ditch to get around the Sheriff's car. His plan was to flank the bad guys should they get that far. Within seconds the deputy and his car responded toward the sound of the automatic weapon fire. This left Roberto somewhat exposed in the ditch, but he remained there because things were beginning to develop fast. In less than a minute a car was approaching the guys real fast, and not seeing the dumpster blocking the road, they almost ran into it. The car skidded to a stop. Automatic weapons were seen coming out of the car windows. One young Mexican guy stepped out of the car with a burst of AK-47 fire on full auto aimed in the direction of the guys in the dumpster.

Claire said, "That was stupid," just as the guys in the dumpster opened up on the car and its occupants. Noel and his men followed suit while Roberto shot the young Mexican in his back, making him drop his weapon and forcing him to try to crawl back into the car which was now full of incoming rounds. This was one of those very odd moments in a firefight when all of a sudden there is a silence that prevails for just a few seconds, like a time-out. It gives people time to reposition to a safer location or reload while watching an opponent's possible movements. The amount of aggression does not change, it becomes more focused but never dimmed during that time. Suddenly there will be action or movement that will justify the next response.

Roberto stood up in the ditch. He motioned that he would check the car by pointing two fingers on his right hand toward his eyes while keeping his left hand with his weapon pointed toward the car as he slowly walked forward. When he got closer, he could hear someone moaning. He also heard the sound of someone in the car chambering a round of ammo from a clip he had just inserted into his weapon. Roberto started to walk backward at a fast pace which signaled to Noel to yell, "Weapon! Weapon!" Once Roberto was no longer in the line of fire, the guys in the dumpster and Noel's men outside opened up again. This time the front windshield of the car blew into the interior, and the rearview mirror fell down into the front seat. FBI and Sheriff's department cars flowed into the area blocked by the dumpster, stopping right next to the car riddled with bullets.

Roberto laid on the road in spread-eagle fashion so no one would shoot him thinking he was a cartel member. The young sheriff's deputy who had manned the roadblock earlier shouted to the others, "He is ok, he is ok. He's one of us, he is ok." When Noel walked up to the car with Claire and Bear Child, they could hear a voice inside identify as being "On Star" asking, if everything was "Ok?"

All six occupants of the car were dead, with no evidence that the six were in this country to do anything legal. In all, ten weapons were recovered. Six of those had empty magazines still in the weapon, indicating they had been fired and were discarded to use the other four weapons that were loaded. There was no female body to indicate the female shooter died in the ambush. Not wanting to share anything with the FBI, Noel informed the sheriff's department deputy in charge to look for a short tunnel in the desert behind the shooter's house. A few hours later a Border Patrol dog found a tunnel where Noel told them to look. John McCall, Larry Bird, and Phil Cloud were out of the dumpster and dry but assumed they smelled bad. One of the young sheriff deputies there asked another deputy, just loud enough for them to overhear, "Why do old people always smell like pee?"

CHAPTER 45

NOEL AND THE GUYS EXPECTED THE FBI TO GET ALL HOT AND BOTH-
ered about not following the warning given to them. Noel didn't care,
but he was concerned about everybody's safety if they were held until
they could have their day in court. He was angered when the FBI instructed him to stay away. That was never his intent. He had been dealt
a blow when Larry was shot and killed, and he wanted to hunt down the
shooter and eliminate her. It was just the way he was built.

Noel's tribe was the Stockbridge-Munsee Mohican people. The
Mohican fought on the side of the British during The French and Indian
Wars. They caught the interest of Robert Rogers, who wanted Mohican
warriors to became members of Rogers Rangers, fighting and killing the
French. They were given specific orders to kill and scalp while terroriz-
ing both the French and Mohawks. Some British officers disliked the
Mohicans and thought them to be lazy and undisciplined because they
did not dig ditches or take orders from the English officers like others
had to. The Mohicans believed that they were there to fight and to kill,
not to dig ditches. And fight they did. In 1774 the Mohicans joined in
supporting the colonies when the Revolutionary War started. Mohican
warriors participated in the historic siege of Boston and at Bunker Hill.
Mohican warriors were also Colonial Army scouts at Saratoga.

Noel fought in Vietnam as a young combat Marine in the 60s. It
wasn't fashionable because this was an unpopular war. The actions that
were required, such as running ambushes at night as a squad leader of
six or seven other young Marines, didn't get favorable press. While under

the cover of darkness and silence, Noel and his men had to surprise and kill the Viet Cong and North Vietnamese Army soldiers who walked into his ambush site instead of being back in the United States in front of a television set watching the late night news. It was his legacy and nature to be a warrior through his DNA. That was all that could be said about Noel Two Horses and his rationale to fight instead of staying away as warned. It brought him into conflict at times as a law enforcement officer and as a detective, but that was Noel Two Horses. He knew he could not offer a defense for his guys or himself, and he knew he had to be cautious in his thinking before speaking to the FBI as the forensic people started work on the shooting scene that his guys were responsible for.

Throughout the day there were numerous interviews, recorded and written. The forensic team shot video and digital records of the car, bodies, and weapons. Measurements were taken to record the exact placement of weapons, bodies, and distance to the dumpster. Fingerprints of the dead and Noel's guys were lifted and recorded, then sent to the various FBI labs. Each body was examined in place, pockets emptied, and items collected. All the bodies remained in place until late that evening while the contents of the two mobile homes that housed the cartel guys were processed. Noel could not recall at exactly what point in this process the FBI agent in charge talked with him, but he had spent a great deal of time on his cell before he spoke to Noel. Surprisingly enough, there was no reprimand. However, there was a warning that charges could be brought against all the people associated with the incident.

It became obvious that someone much higher up in the FBI had spoken to the agent in charge. Noel could only assume that agent was cautioned not to incite another incident like the one Noel participated in with the FBI agent in Casa Grande when one of the FBI assistant directors interceded. At this stage Noel had the feeling he could not risk any more liability. When he and his guys were allowed to leave the area, it was already late evening. His guys had to surrender the weapons they fired that day to the FBI techs before leaving. Noel insisted that everyone grab a room for the evening at the nearby chain motel south of the shooting scene. They could get a meal and a shower while they decompressed.

Some of the guys sat down for their late dinner while others elected to go to bed after a shower rather than join Noel in the dining room. Noel got a call from the young deputy who had been at the scene before the shooting. The call began with the deputy identifying himself and then telling Noel that the Sheriff of Pinal County would like a list of the guys who were with Noel so he could deputize them on paper for the FBI, should it become necessary. The young deputy said it was because he identified Roberto to the FBI in public when he yelled, "He is one of us."

"At the time, I didn't know that Roberto was the shooter who killed one of the cartel members outside of the car during the gunfight. The sheriff wants to protect everyone." Noel asked the young deputy to thank the Sheriff, and he would provide the list of names via text message later that night. This was important information, and Noel wanted to share it with everyone.

The meal now was joyful and full of bravado and made sleeping so much easier that night for those who were battle-weary and tired. Noel handed his phone to Bear Child and asked him to text the young deputy the name of all the guys who were there. After he had sent the text, Claire told him, "You did well out there today, Mr. Bear Child. I would be proud to fight with you any day." Bear Child was embarrassed but responded in a toast toward Claire with his half-full beer glass saying, "Same here, Mr. Blue Crow, same here."

The following day after everyone had checked out, they got together in the parking lot. Noel told them that this time they were lucky, but that the situation was all his fault. "Normally we disappear before the authorities make their grand entrance, but this time we got caught, and for that, I'm sorry." Not one of the guys responded to what Noel said; they understood. Everyone left and began their journey back home. On the way back to Prescott, Claire told Noel, "We don't know what happened at the shooter's house, I'd like to know." Noel replied, "I'll ask the deputy and let you know. Right now they're too busy to entertain answering any of our questions. We need to make ourselves invisible for the time being. I'd really like you and Tim to head down to Mike and Dani's place and lay low. I will take care of Louie for the time being."

Noel told Louie about an emergency plan should he have to leave Prescott for any length of time. Louie was reluctant to sign off on it, but he did after Noel told him it was for emergencies only, and it was highly improbable that it would ever be utilized.

That is the way it went for several days. Noel broke the news to Rebecca that he would be moving into the casino hotel where Louie was to keep him safe. That plan appeared to be ok with Rebecca. She would much rather have Noel in Prescott than elsewhere. Louie would be billed for the services he required, and that was ok, too. Noel's part-time help continued to be utilized for his mystery bookshop. Noel checked the CCTV across the road from Bear Child's old trailer periodically and found it to be only normal traffic to the RV park where it was located.

Claire enjoyed picking up the two horses that Bear Child had acquired and was looking forward to finding a saddle that fit his aged behind. Things looked like they might work out for a while. Claire liked the time on a horse much more than even the cruise he had just taken. Several days in the desert on horseback, helping with the stall cleaning, and assisting with the care of the animals at the stable was relaxing. He enjoyed watching Mike and Bear Child work with the horses at Mike and Dani's place.

Sharing living quarters with Bear Child was ok; it was a nice trailer. Claire was thinking that maybe retirement living in this type of surroundings would be pleasant. It was kind of scary because Claire had not really given any retirement plans room to take hold. He had never even taken any steps to improve his house on the Navajo Reservation which still lacked running water. Maybe he would get a used four-horse show trailer like Bear Child did and enjoy his life going between Noel's place, his place, and other places he would like to explore on horseback.

CHAPTER 46

IN WEEK TWO OF THIS ARRANGEMENT, NOEL GOT A CALL FROM REBECCA. She seemed upset about something, but Noel could not get her to admit that something was going on. "Look, I just called to check and see if all was ok with you and Louie." Finally, she confessed, "I got a strange customer this noon at the restaurant."

"Strange, how do you mean strange?" asked Noel.

"Well, strange, just strange," said Rebecca. "He was about early twentyish, I couldn't tell how tall because he was seated in a booth, and I was busy when he left, so I never did see him standing. He had short, dark hair, and he maybe went 175 lbs. or so. He was in good shape." Noel said, "That is not strange."

Rebecca said, "You didn't let me finish. It's what he said that was strange."

"I'm sorry, that was rude of me."

"Well, apology accepted. He started off by ordering a cup of coffee. Just coffee at our rush hour? He said that the Mexican cartel boss has a wife who pleaded guilty to charges she was running his cartel while he is locked up. Then he said the cartel is now changed, and that they are no longer interested in the killings in Chicago".

"What the hell?"

"Yeah, that's all he said. All I could do was look at him trying to figure out what he meant. I poured his coffee and like I said, got busy. I called you because he must have left right away. He never touched his coffee."

Noel told Rebecca, "Pull your video of him coming into your restaurant and leaving, ok? I need to take a look at him."

Noel was familiar with the leader of the Mexican Sinaloa drug cartel being incarcerated after two previous escapes from jail. He knew that his wife was facing charges of drug trafficking, but the guilty plea she entered was just recently accepted by the authorities. Noel also suspected that the cartel was reorganizing. Maybe that was why the three older cartel guys were knocked off in Chicago by the shooter, who also killed Larry by mistake thinking he was Tim Bear Child.

If what this fellow said to Rebecca was a message to Noel via Rebecca, it sure was a strange method to use. But the more he thought about it, the more convinced he became that this guy was telling her that the shooter was no longer stalking Bear Child. It would make sense because initially they wanted to make sure Bear Child couldn't testify to what he may have heard the old guys talk about. If they were no longer interested in the Chicago killings, they may no longer be interested in silencing Bear Child.

The people who run the drug cartels do a lot of things. They kill, terrorize, extort, kidnap, rape, and anything else that will make money for them. They also know when to cut their losses. Why risk capture of an assassin who works for the cartel if they could just call off an unnecessary hit job? Noel knew he needed to confirm this somehow. Leaving Louie alone at the casino bar for an hour or so in the evening while he reviewed a video of this guy was easy enough to do. Louie enjoyed his cocktail time.

While viewing the video Noel became convinced this guy was a message carrier. He pointed out to Rebecca how his face was concealed both entering and exiting her restaurant. "He is hunching his shoulders and turning his face away from the camera's view. This guy was aware of the camera and avoided having us be able to see him. Not normal behavior for a guy out for a cup of coffee. I gotta pass this on to the feds. I'm not a computer geek, but I think I can do it by putting this on a thumb drive."

Rebecca had a small supply of thumb drives in her back office at the restaurant where the CCTV monitor was, in the event something like vandalism or a robbery happened, and the recording would be needed. She told Noel, "You know, if Louie is being forgiven for all of his sins by the new management of the cartel, why not have Tim Bear Child moved to an inactive status on their things-to-do list?"

"That would be great, but I need to confirm that for his sake," said Noel, adding, "The bastards still owe me for killing Larry, and I won't be forgetting that."

Rebecca offered, "Here is something to think about, I mean, just think about this, Noel. Suppose for a minute that the cartel does not want the gal to continue? I mean, she has screwed it up and almost got caught twice now. Just how many do-overs will the cartel give her?"

Noel thought that Rebecca made sense; she always did when it came to things like this. She had the ability to divorce herself from the things Noel could not. His anger stood in the way while she operated in a calm and cool focused mode. She had a different relationship with Larry. To her, Larry was her manfriend's ward and buddy. Maybe he viewed Larry as almost a kid brother, she did not. Rebecca did not have a lot invested in her relationship with Larry, but she understood Noel's loss and the new emotional void in his life.

There was something about that video, something familiar in that video, but Noel couldn't come to any conclusion as to what it was. He took the thumb drive with him. He thought that if he were near his bookshop, he would do a quick check to see if all was well. When he drove by the big windows of the store, he noticed it was closed. He looked at his phone, and the time display indicated this was because it was one hour past the normal closing time.

Noel called his part-time person to check on things. She told Noel that she did not have the shop open during the day due to a sick child. Noel naturally asked her if she planned on working the following day, and she told him all was good. Noel started thinking that maybe the reason the strange guy went to the restaurant was because he could not find Noel at his bookshop, it was closed. But why avoid the camera at the restaurant if he would have to meet Noel in person at the bookshop? There were no cameras at the shop, but Noel suddenly remembered that there were cameras in the parking facility behind the Saint Gregory Hotel where most of his customers had to park because of limited street parking.

The following day Noel was with the Prescott Police when they reviewed the video of the parking structure behind his shop. On view was the young deputy sheriff from the Casa Grande mobile home park shootout scene walking from his parked car toward Noel's bookshop location and back to his parked car just minutes later. That was what was familiar about Rebecca's video, the deputy's body image was identical to the guy on her video.

The cartel was famous for corrupting law enforcement officers from multiple agencies. Now it was obvious that they had a plant inside the sheriff's department that was responsible for drug intervention in the main drug corridor of the state. Maybe he tipped the shooter in Casa Grande earlier, or maybe he tipped the cartel bad guys and the shooter the other day. Anything was possible. Maybe he didn't worry about being recognized because he may have planned on eliminating Noel, but when he found out he needed to change his plan, he had to hide his face from the camera at Rebecca's restaurant. It was all speculation but easy enough to sort out once Noel had a chance to ask the young deputy in person.

When the police looked at both videos on a split screen at the same time, it was clear that in the parking lot video the deputy had a weapon in a holster in the small of his back, but no weapon was visible in the restaurant video.

Noel had other worries. All the personal information about his guys were turned over to the deputy by text message. His guys were in trouble. They could be picked off one by one as retaliation for killing the six cartel guys.

Noel called each of the men and asked them to be careful after letting them know what the score was. He next asked Claire and Bear Child to meet him in Casa Grande as soon as possible. Claire broke some rather odd news to Noel when he told him over the phone that the young deputy at the roadblock in the trailer park was the same young deputy who drove through the Food City parking lot when he and Bear Child were standing watch on the shooter's apartment in Casa Grande. Noel planned on kidnapping the deputy and sweating him until he got what he was looking for. Claire agreed with him.

Breaking the news to Louie that it was time to kickstart the emergency plan into operation was not that hard after all. Louie was passed out cold, and Noel would not be with him when he came to. Louie would wake on the fourth floor of an Alzheimer ward at a local extended care facility in Prescott. No way to use the elevator or the stairway without a key. Louie would be fed well, and he would be safe and comfortable until Noel or whoever picked him up. Ingenious. Noel didn't know why he didn't think of that before. Good place for Louie.

CHAPTER 47

NOEL TRUSTED THE SHERIFF OF PINAL COUNTY, BUT HIS RELATIONSHIP with the current FBI in Arizona was frustrating for him. However, that did not mean that he would not trust them in this matter. He also knew deep down that he probably would severely beat the crap out of the young deputy who acted as a liaison for the shooter who killed his unarmed friend Larry. He could only imagine what else this guy had done for the cartel people. Noel assumed his only job was to protect the shooter and her drug corridor. Noel called the sheriff to find out if he could arrange a meeting with him. Once that was taken care of, he drove to Florence. On his arrival Noel saw the young deputy using a computer in an adjoining section of the building. Noel assumed he was filing a report or perhaps researching something. But he wished the deputy was drafting his resignation.

The Sheriff of Pinal County was a young, 45ish fellow with a reputation as being a no-nonsense kind of guy, a veteran of law enforcement, and well educated. He welcomed Noel into his small office and offered him a bottle of cold water. "What can I do for you, Mr. Two Horses? I hope it is something related to our friend in the Casa Grande area?" Once Noel began to explain the reason for his visit, the sheriff interrupted him, asking his person in the front office to hold all his calls and to not let anyone interrupt his meeting. "I am going to ask you to leave by our side door when we are through. I don't know if you noticed, but he is just down the hallway, and I hope he didn't see you coming in."

After speaking with the Sheriff and showing him the videos of the deputy in Prescott, the Sheriff agreed to not only arrest the deputy but to take him into custody while he was still in the building. "I am arresting him for smuggling and murder. That way we will have him for at least 72 hours while we refine our charges. I will have to meet with our County District Attorney and the feds." Noel asked the sheriff if he could interview the deputy once he was in custody.

"You're a witness, and I can't answer that right now. I don't want to soil our pants before we can cement our charges."

Noel smiled grimly and said, "Yeah, it's important to avoid that."

"Ok, let me get hold of our FBI and bring them up to speed," said the Sheriff as he got to his feet and opened his office door for Noel. As Noel stepped out of the office, he followed the Sheriff to the side door. After first making sure that the deputy was still on the computer, the sheriff had his captain and another deputy arrest and disarm him. He was immediately placed in a segregation cell.

The deputy knew he was just awaiting the felony interrogation that would soon take place. He was showing no remorse for soiling the badge of trust that was given to him in the United States of America. As a young kid in Mexico, he was questioned by the Mexican police while they beat him and poured a can of Coke down his nose. This department would not strike or beat him like a Mexican police department would do, so he was relatively safe for the time being. He had been assured that he would not be convicted and do hard time in a place far away from Mexico. His safety depended upon not turning on the cartel.

Because there were many fingers of the cartel, the FBI took custody of the young deputy while he was still alive. Three U.S. Marshalls quickly had him flown into Minnesota that night where he would be processed and interviewed. He was driven through the Arizona desert at night and flown out of Tucson after being unloaded at the U.S. Customs location at Tucson International. With the Sinaloa Cartel organization changing, he would be watched 24/7 before they would let his status be downgraded by Washington office bureaucracy. He needed to be charged and brought before the bench within 72 hours of his arrest.

His initial court appearance was done on a monitor in the Federal

Court House in Tucson while he was on camera seated in a chair in Minnesota. The court knew he was transferred as a safety precaution. During the initial interview, he admitted to being in the restaurant in Prescott and to speaking directly to the female partner of a witness. This admission was secured only after he was told he would be an old man before he would be released from federal custody and that he did not fit the profile for the Witness Protection Program in this country. It should be noted that he never asked for an attorney but instead attempted to bargain with the U.S. Government by himself. The most the FBI would offer him was to have Immigration request deportation to Mexico for entering the country under false pretensions and being a party to smuggling.

"After a week of constant interviews and thinking about the offer, he accepted it and cooperated with the FBI. Prior to getting his butt kicked back to Mexico, he has agreed to a meeting with me in Minnesota," said Noel during a telephone exchange with Claire and Bear Child.

"He absolutely refuses to allow Tim in on the interview. I'm sorry, Tim, but I wouldn't be honest if I didn't share this with you or tell you that the FBI has not given me any information about him."

"Well, why would they start now? Not sharing almost got me killed," said Bear Child.

Noel reminded him that the shooter was still at large even if the cartel had changed focus. "Be careful, Tim, that is why you and Claire are there, right? Listen, for the next few days don't worry about me, I'll be in Minnesota, ok?" Without waiting for an answer from Bear Child, Noel disconnected the call. "Just like a fart, he disappears!" yelled Claire.

"Yeah," said Bear Child. "He doesn't linger like a Navajo."

"What do you mean, linger?"

"Asked the insulted Navajo," answered Bear Child. "Noel told me about you."

Claire laughed and said, "Yeah, I'm like a fine wine."

Noel met with the former deputy sheriff in the interview room of the federal prison in Sandstone, Minnesota. He was seated and looked comfortable and well taken care of. The former deputy said, "Well, nice to see you again, can't say I missed you," and then he laughed. Noel also laughed and said, "Yeah, I can imagine. We can chat or get right down to the reason I am here."

"Why, are you in a hurry?" Another laugh.

Noel could tell he was trying to sell the idea he was relaxed and sure of his position, but the phony laugh was a sign of insecurity. Noel didn't take a chair, which made the younger man look up toward him. Noel dominated the room and remained in control by not sitting down. "We got your burner phone," said Noel even though he didn't know if the FBI had the retail cellphone or not.

"Look, it doesn't matter now, her number is on that phone, but so what? That crap was yesterday. You came here to talk about the future, my future. Let's do that, ok?" insisted the crooked deputy.

Noel said very matter of factly, "Sure, here is my problem. Maybe you can help me or maybe I can help you."

"I don't need your help, you wasted a trip. In case you haven't heard, I'm not going to be in prison, I have agreed to being deported to Mexico."

Noel said, "Yeah, that's what I've been told, but you probably wouldn't have made it through your sentence, which was going to be what? 30 to 35 years? Your cartel friends would have cut you a new chin line."

The former deputy laughed and said, "Mexico will be a lot safer, don't you think?"

Noel smiled back and said, "No, I don't think it will be when I leave here today. You may or may not know that I have a friend named Louie Louis who has friends in the Sinaloa boys' club you belong to. You won't be welcomed in Mexico, and you'll find out that there is no place there that will be safe for you."

"Bullshit!" yelled the young man. "You can't do that. You won't do that. You old school guys would be in so much trouble with the law."

Noel walked to the empty chair, sat down in it, and said, "Yeah, you're probably right that I wouldn't, but only because I have no friends in the Sinaloa Cartel. Louie has, and he will. This is what he wants because you helped her after she killed his friend, Larry Figueroa, in

Prescott. He wants her. Give her up, and maybe he will be happy. Maybe you can live to be old school, too."

The younger man thought about this before he spoke, unlike his cocky manner earlier. "I'm not sure I would, but if I do, how would I know he would do what you say he would?" Noel said, "You won't know, but if you want to live looking behind you and around your front door before you go inside, well, that's up to you. If you live to be old school, you'll know he kept his mouth shut about it."

Noel was pushing it and got up to leave when the younger man asked, "Do you know where Dove Mountain is?" Noel said, "You mean the development near the interstate in Marana near Tucson?" The former deputy just nodded his head yes.

CHAPTER 48

WSOCTV.com/news/world
Sunday, June 20, 2021
Gunmen kill at least 14 in attacks near U.S.-Mexico border
By Alfredo Pena
Associated Press

CIUDAD VICTORIA, MEXICO-(AP)- GUNMEN IN VEHICLES OPENED FIRE in the Mexican city of Reynosa on the U.S. border, killing at least 14 people and causing widespread panic, authorities said. Security forces killed at least four suspects, including one who died near a border bridge. The attacks began Saturday afternoon in several neighborhoods in eastern Reynosa which borders the Texan city of McAllen, according to the Tamaulipas state agency that coordinates security forces. Images posted on social media showed bodies in the streets. Authorities did not immediately comment on a possible motive for the attacks. The area's criminal activity has long been dominated by the Gulf Cartel, but there have been fractures within the group. Reynosa is a key crossing point for migrants attempting to reach the United States.

Noel shared the information he had received from the former deputy with both the Prescott Police and the FBI. He figured the FBI had the information from listening in on his conversation, and it wouldn't have benefited anyone to not tell them. Maybe this time they could find the shooter, and he would not have to place his friends in jeopardy again. Noel called Rebecca and asked her to please pick up Louie at the extended care facility. He went into the Tucson area in search of two 30.30 rifles for Claire and Bear Child. He would feel much better if they had the rifles in saddle scabbards while they rode horseback. The FBI lost the shooter on two separate occasions. He did not have any guarantee that they would succeed this time. Noel found a chain operation in Tucson that provided him with the rifles, ammo, and two nylon saddle scabbards. Noel called Uber and had the purchase dropped off for them.

When Noel returned to Prescott, he found out that Louie had surprised Rebecca when she went to check him out of the care facility. Apparently, Louie had lied to the staff and told them that it was his birthday, so they had a party and birthday cake for him. Louie was wearing scrubs and crunching down his second helping of chocolate cake when he saw Rebecca. He motioned her to come over by him and have some cake. She later told Noel that she had a good time, "and the cake was great. Louie loved that place," she said with a big smile on her face, along with a small smear of chocolate frosting above her lips. For that 24- hour stay, Louie had acquired three sets of baby blue scrubs. He started to wear them in the evening in his hotel room when he planned on, "staying in for the evening."

Several days then passed without incident. Noel felt like there was something missing, something not right. Something was out of place, and one evening at dinner he knew what it was. Rebecca said the gal who went on the cruise with them had not shown up for work at her restaurant and had not answered her phone at home for two days straight. Noel assured Rebecca that things would be sorted out, and she would be ok. Rebecca felt odd about Noel's response and pushed him a bit about what he meant by "sorted out?"

Noel said, "What I meant was, it will be fine. I'm sure it is a family issue. Maybe an illness." The following day Noel asked the Sheriff of Pinal County to backtrack on any possible license plate registrations that the crooked deputy may have run prior to the day the group left for the

Mexican cruise. Within minutes he found out Rebecca's employee had her car registration run by the former deputy. When that information came back, Noel immediately called Claire to grill him about his relationship with that gal while they were on the cruise.

Noel left a phone message for Claire. "Claire, you know I don't pry into who you see or don't see since your divorce, and I would never invade your privacy unless it was important, don't you? I need to know if Rebecca's friend grilled you about our current investigation while on the cruise? I know the two of you spent the night together on that ship. Call me back as soon as you can, thanks, Claire." When Claire called back, he told Noel, "You and I were under the microscope. She asked a lot of questions. Don't worry, I didn't let any information slip out to her. She's a nice gal, Noel, but no, I didn't share anything with her."

Noel said, "Thanks, Claire. I'm afraid our little deputy friend must have had Rebecca and me under surveillance and ran some automobile plates in Rebecca's parking lot. When her friend's Hispanic name came back on one of the cars, he probably approached the only gal working there who had dark skin and pulled a cartel extortion move on her, you know, maybe had one of her family members in Mexico held unless she cooperated with him to get information from us."

There was a pause on the line, and then Claire said, "I feel violated, man!" Both he and Noel laughed, and then Noel asked him, "Dirty? Do you feel dirty?"

"Cheap! I feel cheap!" said Claire. Noel gave a deep belly laugh and Claire joined in with his own. Claire then said that he and Bear Child may take the horses and move further north for a few days, maybe to the National Forest outside of Payson, Arizona. Noel thought that might be a good idea.

That evening when Noel told Rebecca what he found out, he began by saying, "I'm afraid your friend probably will not be back in town."

"Why? Is she ok?" Is it her family?"

Noel told Rebecca what he suspected and what Claire confirmed for him. Rebecca remained quiet for the remainder of the evening. In the morning she told Noel that she would be fine. She regretted it happening, and yet she also knew that her friend could have caused a death or deaths. "I will miss her, Noel, but I am glad you guys are safe so far. I hope her family will be, too. Damn that cartel all to hell!" she yelled and left for her restaurant. Noel mumbled to himself after she left, "Damn that cartel all to hell." Noel thought about Larry inside an urn on the mantel of his fake fireplace in his mystery bookshop and repeated under his breath, "Damn that cartel all to hell."

Later that day, Noel interrupted what he was doing at the bookshop and called the FBI out of curiosity. He wanted to find out what kind of shoes the FBI found at the former deputy's house or apartment. When an FBI forensic tech sent him photos of the various shoes, Noel compared one FBI photo to the photo that Claire took with his cellphone camera inside the escape tunnel in Casa Grande. The two photos showed the exact same circle pattern on the sole of the shoes. This deputy had been inside the tunnel before the FBI were there that day, indicating he had used the tunnel to communicate with the shooter. Noel passed this information on to the investigating agents with the hope it would strengthen the case against the deputy so that the deportation would be withheld, and he would be prosecuted instead. Being in the country illegally and being a party to smuggling were not ironclad offenses that would send him to prison unless the feds had a good case against him. His personal shoes would help seal his fate on being a party to a smuggling charge and maybe even conspiracy to commit murder charges if they were to lay it on him.

Waiting for the FBI to capture or kill the shooter in her Dove Mountain location near Tucson was a process that seemed to take forever. Finally, Noel got the phone call he had been waiting for. The FBI had engaged the shooter in a gun battle and possible hostage situation in the middle of the Dove Mountain development. Units of the Pima and Pinal County Sheriffs' offices responded to the location with snipers and hostage negotiators. Within hours the local media had the development surrounded with news vans and announcers walking around the cordoned-off neighborhood. Two Phoenix area television stations had choppers overhead and the Tucson Police had an aircraft up as well.

Noel watched the events unfold on a small television he had under the counter in the bookshop. "Nobody has been shot as of this time," one of the local news people announced on the air while another several feet from her announced that, "Reports indicate no one was transported from the scene but many are expected in local hospitals should they be shot or killed." Noel was waiting for some station to announce that, "Many have been shot on the way to local hospitals in the area of the shootings." Anything to give the viewing public the impression they had up-close and mostly confidential information as to body count, and who might be shot. "The breaking news is the shooter is described as Hispanic, a female, and a resident of Dove Mountain. She is also an amputee according to our sources. One neighborhood source described her as being disabled and obviously missing a limb from the way she appeared to walk. We will have more as this situation develops," promised one station anchor person.

Noel said out loud, "Great, now someone will start a Go Fund Me page for the shooter." As the day moved toward the evening coverage, it became clear that the FBI had called in additional help from the number of nondescript cars parked in front of the television vans. "No additional information or evidence has been presented indicating a hostage situation is taking place at the moment," one news person reported while showing a video of her asking a uniformed officer where the snipers were located. One news wizard told his audience, "The number of gun deaths in this country is staggering, and everyone hopes this will end with the hostage taker getting the help she so obviously needs."

Noel was positive that the cartel shooter was hoping for that as well. However, he doubted she would receive that right away. One person who lived in the neighborhood identified as a member of the Neighborhood Watch was being interviewed on camera saying, "I pray that we don't have another neck-kneeling cop situation here like they do in larger cities. We have churches here and a professional golf course to die for. I mean, not literally, but you know." Noel just took it all in.

People had been evacuated from their homes and left to wander around the development. A person who drove up to the neighborhood in an RV to make a bathroom available to those displaced homeowners was arrested when it was discovered that the Good Samaritan had rerouted the vehicle's backup camera to that bathroom.

At approximately 8:00 P.M. movement was seen inside the home, and things started happening. The front door was opened a crack; one person stuck her head out of the door and slowly stepped out with another person in tow. In a matter of seconds both people were standing on the front steps of the home within clear sight of all the snipers dispatched there. One officer could be heard yelling, "Put your hands up! Put your hands up! Put your hands up, damn it!" Another officer was heard yelling, "She's an amputee!" "She's an amputee!" Obviously the two people were women or looked like women, but it was hard to tell because of the lighting around the home. The blinking on and off from police and news chopper search lights made the scene almost 1960's strobe light in appearance.

Both women were made to lie on their stomachs while the front of the house immediately became swamped with officers in riot gear. One cop was pushing an empty wheelchair toward the two women. A caravan of ambulance crews rushed toward the driveway of the home, but only one made it to the garage area. The rest parked behind each other, blocking the first ambulance there.

It was just a few minutes before someone took charge of the scene. The mob of officers was cleared away from the yard while FBI agents took the two women into custody. Others in forensic attire waited for the swat folks to clear the home itself of any unreported occupants and/ or tunnels. The two unmarked FBI cars that contained the women were swiftly swept from view of the various television camera crews there while joining two other unmarked FBI cars, enroute to Tucson no doubt. Noel felt sure that if there were any weapons in the home that could be traced back to any of the cartel murders in Chicago, and if the shooter could remain alive while in custody, it would mark the start of one of the longest court trials in history. Larry probably would not see any justice for several years.

It was just a matter of a day when both women were moved. One woman went to California, and the other was sent to some place in Minnesota. Both women asked for Mexican Consulate intervention. Surprisingly enough, it was taken under consideration. Even Noel knew that digging tunnels in Arizona was not a felony, so he waited patiently for the FBI forensic team to make its report once he learned that there was a handgun recovered inside the home. According to Noel's sources in the FBI Lab, the weapon did not have any direct connection to the by-now famous Chicago killings, but it was a forensic homerun for direct linkage to the Larry Figueroa murder in Prescott, Arizona, earlier in the year.

Noel was overcome with relief and joy at the same time. He kept himself busy calling people to let them know what had happened. A major event had taken place in his life, and now a situation happened that may have brought him a step closer to being repaired. This had the possibility of making him whole once more.

Chapter 49

Each year thousands of people in North America stand trial for murder or some other felony. Trial by jury is very strenuous for all concerned, not just defendants. Defense attorneys, prosecutors, families of victims, and victim's friends all participate in the grueling process. The people who have no stake in the outcome hurt, also. Noel knew that Tim Bear Child was on pins and needles, but his interest was a clean record and reputation, while others who were close to Larry would never get their friend back.

Noel got word from the FBI that the shooter wanted to speak to him in person. This surprised him because he was getting ready to be sworn in as a witness. Noel had to think long and hard. He had a lot of hatred in his heart. but eventually he did agree to meet with her.

Flying into Minnesota late one evening, he caught a cab to the closest hotel to the federal facility that was holding her. However, he thought better of it while enroute and had the driver turn around to find a hotel near the airport. If he were a cartel shooter, maybe having a witness disappear before trial might pay off, so why take any chances by staying at a place close to the facility where the shooter was currently locked up? The shooter requests a visit, the witness complies, does the dumb move of being close to the shooter, and he disappears. Noel might be overthinking it but that was ok, the cartel was real and so was death. The following morning Noel skipped the great free breakfast that is served in airport hotels. Instead, he just had black coffee. After clearing security at the federal facility, he met with the shooter.

To his surprise, there was an interpreter present. It never dawned on him that she didn't speak English. Well, maybe she did but preferred Spanish. She sat still while the other person introduced her to Noel, and then the visit started. She had long dark hair, wore a short-sleeve orange jumpsuit with a long-sleeve insulated top underneath, and socks with shower shoes. The woman had beautiful eyes and facial features that were no less striking. Her hand was missing, but at the end of her wrist was an orthopedic device that looked strangely like a large cup. He didn't want her to notice him looking, but he couldn't resist and had to take quick glances at it. She instructed the other person, an older woman, to give her a cigarette which was lit and passed to her. This was odd in this type of a facility, but apparently not for this person who appeared to be getting more benefits than most in lockup.

She began by telling the woman to tell Noel she wanted to thank him for meeting with her. It turned out that one reason for the meeting was to learn more about the man who successfully stalked her. Noel responded by telling her, "You were very hard to find." Through the interpreter she told Noel, "I was living in the open; only those who wanted me could not find me. I also wanted to tell you that sometimes people make errors, terrible errors, and that may have been the reason innocent people got hurt. That may have been the case in Prescott. You have to forgive me when I speak in vague terms, but your government listens to my conversations with the hope of catching me making guilty comments."

Noel did not respond to her statement about Larry being shot by mistake but instead asked her why Mexico would consider her plea for help to the Mexican Consulate in Tucson. She responded with a smile, "Well, I am a Mexican citizen, and my detention could be another mistake. I am challenged by being a female, and a crippled female in our world is at a big disadvantage," she said while holding up the arm that had the missing hand. "I have to take income where I can and find help where I can. Sometimes one must adapt and take work that is not pleasant. Does that make me unpleasant?"

Noel answered, "Of course not, but some German people thought Hitler was pleasant."

She smiled again and said, "But to answer your question, maybe someone in my consulate will be instructed to assist me?"

"You know, Mr. Two Horses, there is research going on in Israel. They are using genetically engineered e-coli bacteria to locate landmines. When the e-coli is spread over the mine fields, the bacteria will adhere to these landmines and emit invisible vapors. The landmines light up like little fireflies do and give the appearance of glowing in the dark. The reason I am telling you this is because I donate money to the organizations that help sponsor this research. I am not comparing myself to Princess Di, who, as you know, had very strong feelings about abandoned land mines and what they do to children living in countries at war. But I have to ask you if that is something a terrible person would do, contribute money to research that would make this world a safer place for children?"

Noel told the shooter, "I won't comment about your humanity or lack of humanity, and I am not a microbiologist, but I can detect invisible vapors, and you do not pass the smell test. I assume maybe your generosity is directly linked to your injury as a child and the lack of control you had at the time in the decision made to shoot your family that night on the border. But that could be, well, just an educated guess. Why don't we get to the point of this meeting? I will not be on your jury, so why did you send for me?"

Before she answered Noel's question, she instructed her interpreter to leave the room. She waited for the door to close before she began.

"I am glad you brought my being shot into our conversation. I may not have a jury in this country, I may become another international incident again and have to return to Mexico." Noel was shocked to hear her flawless English. He replied, "That may be be true, but I would not count on it."

"How did you find out my name was Alita Lopez? You appear to be good at what you do."

Noel told her the story of her childhood print on a painted piece of clay and how it was linked to her name. She leaned in toward Noel and whispered across the table, "That may not stand up in court, but you actually may not have to testify to that."

Noel asked, "Why would that be?" and the shooter replied, "I can make you a very wealthy man within the next 24 hours. Think about it."

Noel did think about it. He discovered that she wanted him to be in Minnesota in person so she could bribe him. Whispering to him in person, out of range of any recording device, did not work. Noel did not respond to her; he looked at her, stood up, and walked toward the door. The correctional officer let him out, and he returned to his rental car. If nothing else, he had the satisfaction of knowing she was in limbo right now. He wanted her to go to hell, but for now he had to settle for limbo. The trip to Minnesota was an expense he would eat, but he now was convinced that Larry meant nothing to her. The cartel shakeup cost many families the lives of their loved ones. The Mexican drug cartels do not care. In this case, the cartel could arrange to have her pulled from the U.S. before she even got a court date for murder. Noel noted that she never mentioned having legal representation, public defender, or an expensive defense team of attorneys. She probably was well-connected to a drug lord who did not want her eliminated.

Noel drove his car back to the airport. While waiting to board his flight, he became thirsty for a cold beer. Noel walked over to the closet bar inside his terminal concourse and sat down at a two-person table, facing the small bar. Nearing the end of his drink Noel spotted a young guy heading directly to him, aiming at the empty chair at the table. The young fellow said hello to Noel and told him he wanted to grab a waiter. He asked if Noel would watch the backpack that he just removed from his shoulder and placed on the empty chair? Noel smiled at him but got up and left as soon as the young guy turned around. Noel was in the concourse watching the guy from a distance as he drank his beverage. After just leaving a cartel shooter and not responding to her request, Noel was not about to let an unknown person leave a backpack on the chair in front of him with instructions to watch it. He saw the young guy leave the small airport bar and head down the concourse in the opposite direction of Noel's location.

Noel had seen enough in his life to know it pays to use caution. Booby traps have that name for a reason, and Noel had seen his share of booby traps to last a lifetime. One day while on an operation in Vietnam, his platoon had stopped to take a timeout while moving with full combat gear and a machine gun team in 100 plus degree temperatures. That meant, in addition to normal combat gear, they were carrying heavy cans of machine gun ammo as well. The area where the platoon was operating was laced with booby traps and underground tunnels used by the enemy. They were in a clearing of sorts, surrounded by small palm trees. The platoon took up positions around the perimeter in the event an attack would take place. Two of the guys from his platoon found a tree and slid down the trunk of the tree back-to-back to rest when the entire tree suddenly exploded. If Noel were to go back to living under booby trap conditions, he knew it would only be for a short while. He had already lived with startled reflex issues since Vietnam anyway, responding by jumping or flinching at sudden loud cracking sounds.

Looking back on it, Bear Child had been living under those very same booby trap conditions since he moved to Arizona. He had physical support from Claire, and part-time support from Prescott Police Officer Randal and Noel himself from time to time, but it was Bear Child who took the initiative to be his own guardian. On the other hand, Noel had Louie who operated under the herd mentality rule. It was another person's responsibility to protect Louie.

When Noel returned to Prescott, he found out that Louie had struck out on his own and wished everyone a fond farewell. Rebecca could not contact Noel while he was in the air, so she saved the information until he arrived. Louie had apparently made another call to his old cartel friend and found out he was "Free again!" according to Louie. As much as Noel hated Louie calling those people, it did come in handy to have him able to do so when information needed to be mined in Mexico. The obvious problem was he never knew what Louie told people in Mexico.

Noel invited Claire, Bear Child, and Rebecca to join him for dinner at the St. Gregory so he could share what the shooter was after and to let them know more about her. He also wanted them to be able to celebrate Louie's departure for the time being. Louie was becoming a frequent flyer with Noel and Claire, and they knew deep down in their heart of hearts, he would return someday. Like the flu or a hangover, Louie would resurface.

Noel thought it was good to see Bear Child at dinner and to be able to let him know that he could finally make plans. Noel was the last one to sit down at the dining table. Rebecca was spreading her linen napkin onto her lap when Claire made an announcement that if all went well, he was going to go back on another Mexican cruise as soon as he could. The party began to order before-dinner drinks when Noel said, "I hope you can enjoy it this time, Mr. Sauvé. I know you only enjoyed a little of it because of Louie and your ladyfriend's demands."

Rebecca suddenly said, "Oh, Claire, I am so sorry I asked her to join us, I didn't know she would pressure you for information."

Claire answered, "That's ok. You know, I want to believe she only did it because she was being threatened."

Rebecca said, "I hope she is alright but most of all safe."

Bear Child and Claire raised glasses to that and clinked them together.

Noel said with a smile, "I hoped she was alright, too, Claire."

Claire responded with a low mumble, "Sir, I never kiss and tell."

Rebecca did not hear Claire, so she turned to Noel and asked him, "What did he say?"

Noel told Rebecca, "Only God can tell."

The waiter took his time taking every order and pitching the same special to each person at the table. When he finally left the area, Noel said, "Ok guys and gal, this was probably one of the most interesting transformations I have witnessed in this business yet. First of all, this woman is drop-dead gorgeous." Noel told them about the interpreter being present initially but then dismissed. He spoke of her command of the English language after Claire commented on his understanding she was from Mexico and was a Spanish speaker. "It was all a plot to get me to say something out loud while assuming she did not speak English. Or she did not want the interpreter to hear her speak to me in English, reference the bribe."

"You got a bribe?" asked Rebecca. "She flew around the country shooting her own cartel people and killed Larry right here in Prescott, and she had the gall to give you a bribe?"

"No, no, no, I don't have a bribe, I didn't take it," explained Noel. "She offered me a bribe, I didn't take a bribe."

"What kind of bribe?" asked Claire.

"She told me she could make me a wealthy man within 24 hours," answered Noel, "implying if I did not testify for the prosecution."

Noel also told the group about her request to the Mexican Consulate which indicated that the cartel is well connected there. He went on to share her explanation for contributing to an organization that helps to finance Israeli research on landmine location using E-coli bacteria. "This was explained to me in detail to help prove she was also a humanitarian." "Oh, a killer humanitarian?" asked Bear Child." "Apparently," said Noel. "It was all B.S."

"She never admitted to shooting Larry. 'Sometimes people make terrible errors' was her explanation for Larry's death. On the upside, she thought or lead me to believe that she thought we did a great job in stalking her, and we knew our trade." The entire group raised a glass to that. "Interestingly, she appeared to be fascinated with how we discovered her name. I think when I told her about her childhood handprint, she must have felt confident it would not stand up in trial because she got arrogant again. This made me believe that we were dealing with an extremely intelligent person, not just an ordinary hitman from Mexico. She knew the rules of evidence and apparently is not represented by legal counsel."

"That might be her downfall," ventured Claire.

"I think she believes the cartel will get the Mexican Consulate to act on her behalf," cautioned Noel. "We will have to be open-minded enough to expect and accept it. I'm confident the cartel is finished hunting Tim. It's just the way it rapidly evolved with new people taking the steering wheel down there."

Bear Child commented, "Not worth killing, huh? Neither Louie nor I are worth killing?" He said this while laughing out loud.

Claire said, "Don't feel bad, we like you guys. Your mom probably still likes you."

CHAPTER 50

The Arizona Daily Star
Sunday, June 27, 2021
Mark Stevenson
Associated Press

Disappearances rise on Mexico's highway of death

MEXICO CITY-AS MANY AS 50 PEOPLE ARE MISSING AFTER SETTING OUT on three-hour car trips this year between Mexico's industrial hub of Monterrey and the border city of Nuevo Laredo on a well- traveled stretch of road local media have dubbed "the highway of death." Family members say the simply vanish. The disappearances, and last week's shooting of 15 apparently innocent bystanders in Reynosa, suggest Mexico is returning to the days of the 2006-2012 drug war when cartel gunmen often targeted the public as well as one another.

Most of the victims are believed to have disappeared approaching or leaving the cartel-dominated city of Nuevo Laredo across the border from Laredo, Texas. About a half a dozen men have reappeared alive, badly beaten, and all they say is that the armed men forced them to stop on the highway and took their vehicles.

What happened to the rest remains a mystery. Most were residents of Nuevo Leon state, where Monterrey is located. Desperate for answers, relatives of the missing took to the streets in Monterrey on Thursday to protest, demanding answers. Nuevo Laredo has long been dominated by the Northeast Cartel, a remnant of the old Zetas Cartel, whose members were infamous for their violence. Officials in the early 2000's were often quick to repeat an old belief that "drug cartels only kill each other, not innocent civilians." That argument, "that they only kill each other" is not heard so much according to Mexico security analyst Alejandro Hope. He said the highway disappearances and the June 19th events in Reynosa when gunmen from rival cartels drove through the streets, randomly killing 15 passersby-were reminiscent of the attacks on civilians during the 2006-2012 drug war. In 2018, a drug cartel in the western city of Morelia tossed hand grenades into a crowd during an Independence Day celebration. In 2011, cartel gunmen in Tamaulipas abducted dozens of men from passenger buses and made them fight each other to the death with sledgehammers, either as a recruitment tool or for entertainment.

Claire had discussed calling it a wrap with Noel the next morning at the bookshop over coffee. He said, "As a precaution, Tim is moving his smaller trailer out of the RV park and putting it up for sale. He wants to find a spot just north of town, maybe Chino Valley. I think he will be fine. He seems to be well-grounded right now. I think I'm going to head out as well."

Noel Told Claire, "You know you don't have to, right? You are welcome to stay for as long as you like. Were you serious about doing the cruise again?"

"Yeah, I was serious," said Claire. "You know I enjoyed it and liked the way it was organized."

"Relaxing, huh?" asked Noel.

"Yeah, that and the fact I haven't taken that type of affordable adventure when I could have before. I mean, I don't want to miss any more of that while I can still do it," explained Claire.

Noel said, "When you put it that way, I guess it makes sense. Maybe I'll follow up on that myself. I always pictured taking adventure and beating it into submission. Maybe I should have just enjoyed the good things about it?"

Claire admitted to Noel, "Same here, I guess we had to have control. Old habits don't break easily."

Noel thought for a minute and said, "Maybe it was survival, control ultimately meant survival for you and me. Well, me anyway."

Claire said, "No, me too. I'm guilty of that. I want to change that, I want to enjoy things."

"Who the hell knows?" asked Noel. "Maybe it was Larry's death at the hands of Super Bitch that did it? Maybe that got us philosophical in our old age. Questioning our own mortality. I have better things to do."

Claire told Noel, "You know, you teach college, you have a mystery bookshop, and run the P.I. agency. You function and remain anchored. I'm not that occupied. I think I'm at that stage where I'm burned out or close to it. I need a view from a different location. I like what I saw on that cruise."

Noel could not respond to what Claire was telling him. Instead, he told Claire, "I haven't had the time to figure out what your share of the billing is for Louie and Bear Child this month. But if you'll give me a few hours to do it, I'll make sure you have it in cash." The men agreed to get together in two hours at Rebecca's restaurant. Claire would gather up his things at Noel's house and meet him at the restaurant. Within that two-hour window a lot of things ran through Noel's mind as he got Claire's money ready for pickup. Noel reflected on what Claire said. There were things that did keep Noel grounded, and those were the things he valued: His relationship with Rebecca, his teaching position, his bookshop, and the investigative agency he operated.

Noel got a surprise telephone call from Sargent Henry of the Prescott Police Department letting him know that the District Attorney for Yavapai County was seating a State Grand Jury to indict Alita Lopez for the murder of Larry Figueroa and the attempted murder of Tim Bear Child. This was an obvious attempt to get her arrested for Larry's murder before the Mexican Consulate could interfere and get her out of the country. That all of this was going on with scant interest from the FBI didn't make sense, and Noel wanted a response from them. Sgt. Henry was able to calm him down when he informed Noel that the FBI were the people that wanted the Yavapai County District Attorney to seat the Grand Jury. This way the FBI would not be the people who would create another international incident. Politics is sometimes more subversive than those in society who commit offenses for a living.

In the end, there was not any international incident whatsoever when, during the transfer from the Yavapai County Jail to the County Courthouse in Prescott to stand trial for the murder of Larry Figueroa, she was shot and killed by an unknown assailant. Forensic evidence indicated that the victim died from one shot to the head from a 30.30 caliber weapon, based on lands and grooves that matched that of the 30.30, the winchester rifle manufactured in America and sold nationwide to thousands of hunters and sportsmen for over a century. The forensic finding also revealed that, because of the severity and location of the wound, death probably occurred on impact. Noel decided not to mention that he had purchased this same weapon for Claire and Bear Child during the time they were avoiding the cartel shooter.

Further north Bear Child was looking at the property he purchased in Chino Valley. There would be room for his horses and a place to have a tack room and hay storage. He wanted to sink a well but that was only because the land was being sold with the use of a shared well. There was a brick house on the property that offered Bear Child a kitchen, two bathrooms, two bedrooms, and a den. He hoped his friends and family would visit him there. He also wanted a place for his mom when she became more elderly. Bear Child couldn't know that he would lose his mother a few months later when cancer took her life as it does to millions of people worldwide.

Bear Child was able to finish his studies and graduate as he had planned. During his academic period, he assisted Noel Two Horses with the case that he was working on with Noel prior to Larry being killed. Together they brought back evidence to the two tribes that had retained Noel's services to track down their missing girls and women.

Bear Child had met a young Yavapai Apache woman who was also attending the same college as he did. The two of them became a romantic couple on campus, but Bear Child never let his mind wander away from the Mexican cartel that wanted to kill him, so he always lived his life with caution.

He depended upon his five senses, his understanding of technology, and good luck to live a whole and satisfactory life. He never married nor did he father any children because he did not want to bring a child into this world.

ABOUT THE AUTHOR

RICK CHURCH IS AN ENROLLED MEMBER OF THE STOCKBRIDGE-MUNSEE Mohican Nation. He is a Vietnam Marine combat veteran and former state trooper and Police Sergeant. Rick is also a graduate of the FBI Academy Command College Quantico and has a master's in forensic psychology. He was a Special Agent in undercover narcotics for the Department of Justice and an investigator for a CIA contractor.